UNTAMED HEART

Gemma Morr has worked in book marketing for twenty years, connecting imaginations with the worlds in which they belong. She currently lives in Hampshire with her husband and two children. *Untamed Heart* is her debut novel.

UNTAMED HEART

GEMMA MORR

PAN BOOKS

First published 2025 by Pan Books
an imprint of Pan Macmillan
The Smithson, 6 Briset Street, London EC1M 5NR
EU representative: Macmillan Publishers Ireland Ltd, 1st Floor,
The Liffey Trust Centre, 117–126 Sheriff Street Upper,
Dublin 1 D01 YC43
Associated companies throughout the world

ISBN 978-1-0350-7625-3

1 3 5 7 9 8 6 4 2

A CIP catalogue record for this book is available from the British Library.

Typeset in Granjon by Six Red Marbles UK, Thetford, Norfolk
Printed and bound in the UK using 100% Renewable Electricity by CPI Group (UK) Ltd

MIX
Paper | Supporting
responsible forestry
FSC® C116313

Visit **www.panmacmillan.com** to read more about
all our books and to buy them.

For Rich, Thomas and Alex. It always has been,
and always will be, for you.

The *Untamed Heart* Playlist

'Worst Way' – Riley Green
'Home' – Good Neighbours
'Bed Chem' – Sabrina Carpenter
'Lose Control' – Teddy Swims
'Ain't No Love in Oklahoma' – Luke Combs
'Get Good' – St. South (Infinitefreefall remix)
'You & Me' – Disclosure & Eliza Doolittle (Rivo remix)
'Doublewide' – Gabriella Rose
'Something in the Orange' – Zach Bryan
'Homesick' – Noah Kahan
'Daddy's Mugshot' – Laci Kaye Booth
'Tennessee Whiskey' – Chris Stapleton

CHAPTER 1

It was 6.15 a.m. and I was sweating like a nun at a *Magic Mike* show.

My phone lit up *again* as I attempted to hoist my work bag onto my shoulder without creasing my shirt. My front door slammed shut behind me and I winced at the noise in the silent hallway.

'Hi, Cressida,' I said, squashing the phone against my ear, desperately hoping I hadn't woken anyone up. My long working hours were already a talking point in the building. Between lovely Mrs Peterson next door, genuinely concerned that I was mid-burnout, and the passive-aggressive notes from the guy opposite, I was one early morning or late night away from an intervention. But, as my manager Cressida was about as warm and understanding as your average dictator, I forced my voice into corporate mode, burying the exasperation in my tone as I reached the outside door. 'I'm on my way, won't take much long—'

'Yup, yup, I know – look, Lottie, can you pick up the coffee order on the way in? I wouldn't normally ask but the whole team's on their knees.' I bit my lip. Why was she saying this like I didn't already know? As if I wasn't one of them? But I kicked my thoughts into the background and quickly opened the notes app, trying my best to keep up with the list of drinks she reeled off. As she finished, she paused before adding, 'Oh, and Heather from HR has scheduled a 9 a.m. in your diary, just so you know.'

I slowed, turning off the path from my building and onto the main street. My new shoes, an unexpected gift from my boyfriend Kyle just the previous weekend, were already beginning to pinch and rub.

'Okaaay,' I replied, completely lacking the balls to ask why. 'I'll be there as soon as I can.'

She hung up before I'd finished speaking, just as she usually did. Staring at the blank screen of my phone for a moment, I fought the urge to mirror the scream of a 747 flying overhead as it cruised down towards Heathrow. Refusing to acknowledge the growing pain from my toes, I carried on up the street towards the tube station, almost breaking into a jog, despite the 4-inch stiletto heels. I figured they were worth it – beautiful, made from eye-wateringly expensive Italian leather. Kyle had stared at my legs, his eyes inching up my body as though he wanted to devour all of it. Slowly. I smiled to myself despite everything. He could be exacting, yes, and sometimes a bit of a snob, but *sweet Jesus* that man was HOT. Plus, he'd made me promise I'd wear them tonight for drinks and dinner. I couldn't let him down; that would only bring out his moody, snarky side, and that was more than I had the bandwidth for at the moment.

As I forced myself to take a deep breath, the caustic scent of exhaust fumes and weed hit the back of my throat. I couldn't quite suppress a wistful glance at the source of the illegal smell as I passed the two student houses tucked at the end of the street, likely still going from the previous night. Imagining Kyle's disgust, I reminded myself that all of that was behind me now – there was no room for messing around any more, no room for failure. I snapped my head up and aimed for the entrance to the tube, for my extremely hard-won job on the Bowers & Johnson graduate scheme, and for everything I now had.

The temperature gradually rose as I descended on the escalator with a handful of other tired, blank-faced commuters, and I was beginning to sweat. Huge fans circulated the stagnant air at the bottom, giving everyone with long hair a Medusa-like appearance as they passed by. I knew my own wilful dark curls, hastily straightened just fifteen minutes earlier, wouldn't hold. The tips were already threatening to twist and I cursed the unseasonably warm early May weather, my shoes, the tube *and* my job.

Finally on board, as we rattled east and drew closer to zone 1, the carriage filled. I gave up my seat to a pregnant lady as we got to South Ken, her grateful smile just about making up for having to squish myself into the sweaty armpits of two tall, highly perfumed City boys.

Forcing my mind to head for my happy place, the rest of the journey occurred largely in the countryside where I'd grown up, at the riding stables where I'd spent most of my time as a teenager until I'd left home for university – just me and a couple of close friends, shovelling the shit produced by about thirty horses. In exchange, I rode most days through the surrounding countryside of rolling hills and forests, free of people, of responsibility and of overpowering, overpriced cologne. Often I'd listened to audiobooks as I worked, measuring out the horses' feed into buckets, or taking apart bridles to give them a thorough clean and polish. Sometimes I'd even taken my books up to the stables and snuck a read in the tack room, the comforting smell of supple leather and sun-warmed hay infusing the memory of the stories.

As I made my way off the tube at my stop and wound my way up to street level, I realized I couldn't remember the last time I'd read or listened to anything. Work and Kyle took up so much of my time that anything else other than exhausted sleep felt like nothing more than a vague memory. Had those years at the stables been the happiest time of my life? If so, was it all downhill from there?

Before pushing my way onto the street, I pulled out my phone and checked my reflection. It revealed the true mess that my expensive clothes and make-up couldn't disguise. Wide blue eyes now watery with exhausted frustration, overly pink cheeks contrasting with my otherwise pale, freckled skin. As for my hair . . . the ends had now bounced upwards, creating a curly chaos. My best friend Hestia had once described it as perfect surfer-girl hair, adding, 'You know, if you had any chill at all, you could totally pull it off.'

She hadn't meant it to, but it'd hit a nerve. Would I ever be able to relax? Could I afford to do that and be the success I needed to be?

My phone lit up again with more messages – two more coffee orders.

Apparently not.

Swallowing down choice expletives, I propelled myself towards the only café in this section of zone 1 that Cressida hadn't declared 'fucking abysmal', and considered the years I'd spent studying, the months I'd spent cramming for my finals, the sheer effort and tears that'd gone into applying for the scheme – endless interviews, aptitude tests and team exercises. To get her and the rest of the marketing team coffee.

There was no way in hell that Kyle would have to fetch coffee for his team, but perhaps that was the difference between a marketing assistant at a law firm and a junior analyst at J.P. Morgan. Or maybe because his father was on the board, or just that he had the right accent and a signet ring.

I mentally slapped myself, knowing I needed to knock it off. Maybe I needed coffee too, way more than I thought.

Finally reaching the door of the café, I pushed inward on the long brass handle, but nothing happened. My frantic momentum almost propelled me through the glass, my eyes directly in line with a piece of paper taped to the inside.

'*Closed due to unforeseen circumstances on Tuesday 7 May. See you again soon!*'

Oh. *Fuck.*

Cressida was exacting in the extreme, but the only other option without a significant walk and three more blisters was the Starbucks just up the road. Bowers & Johnson was part of a sea of steel and glass offices that swallowed the older stone buildings in their shadow and didn't leave much room for anything else. We had our own café in the building, of course, but it wasn't open until later. Because reasonable people don't require caffeination at their office before 7 a.m.

Praying to any and every god, I jogged to Starbucks, rationalizing that turning up with some kind of coffee was better than none. I offered up eternal servitude, my new car – hell, my unborn children – for Starbucks to be open.

It was. Thank fuck.

The barista's eyebrows rose as I barrelled in, groaning in relief and reeling off my order before I'd even reached the counter, grateful that it was empty.

'Are you sure you need coffee? We have some herbal options?' he said, a half-smile on his mouth as he added the order to his screen. I paused, mid-list, ready to narrow my eyes or poke his out when he winked. 'I'm just saying, girl, you look like you need a Xanax, not caffeine.'

The sheer ridiculousness of the moment hit me and my mouth twitched.

'You got a cold foam Xanax? I'll take a Venti.'

He laughed, shaking his head.

'I'll fix you up,' he added, nodding towards my phone, the list open on my notes app. 'Give me the rest of it.'

I read out all eight drinks, then watched as he prepped them quickly, tapping my company card and collecting the receipt.

'So, why's a pretty girl in a beautiful suit with a bag to die for' – he nodded at my new Bottega Veneta, another ridiculously lavish gift from Kyle – 'having to fetch drinks for a whole bunch of people? You look too good for that, honey.'

I smiled. It felt hollow, but I knew he was trying to help.

'I'm just the assistant and my boss is . . . well, she does things in her own way. It's a great job, though, I'm just glad to have it.'

'They give you a clothing allowance?' he asked, finishing up the last two cups and arranging them all into two trays, carefully balanced inside a large carrier bag.

I shook my head. 'Boyfriend in investment banking.'

He laughed, hand covering his mouth.

'You come back and let me know if he's all right with you bringing a friend out to shop on his card, okay?'

It was my turn to laugh, the idea of Kyle's well-mannered bewilderment at me swanning around Harvey Nics with my new barista best mate setting off a feeling of mild hysteria, quickly stymied as I realized the time.

'Deal. I'll be back for the Xanax later.'

'You got it, sweetie,' he called, waving me off as I somehow made it back out onto the street without dropping anything or twisting an ankle.

Eventually, like a desert mirage, the main entrance to the office appeared, the security guard opening the side door to allow me through without having to navigate the revolving one.

'Can I give you a hand with anything?' he asked politely, holding out a hand towards one of the bags with the coffees inside.

'Ah no, don't worry – thanks so much, though!' I lied as I struggled in, determined to make it up to the seventh floor without help. Almost defeated by the barriers, knowing my pass was buried in my handbag, the building's night manager opened the one nearest to me. She nodded, her expression knowing, as I mumbled more thanks, using my elbow to stab the lift button and finally stepping out at the almost silent open-plan office.

'Lottie, we're in the boardroom. Get a move on, would you?' a voice called out across the expanse of empty desks.

'Be right there,' I called back, almost whimpering at the sharp stab of the blisters, promising myself the sad reward of plasters for my feet after delivering the coffee.

Hurrying over, I opened the door with my hip and set the coffee down on the side counter. The main table was covered in laptops, a presentation slide on the big screen at the back and Tom, the marketing director, and Cressida's boss, giving instructions for amends.

'Did you really go to . . . *Starbucks* ?'

Cressida's face was aghast, as though I'd just presented a brace of severed heads.

'Carrelli's is closed today,' I replied quietly. 'There was a note on the door. I thought arriving with no coffee would be worse.'

Tom quirked an eyebrow.

'Right,' she said, pinching her brow. 'And you didn't go over to Notes on Victoria Road because . . .'

'Oh Cress, give it a rest.' Tom gestured me over with his hand, shaking his head. 'She's trying. It's just coffee. We can go out after we've delivered this.'

I passed him his drink as some of the others came over to help themselves, not daring to catch his eye or hers, fear suppressing the internal seething. Cressida huffed, flicking her perfect, poker-straight blonde hair over one shoulder. It was the colour of champagne, contrasting with the sharp black skirt suit and blood-red lips.

'Well, I can't drink that slop,' she snapped, grey eyes piercing mine. 'Could you get me a bottle of water, if you can manage it? It's in the small kitchen by the double doors.'

Her voice was slick ice, every other gaze and reaction from the team sliding off her to me. The passive-aggressive directions to the kitchen we used every day threatened to bloom across my cheeks, so I left before they could.

Feet still on fire, I marched to the kitchen and snatched a glass bottle from the fridge, delivering it to the boardroom as quickly and silently as possible. No one so much as looked up, Cressida actively ignoring me and the rest engrossed in making the final tweaks to the slides I'd spent the last week creating.

Finally, tears rising, I took off the torturous shoes outside the meeting room and hobbled to the toilets. In silence I peeled and stuck plasters on both feet, grimacing as I slid the shoes back on. Then, sighing, I pulled myself together and scraped my now rampant curls back into a tight bun, reapplying my make-up to calm myself, as though painting on my composure.

Back at my desk, I tried to settle myself, methodically making a list of tasks and highlighting the ones that absolutely had to happen that day. Working through my emails, I eventually came across the one from Heather, as Cressida had mentioned. It was weird — very vague but also very definite in its tone. The meeting was scheduled for an hour at nine, and even more strangely, my diary was clear for the rest of the day.

Frowning and checking Cressida's calendar, rammed full after nine, I tried to think of a time when I hadn't been in near constant meetings. It must be the effect of the board coming in today, the whole reason for the presentation I'd been prepping and the latest excuse for making me work twelve-hour days. I refocused on my list and, headphones in, I let Dolly soothe my frayed nerves.

The office gradually filled around me, more fixed expressions and shadowed eyes than I'd noticed before. Giving the occasional nod and smile to people I knew, I wondered if it'd always been this way, or whether today was somehow different. It *felt* different, but I had no fucking clue why. Neither Cressida nor the rest of the team came back over to the marketing department, but I was more than grateful for the reprieve.

Just before nine, clutching my laptop and phone to my chest like a shield, I entered the meeting room.

Heather from HR looked up, a tentative smile forming. Sitting opposite her at the round table was Cressida, sporting a very different kind of smile.

'Hello, Lottie,' Heather said, gesturing to the empty chair nearest the door. 'Have a seat.'

My own rictus expression froze in place as I sat down, laptop all but sliding out of my instantly sweating palms and onto the polished walnut wood.

Was this about the coffee? The first missed call this morning at five thirty? I hadn't meant to turn my phone to silent last night, but Hestia's drunk messages had been endless.

'You're probably wondering what this is all about, I imagine?'

Heather's expression was guarded, her eyes still and measured. I nodded, swallowing as Cressida's head tilted to one side, as though she was enjoying whatever was unfolding.

'Well, I won't draw it out, but you might've heard that market conditions are tough at the moment, what with all of the various global challenges we're facing.' She paused, clearly expecting some kind of response. When I offered nothing, my head blank and my heart beginning to pound in my ears, she continued. 'So unfortunately, we're having to make a difficult call across the business, in multiple departments, to let a small number of people go at a certain level.'

The silence in the room between us was absolute, broken only by the sound of a phone ringing somewhere down the corridor. A hollow feeling opened in my stomach, as though someone was busily vacuuming the contents out, leaving me reeling. I knew I had to say something, even as the same prickling feeling behind my eyes threatened again.

Cressida lifted an eyebrow, the corner of her mouth curved in challenge.

'I see,' I breathed, focusing on Heather, her careful neutrality easier to navigate.

'Unfortunately, that does include your role. It's not a reflection of your work – Cressida assures me that everything you've done has been largely satisfactory. I can walk you through the practicalities, of course, but this is your one week's notice.'

Largely satisfactory? Almost a year of back-breaking, exhausting slog, delivering everything asked of me and more, on time – no, early – for 'largely satisfactory'?

My stupor shattered as I looked over to Cressida's face, the same vindictive expression I'd shed tears and lost sleep over present once again.

'I can appreciate that it's not easy to be made redundant, but you'll receive good references and I'm sure will have no problem finding another role. Do you have any immediate questions?'

'No,' I said quietly, instead keeping a handle on the tears that threatened, resolving that I would be absolutely damned if I let Cressida see me upset again.

Heather nodded, rising to standing.

'I'll need you to prepare a handover for the team,' Cressida drawled, stretching like a cat. 'Then you're free to go.'

I paused as I stood, keeping my face blank. My temper was rising, something I worked hard to keep a lid on, especially amongst the unflappable lawyers around me. As I opened my mouth to agree, another glance at her bored, lazily amused expression choked the words that had been forming.

'Oh no, I'm sure that's not necessary,' I said instead, savage joy stirring at the surprise in her eyes. 'You'll figure it out. I know how anything less than excellence won't fly in your team, Cressida. My notes would only be *largely satisfactory*, so it's probably better if you do them yourself.'

I did my best to stalk out of the meeting room without hobbling, clamping my hands around my laptop to prevent myself from flipping her off.

CHAPTER 2

I held it together until I'd left the building.

Then as I walked down the now bustling street, my head held as high as possible, I let myself cry. With no idea where to go, I wandered past the Starbucks I'd been so relieved to see, so desperate to please Cressida, when she'd known full well what was going to happen.

Frustration, fear and anger all took turns at spurring me forwards, and I didn't even notice the sting from my damn shoes until the right one felt damp. Pausing mid-stride to glance down, I could see a rivulet of blood snaking from my heel, the lining of the shoe now ruined.

I forced myself to take a breath, and crossing the road, hailed a cab.

'Where to?' he asked as I climbed in.

'Covent Garden,' I blurted, thinking only as far ahead as finding some other shoes and my date with Kyle later this evening. We were meeting early at Christopher's, his favourite bar near the Opera House. He hadn't said why, but he loved to surprise me, so I hadn't asked. At least there was that.

But the closer we got as the taxi wound through the congested streets, thrumming with purposeful people, the more uneasy I felt. Somehow, I couldn't imagine telling him about what'd just happened, couldn't picture his reaction.

By the time the cab dropped me off outside the Zara on Long Acre, my stomach was a butterfly-ridden mess. Kyle was the life and soul of every situation, his easy, roguish charm and lazy smile turning every female head. I'd been one of them, a year or so after I'd arrived in London, fresh from uni. Introduced by a mutual friend in one of the City bars, we'd immediately hit it off. In fact, I couldn't think of a situation where we'd had to navigate something like this until now, approaching our one-year anniversary.

I walked into the store, scouting for shoes but my mind churning. Ignoring the niggling voice in the back of it, I called the one person I knew would say exactly what I needed to hear, however hard that was.

'It's me,' I said as the ringtone cut and she picked up. I kept my voice low amongst the few tourists shopping around me. 'I've just been made redundant.'

There was a pause, then what could only be described as a high-pitched yell, then a celebratory cackle.

'You're free! Ding dong the fucking witch is dead!' Hestia exclaimed. A murmur of voices in the background and some obscure indie EDM confirmed that she was at work. Recently qualified as a tattoo artist and with an attitude as bold as her designs, she'd just taken the plunge and opened her own studio. 'Oh Lots, I know you're probably feeling gutted but honestly, I couldn't be happier. That boss of yours – what was her name? Cretin? Whatever – she was a fucking asshat, and the hours they made you work were insane. Are you freaking out yet or are you doing that weird stoic, icy-calm thing you do?'

'Icy-calm,' I replied, hearing how dull and blank I sounded compared to Hestia's natural effervescence.

She laughed, then apologized to someone in the background.

'Listen, I'm mid-ink – let's meet up later? I've got a client until seven-ish, but dinner after, maybe? Or come to mine?'

Suddenly wishing I could ditch my date with Kyle to cry and

bitch about Cressida with Hestia, I told her I wouldn't be able to make it.

'Well, tomorrow then?' she replied, as the buzz of her needle started up. 'Or if the surprise date is boring you to death at the bloody opera again then develop a headache and come over here, okay?'

'Got it. Thanks, Hes,' I said, fighting back a fresh wave of tears. 'Thanks. I knew you'd say the right thing.'

'Listen, chin up for now and save your breakdown for me – you know I love pretending to use my useless degree. Love you, Lots. It'll all be okay. Worst comes to worst, you can be my coffee bitch instead.'

I hiccupped a laugh, lovingly telling her to fuck off as I hung up. Pouncing on a pair of soft-looking ballet flats in my size, I was hit once again by our random but fortuitous meeting on campus at Bristol uni. It had been simultaneously one of the most mortifying yet most wonderful moments of my life, and as I paid for the shoes and wandered back out onto the street, I lost myself to the memory. To when, in a desperate bid to meet people and fit in, I'd been persuaded to assist the student union with promoting safe sex in freshers' week.

Handing out condoms on campus.

Dressed *as* a giant condom.

Hestia, already the ringleader, had rounded the corner of the library with a new group of friends from halls, and, unable to see properly out of the costume, I'd promptly tripped right over her feet.

She'd stumbled, landing on top of me as condom packets rained down on us like confetti from the bucket I'd been holding.

'Oh fuck,' I'd groaned as we untangled ourselves, listening to the laughter around us, other students stopping to survey the chaos. I could feel my mortification growing with every second, the only crumb of comfort in the anonymity of the costume.

There was a pause and her head turned from me as she sat up and shook out her long black hair, strands of flamingo pink peeking out from underneath. My instant impression was that of meeting Goth Barbie, with stunning blue-green eyes and full lips, both painted black, the freckles smattering her nose over-emphasized with eyeliner.

'Good job you were wearing protection,' she murmured, turning to me with barely concealed amusement, those bright eyes sparkling in a way that would for ever come to define her in my mind.

I couldn't help it – I snorted with laughter, the shit joke and ridiculous situation fully dawning on us both.

She joined in, shoulders shaking as I tried, fruitlessly, to wriggle into a seated position, which only resulted in me producing a demented breakdance move on the concrete.

'Oh God, stop,' she gasped, tears gathering. 'I can't breathe, I'm going to piss myself.'

Caught between mild hysteria and utter humiliation, I tried, one more time, to roll onto my side and bring my legs up.

'What the fuck is going on?' a male voice said, vaguely registering as the student union supervisor for the campaign. 'If you've damaged that costume, you'll have to pay for it.'

'Here,' said Hestia, still laughing, a warm, firm hand gripping mine. 'One, two . . . and up.'

I tried to steady myself, but ended up wobbling into her again, causing us both to giggle again alongside the fresh peals of laughter from the people around us, mercifully hidden from my view.

'Sorry,' I replied.

'Are you serious? What the fuck for? I haven't laughed this much since my dog dry-humped our local MP on national TV.' She arranged the eyeholes in the costume to align with my actual eyes. 'True story. I'm Hestia, by the way.'

'Lottie.' I blushed.

The supervisor had approached and was standing over us, open exasperation on his face. 'Are you drunk or something? Get the costume off and take it back to the union. I haven't got time for this.'

But before I could answer that I was not nearly as drunk as I wanted to be right now, Hestia stuck out her hip, eyebrow raised.

'Here,' she said, scooping a couple of condom packets off the ground and pressing them into his hand as he stared, eyes widening. 'Sounds like you could do with getting laid. Chill the fuck out, bro. It was an accident, she could've hurt herself – isn't it your job to make sure she's safe while she's carrying out work on behalf of the student union?'

'Fucking preach,' I agreed, my voice muffled inside the condom.

Before he could reply, she'd served the most imperious glance I'd ever witnessed, then put her arm around my shoulders and helped me shuffle towards the nearest toilets, thankfully just inside the library building.

'What a prick,' she huffed, not bothering to keep her voice down, attracting yet more stares before we finally reached safety. I directed her to the zip at the back of the costume and emerged a minute later, sweaty and ruffled, my cheeks pink. 'Huh,' she added as I adjusted my T-shirt. 'How the fuck do you look like that after rolling around in a giant condom?'

I frowned, glancing from her surprise to the mirror.

'What do you mean?' I asked, seeing only a humiliated mess, my curls in a nest, last night's mascara now smudging in the corners of my eyes.

She ignored me, tilting her head for a second.

'You're not gay, are you?' she asked, as simply and honestly as if she was asking me whether I took milk in my tea.

I smiled, liking this girl more and more each second.

'Sadly not,' I replied, trying to comb through my hair with my fingers, making it worse if anything.

'Worth a shot.' She shrugged, arranging herself in the mirror too. 'I'm bi, mostly guys so far, but . . .' Her eyes flicked to mine, assessing me, before creasing as she smiled. 'Well, if you're sure. Friends it is.'

'Did I hurt you at all? Are you sure you're okay?' I asked, gathering up the wretched costume and checking for rips. Thankfully there were none; a welcome result given the state of my bank balance.

'No, I'm not,' she replied, helping me with the costume and then linking her arm through mine as we carried it back out. 'We need to go out and get wasted. Immediately.'

I laughed, her carefree vibe contagious. We walked over to the student union, my old, yard-worn trainers falling into step with her battered DMs.

'Okay, okay, but one of the nasty, cheap bars — I haven't got much at the moment. I need to get a job—'

'Oh, do fuck off,' she said, patting my hand as we ceremonially dumped the costume inside the reception area. 'With a face and body like yours? We're not paying.'

And before I could scoff at her imagined success, within the next twenty minutes we were deep into the first of many free drinks of the evening.

That night, we told each other everything, from my struggle with this first week of city life, to her true passion for art and tattoos, some distance from her choice of a psychology degree. My choice of business intrigued her, and she frowned as she tried to connect her building impression of me, a clumsy ex-condom with a passion for horses and books, with spreadsheets and suits instead.

But unlike our choice of studies, those early moments of our friendship felt just right; like a padlock, opening to the only correct combination in 40,000 variations. We were the right answer, the satisfying click.

I realized now, some six years later, how far removed from that sensation every decision since then had felt.

———

The rest of the day passed in a hazy fog. I gave myself chores, taking myself from minute to minute, hour to hour, knowing I just had to last until five thirty. First, I found a chemist and patched my foot up properly, then a hairdresser with a free slot to wash and blow-dry my hair, and tame the chaotic curls into something sleeker. I browsed in a bookshop for longer than I ever usually allowed myself to do, buying a new romance by an author currently blowing up on social and settled into a nearby café to read. I just needed to make it until Kyle arrived. Then I could forget it all for a while.

Except, by the time five thirty rolled around, the soft light of early evening casting shadows across the cobbles, my nerves were jangling. I'd done what I could to look good at least, and I'd even rehearsed how to tell him what'd happened. But the moment his long, lean frame strode into view, hand sweeping back his burnished blond hair, I chickened out.

'Have you been waiting long?' he said, swooping down to press his lips onto mine, the sun catching the green flecks in his hazel eyes. 'I got away as soon as I could. Bit of a heavy lunch, if you know what I mean.' He winked. 'You know how Henry necks Bolly like it's Evian.' I smiled, suddenly unsure of what to do or say, the weight of my news flattening my words. 'Christ, what's with the shoes?' he added, standing back, face aghast. 'Thought you were wearing the new ones? Doesn't do your legs many favours – you know how I love your legs.'

I opened my mouth to explain, protest – anything – but, hand on my elbow, he propelled me inside the bar with him, his other hand giving my ass a squeeze.

'Listen, I've got a confession,' he began, a sheepish smile breaking out that melted my growing irritation. He was somehow still tanned from his family's Easter skiing trip, and his chiselled profile and sharp suit were utterly distracting. Dimples formed and his eyes lit up as he recognized my expression. My heart gave a stutter, not ready for another surprise today. 'We can absolutely get some drinks, but we're being gate-crashed, I'm afraid – and then I've been roped into dinner with Henry et al. Some of our US partners have flown in today and we've got to show them the town, the usual.'

I raised my eyebrows.

'Gate-crashed?' I asked, looking around, but not seeing anyone we knew. The bar was filling up with pre-theatre drinkers, loud, braying voices and the clink and pop of champagne flutes and bottles.

'Ma and Pa,' he replied quickly, raising a hand towards the bar staff before I could reply. He ordered for us, his pedantic choices – 'No, not Gordon's, Christ – Hendrick's. And no lemon for her – no, the chilled glasses' – earning him sidelong glances from the group nearest to us. The two women had already gone from listening to his order to outright ogling.

I felt myself sink even lower. There was no way I could tell him about the job now – the thought of it being picked over by his parents was more painful than the damn heels had been.

'Right, okay,' I sighed, leaning on the bar and recalibrating. 'When are they getting—'

'Daaarling!'

A shrill voice echoed behind us and as Kyle handed me a martini, he was enveloped by his mother. Marina Montgomery was . . . a special breed of woman. 'Christ alive, the devil literally does wear Prada,' Hestia had hissed to me once on meeting her.

'Do you think they insert the sticks up that type early on, or is it something that happens once they get married?'

As I took a laboured sip of my drink, Marina turned to me.

'Oh Charlotte, how lovely,' she said, stooping slightly from her heels to kiss the air near my cheeks, her own height dwarfing me. She wrapped her bony fingers around my arms, the cloud of Chanel Nº 5 that surrounded her threatening to choke off my air supply.

'What a nice surprise,' I lied, plastering my corporate smile back on, replicating the greeting with Dominic. A thirty-year window into Kyle's future, his father had almost the same hair, now receding and as grey as it was blond. The same handsome face beheld us both, eyes crinkling.

'Looking smart, old chap,' he said to Kyle, shaking his hand. He beckoned the bar staff with the same gesture as Kyle had used.

'Oh yes, I do like this,' Marina added, French tips grazing the lapels of Kyle's jacket. Standing between us, her body was angled towards him as if to cut me out.

'Lottie chose it,' he said, giving me a dazzling smile, working hard to keep me onside, knowing just how little I would be enjoying the presence of the gate-crashers.

Marina turned to smile at me, but it didn't reach her eyes. I braced myself.

'Oh . . . yes,' she replied, glancing at my handbag before looking back at Kyle. 'Excellent taste, clearly. Expensive, too.' They tittered at her joke, my excellent choice of boyfriend. My smile felt fixed, as though held by setting spray. 'Just as it should be. Nothing wrong with aiming high, is there, Charlotte?'

And there it was.

If passive-aggressive digs were a sport, Marina would be the most decorated Olympian of the last millennium. I took a gulp of the martini, accidentally finishing it.

'Steady on, old girl,' Dominic guffawed. 'Quick out of the blocks, I see. Rough day at the office?'

I nodded, placing my glass on the bar for the staff to take away. Kyle's expression was quizzical.

'So where are you going this evening?' I deflected, turning towards Dominic instead.

'Oh, don't ask me, I'm just the passenger. What is it, Marina? *Carmen*? Imagine I'll be asleep by the interval.'

'*La traviata*,' Marina corrected as Kyle handed her a glass of champagne. 'At the Royal Opera House, of course. Didn't you go recently, darling?'

She turned to Kyle and the conversation switched to the performance we'd seen on our date the previous month. As they went into detail about the singers, then on a tangent to people they knew – some story about a yacht sinking off the coast of Italy – I subtly fished my phone out of my bag.

PLEASE tell me you can still do dinner later? I messaged Hestia, waiting for her reply, but knowing she'd be unlikely to respond whilst with her client.

'. . . I mean I know it's terrible,' Marina said, hushing her voice. 'But really, it's all so gauche, isn't it, flitting about on these boats. Asking for it, if you ask me.'

Kyle nodded, but his eyes were on me, his unspoken question about my rough day as clear as Marina's hatred of me. My crime had been and would always be the difference in our backgrounds, my ordinary, middle-class family, attendance at a state school and absolutely no friends or family of 'note'.

As I watched Marina drone on, her face merged with Cressida's in my mind. The martini swirled my emotions.

'Sorry to interrupt,' I blurted. Marina turned to me in barely concealed astonishment. 'I'm afraid I'm going to need to run.' Kyle frowned, his mouth opening. 'Dinner with my friend, I completely forgot,' I added, before he could continue.

'At least finish your drink?' Dominic started, placing another martini in front of me. 'Shame to—'

Fighting back temper, tears, a whole vortex of chaos in my mind, I picked up the fine crystal stem and knocked it back in one.

Marina's mouth fell open in tandem with Kyle's.

'Great to see you,' I said to no one in particular, placing the glass down carefully and backing away.

'Lottie?' Kyle said, stepping out of his mother's clutches. 'What—'

'I'll call you tomorrow,' I replied as I turned and walked out, breaking into a run as I hit the pavement and taking an immediate left around the back in case Kyle tried to follow me.

Fuck, fuck, *fuck*.

YES! Get over here now, was Hestia's reply to my message as I checked my phone, almost breaking into a sob as I reached the tube. My hot tech start-up guy is here and I'm tattooing his thigh. I should be live-streaming this on OnlyFans, I'd make a fucking fortune.

I all but ran into the station, relief at my escape mingling with dread. What the hell was I doing?

CHAPTER 3

The door to Hestia's studio, The Inky Hearth, was ajar when I arrived.

'Can I come in?' I shouted, checking my face in my compact mirror one last time. Reapplying make-up on the tube was not my forte. I scrubbed at a smudge of eyeliner, sighing.

'Yep, we're in the back,' she replied, the whirr of the needle just audible over the music. *Nine Inch Nails*, I thought, remembering it from our time as roommates.

The interior was as moody and intense as the song, the walls a deep blue-black, contrasting with the vibrant pinks of the Japanese cherry-blossom mural surrounding the window opposite, a train rattling over the tracks behind. The studio fitted right into Shoreditch, the edgy other end of the spectrum to my City world of marble, suits and fake smiles. I realized I was at home in neither, my own corner of London yet to be revealed to me, if it ever would be. Perhaps my mum had been right: you can take a girl out of the country . . .

Through the doorway into the second room, Hestia looked up and smiled.

'Scott, this is my friend Lottie, the hot one I was telling you about.'

She winked, but before I could scowl, I realized what was

underneath her arm. A very round, sculpted butt-cheek clad in tight boxers.

'Hello hot Lottie,' he replied, face down in the black leather, his voice muffled against the bed. 'Don't mind my ass.'

'Bloody hell,' I muttered, trying to look anywhere except the bed as Hestia laughed. I didn't think of myself as prudish, but around Hestia I sometimes felt like Mother Teresa.

'Heard you lost your job,' Scott said and my eyes narrowed. Hestia kept her eyes on his skin, the corners of her mouth uplifted.

'Mm-hmm,' I replied, determined not to discuss my life with a stranger, even if he did have a peachy ass.

'Come work for me,' he offered, trying to turn his head so he could face me. His hair was long, a deep brown, almost black, like mine. 'What do you do? Marketing? Always need decent marketing people.'

'You only employ hot women,' Hestia murmured, concentrating intently as she honed in on a detail. The tattoo was a snake, curled around some kind of foliage. 'Lottie's too good for you. Definitely hot enough, but way out of your league.'

He snorted.

'I've sued people for saying less, you know,' he replied, still trying to turn to look at me. 'I mean, you're right, I do, but still.'

'And I could be very tempted to change this design into a pig,' replied Hestia, nudging him as she sat up for a moment, straightening her back. Bright cherry-red hair spilled over her shoulders; her kohl-lined blue-green eyes sparkled. 'Keep still – one last bit and we're done for today. I need to take Lottie out and get her wasted.'

Exhaustion suddenly threatened to take over and I grabbed the spare chair next to the other, empty bed. Hestia glanced over at me, her eyes reading my expression in seconds. The smile from their banter still on her lips, she leant towards Scott again, touching the needle to his skin, focusing intently for a few seconds.

'There, all good. Outline's done – only one more session now.'

I watched as she packed away and Scott shifted, stretching. I realized how much I wished I could be as easy with people as she was, to be able to be myself, even at work. My work clothes felt like a cage, the ends of my hair as limp and frazzled as my thoughts.

'Hi,' Scott said, looking up at me. 'She's right. You're gorgeous, Lottie – nice to meet you.'

I shook my head, trying not to blush.

'Thanks. I'll umm . . . wait out there,' I replied, catching Hestia's eye and mentally threatening all the ways I would make her pay for this.

Their combined laughter, although not unkind, only served to dampen my mood further. My phone buzzed.

I'm so sorry about tonight, Kyle's message read. I swear I'll make it up to you. Date to end all dates next week? Are you sure you're okay?

I stared at the screen, my thumb hovering over the reply but typing nothing. His second message followed. I'll call you tomorrow, get some sleep. Love you x

'Right, let's get you drunk,' Hestia announced as she strode in, Scott following. 'And no, you're not invited, Scott. We need to discuss your exposed ass in private.'

———

Guilt surged as Hestia brought over a third round of drinks, tongue sticking out of the corner of her mouth in concentration. Her ripped Fleetwood Mac T-shirt, black denim shorts, fishnets and silver Doc Martens fitted this place perfectly, one of the last genuinely grungy bars in a street otherwise swallowed whole by gentrification.

'You should have seen me with Kyle's parents, Hes. I downed my martini. Not a dainty sip, I knocked the whole thing back, all £20 of it. Marina almost had an aneurysm.'

Hestia barked a laugh, handing me a long glass and clinking hers against it.

'Fucking right, that woman would turn anyone to hard drinking. Listen, you've got to stop beating yourself up about acting the way you feel – it's totally justified! You got made redundant from that place, despite all your hard work, and then that bitch turns up and begins the pass-agg parade. I'm just pissed you didn't throw it in her smug face.'

I knew she was right, but I felt stifled. I can't upset Kyle's mum without upsetting him and after his message, I was starting to feel like a complete ass for behaving as I had.

'I couldn't even tell him about the job,' I replied, sipping on my drink, pulling a face at the paint-stripping gin. 'Totally chickened out. And not just because his parents were there. I just couldn't picture his reaction, you know? I think part of the reason he's with me is because I'm on an ambitious career path, like him. Or at least I was. What's he going to say when I tell him I couldn't get a year beyond the bloody graduate scheme?'

Hestia pursed her lips, a sure sign she was keeping her thoughts to herself. For once.

'Look. You know I'm not Kyle's biggest fan,' she began carefully, waving away my narrowing eyes, 'but he's clearly into you, right? It's been, what, a year now? In all likelihood he'll be supportive. I mean, his lot are all nepo babies – he's more likely to get you a better job at his dad's firm than judge you. Everyone's either screwing the boss or their son in that world. Come on, tell me I'm wrong.'

She raised her eyebrows above her own drink, daring me to disagree. A flash of light from the dancefloor highlighted the tattoo on her neck, flames licking up to her jaw, as though her passion had burnt through and branded her skin.

I couldn't disagree. She was right, as usual.

And it made me queasy.

'What about you and Cal?' I asked, deflecting. She smiled, but let me get away with it. The complexities around her on/off boyfriend and business partner could've filled a week's worth of conversation, and I felt bad that, what with my recent schedule and Kyle, I hadn't asked her about it lately.

She shrugged, crimson lips pursing. That was the first hint of her true feelings; the hesitation and sip of her drink were the next. Hestia was easily the most open, blunt and big-hearted person I'd ever met, but when it came to the really deep feelings, the ones that mattered the most, she kept those well guarded.

'Oh fuck, I don't know,' she sighed. 'I love him, I do. We've been together so long now, he feels more like an extension of myself, you know? But . . . maybe it's because we're in business, running the studio, living together . . .' She tailed off, sipping again when she couldn't express what she felt.

'You're a long way from the reason you got together, right?' I offered, watching as she held my eyes, considering. 'It's not exactly romantic, is it? Working 24/7 and having to live other roles before being a couple. You need more connection than that, Hes.'

'Lottie Wright, you're an old soul,' she replied after a pause, her voice gentler. 'Sure you don't fancy a gay awakening with me?'

I laughed, half spraying her with my drink at our longstanding banter. I'd never let her forget that she'd all but propositioned me in the toilets, when I was still half dressed as a condom. She'd repeated it at least once a year since, usually saving it for the least appropriate moments, for maximum reaction.

'Girl, your mighty rack is wasted on me,' I smirked, saluting her chest. 'But I will always love you more than anyone else ever can.'

She smiled, fading as her face became serious again.

'How do we know when it's right? In a relationship, I mean?' she asked, staring at her drink, swilling the contents. 'Does anyone ever really know when they've met someone they love? Or if they're fucking *in love*, whatever that is? Sometimes I feel like

Cal and I were just all fire and passion to begin with – I mean, Jesus, we didn't stop fucking for a solid month,' she noted, smiling briefly at my look, the one that confirmed I'd heard most of it in the next-door bedroom. 'But it all just went so fast, and with the end of uni . . . Maybe if we'd met at a different time, had had less pressure to make a call on the future . . .'

I put my hand on hers. 'What are you always telling me? What's for you will find you. Right? Like this bullshit with my job. If you and Cal are meant to be, then that's how it'll turn out. And I guess, maybe, if you find love, a soulmate, whatever the fuck you want to call it, you'll know.'

We both realized it at the same moment. That if what I'd just said was true, then the only relationship either of us could apply it to was our own.

'Fuck.' Hestia sighed, offering her glass up to mine again. We clinked and then both took an overly large gulp. 'Well, however things pan out, at least you don't have to work with Kyle.'

'True,' I agreed. Then, 'I'm just going to have to apply to a load of other places,' I went on, inwardly groaning at the thought of completing application forms and revamping my CV.

'There's always Scott,' she replied, smiling. 'Nice ass, right?'

I tried not to return the smile and failed.

Hestia squeezed my arm. 'It'll all work out. You like the actual marketing side of it, so maybe look out for a job in a more interesting industry? Become an influencer!'

She slapped the table as though some kind of epiphany had blasted through her thoughtful reverie.

'Yes! Oh my God, Lots, I could SO see you doing that – you're Insta perfect, you know what you're doing, always immaculate . . . there'll be a ton of brands that'll want your face plugging their stuff. Do it!'

My heart lifted at her enthusiasm, her crooked grin and wide eyes.

'Thanks,' I said quietly, my voice almost lost under the music and the voices in the bar. 'You're the best.'

'I know,' she giggled, reaching over and kissing my cheek. 'Why don't you go over to Kyle's place, get it off your chest and tell him you'll be making millions by the summer flogging beauty products? Plus, you'll very likely get laid too and frankly, you could do with it.'

I broke, dissolving into alcohol-giggles, leaning on her arm as I tried to stand.

'Okay, okay, enough. I'll do it.'

'Atta girl,' she replied, gripping me with equal fervour as we swayed over to the door. 'He's not my type but I've got eyes. I bet he looks even better with his suit off. Go enjoy yourself.'

We walked our separate ways, the impression of her warmth lingering as I attempted to keep a reasonably straight line down the road. As the length of my journey to Kyle's place in Battersea dawned on me, I turned and lifted my arm to hail a cab – then lowered it a second later. I was unemployed; time to act like it.

Back on the tube, I wound my way back west, gently numb thanks to the alcohol. Vaguely I thought about food but dismissed it. What I needed was support, arms to lean into and take the weight. By the time I reached Kyle's road, a solid twenty-minute walk from the station, my feet were on fire and the slow throb of a headache was beginning to pound behind my eyes.

The tall, Edwardian terrace glowed white in the amber lamplight, each house slightly different but all well kept. Neatly trimmed trees and ornately tiled paths led up to every one, millions of pounds' worth of cars lining either side of the road. As I drew closer to Kyle's house, a graduation gift from his grandparents, I craned my head to check for lights on inside. None.

Steeling myself, I opened the gate and walked to the front door, heart sinking. Shit. He was still out. Checking my phone and noting the time – 11.43 p.m. – I paused. He was always saying how he was useless after eleven anyway, and with work tomorrow, it wouldn't be long until he was back.

Sighing, I lowered myself onto the steps by his front door and sat there in the shadows trying, for the millionth time, not to feel bitter or paranoid about my lack of key. It was a small thing, but somehow it mattered more than I wanted to admit. And now, alone in the creeping cold with my head and heart wrung out, it loomed over me: the memory of offering my key to him, feeling as vulnerable and small as it was possible to feel, the fleeting panic in his expression that he tried so desperately to hide.

He'd explained, reasoned it out, even become tearful about his own fears around commitment, the significance of giving me a key. And somehow, for reasons now buried or unreachable in the back of my mind, I'd let it go. He cared for me and that was enough; his gifts and gestures were relentless proof.

'Christ, what did he do?' was all Hestia could say when it began with the first designer handbag, then the ridiculously over-the-top bracelet from Boodles.

I'd rolled my eyes, both of us all too aware where Hestia's deep-seated prejudices came from – a rocky upbringing, her mum bullied and coerced by Hestia's stepfather. It coloured her view of relationships, especially given her bisexuality. As far as Hestia was concerned, women were far superior and many straight men were the lowest of the low, to be trusted only in exceptional circumstances.

Stifling a jaw-cracking yawn, I pulled my knees in and rested my chin on them. So much had shifted in the last twenty-four hours. Kyle would be home soon, he might even be in a cab right now. As my eyelids drifted shut, the sound of sirens in the distance and strains of music from the pub at the end of the road lulled my consciousness into sleep.

———

The laugh was bright, a peal of bells in the silence. My tiredness fought it, but the chilled night air prickled my skin, forcing my eyes open. A jolt of pain through my neck, the product of my awkward slump against the wall, yanked me into reality.

Swearing to myself, I checked my phone.

2.45 a.m.

I frowned, blinking at the screen, holding it closer as though the numbers would suddenly make sense. How the hell was it almost 3 a.m. and he wasn't home?

A second, deeper laugh sent an entirely new sensation across my skin, hairs rising as my eyes widened.

I tried to stand, legs wobbling as I rose. Reaching out to place my hand against the wall, I craned my head to see down the street.

There, walking towards the house, was Kyle.

One arm thrown casually around a woman's shoulders, her long blonde hair spilling over his chest, his other hand reaching over to her smiling face, pulling her chin up towards him as he leant in to kiss her.

I forgot how to breathe, my fingers turning into claws against the cold bricks. Instinct propelled me forwards, away from the front door and down the side of the house, into the narrow passage between the wall and hedge. Deep shadows held me as my insides threatened to fall apart.

Their sounds mingled as they reached the path, the words and footsteps blurring together over the thundering of my heart. I let myself fall into a crouch, unable to draw enough breath to stay standing.

'. . . I don't know, oh God, maybe it's in my other bag. I couldn't bring it though, they'd know . . .'

Her voice was velvet, a silky American undertone with British pronunciation. Kyle laughed again.

'Here it is,' he said, a softness to his words that punched my gut.

Risking discovery but unable to stop myself, I peered around the house. They stood just off the street, using the nearby street-light to look into her handbag. Smiling, eyebrow arched, Kyle drew out a key.

Her key.

To his house.

She shook her head as he kissed her nose, the intimacy of the moment yanking me back into the shadows with a ferocity that shocked me.

'Thank you, baby,' she whispered as they drew closer, their soles shuffling on the steps. Blankly I wondered if I'd left anything of mine in the house, whether they'd see it. Whether it would matter. 'At least I left my pyjamas from last time, huh?'

'No need for those,' he growled as the scrape and click of her key pushed into the lock. 'Completely superfluous.'

She giggled as the door opened, light from the hall lamp spilling out onto the path. I caught her perfume then, as recognizable as the need in his voice, the expression I knew he would be wearing. His fingers would brush her hips or waist, his eyes already making light work of any buttons.

Chanel N° 5.

The same scent his mother wore.

A savage urge to laugh overwhelmed me and I bit down on my fist to stop it. I pictured telling Hestia, forced her face into my mind instead, her reaction. *That guy is such a fucking basic Freudian stereotype.* Anything to not be here, the interloper in the dark, hiding like a frightened animal.

The door slammed shut, cutting it all off. The light, their words, her smell.

I kept my fist in my mouth as the tears fell freely, running across my fingers and pooling at my wrist.

My knees protested, their stress overwhelming the rest of me. Pulling myself up, my fingernails digging into the brick, I realized I couldn't feel the cold any more at least. But standing in the shadows, looking out at the street, a bigger realization threatened to make me feel everything all at once. The sheer scale of rejection in only twenty-four hours.

'No,' I said to myself, jumping at the sound in the quiet. I refused to process all of this now.

New plan. More alcohol.

Maybe some fried chicken.

As I walked out of the shadows, across the path, I knew full well that Kyle would be way too busy to look out of the front windows and see me. I paused, turning onto the street, resisting one last look at the house I was never quite let into.

Icy-calm mode activated once again, I cut the shortest possible path to the nearest twenty-four-hour store, the only thing now open. Their selection of alcohol was unbearably *Kyle*. The wines I'd seen in his rack, Bollinger and Pol Roger behind the counter; even the small German beers he preferred. So I chose the cheapest, least Kyle thing I could see: a small bottle of tequila.

Walking slowly down empty streets, sipping and wincing intermittently as the tequila scorched a path down my throat, my subconscious whispered words of warning. Alone at this time of the morning, barely anyone around . . . A bus stop came into view, the number of the bus that went right past my flat due to arrive. Three women were perched on the plastic bench already, chatting and laughing. I gave into the sensible half of my brain and walked up to it, keeping my head down and staying back. Within seconds their noise had petered out.

'You all right, babe?'

I looked up, just as the bus rolled into view. One of the women stepped towards me, her frown marring her immaculate make-up, a black silk bomber jacket over a denim jumpsuit. Her two friends hung back, concern on their faces too.

'Umm, yeah,' I mumbled, wondering if my mascara had run. Quickly swiping my finger under my eyes, I realized my whole face was wet, that I had somehow been crying without realizing. As the bus arrived, they went back to their conversation and we all boarded, finding seats as the driver pulled away. Sitting a few rows in front of them, I felt their eyes on me between the snippets of their conversation as the bus looped through the south London streets, finally trundling along my road. I pressed the bell to get off, risking a glance at the girls as I stood, the sway of my movements not entirely due to the bus.

A small smile was on the jumpsuit girl's face. Not one of judgement, just concern.

I tried to smile back, but my face crumpled. Tasting tears, I stepped off into the dark as the bus roared away, the warmth of the fumes dissipating into silence. Crossing the road to my flat, I realized that it was likely the first kind gesture without motive that I'd experienced from anyone, other than Hestia, in weeks. Months.

The life I'd thought I'd built here no longer existed.

It was empty. Just like my heart.

CHAPTER 4

It wasn't until I was on my second peppermint tea, a dry cracker from an hour earlier apparently staying down for now, that I felt brave enough to make a call.

As the phone began to ring at the other end, I rubbed my temples, closing my eyes to the weak sunlight filtering in through my kitchen blinds.

'Oh, hey honey,' my mum said as she picked up, surprise in her tone. Her soft American accent, chiselled away by over thirty years in the UK, always sent me straight back to my childhood. 'This is a nice surprise! I thought you'd be at work. Are you having a day off?'

I bit my lip, realizing how long it had been since we'd spoken. Really spoken.

'Hi . . . yeah, sort of.'

My voice wobbled and I kicked myself.

'What's going on? Are you okay?'

I could picture her in our family home, likely on the small floral sofa in the kitchen-diner, a coffee on Grandma's old side table to her left, her Kindle or a newspaper to her right. The radio would be on, Radio 4 at this time of day – she loved *Woman's Hour*.

'Umm . . . no, not really,' I whispered, a thick sob rising up and spilling out. 'I've been made redundant. I don't have to work my notice period, so I'm just at home.'

'Oh sweetie, I'm so sorry. What happened? Listen, do you want to come home for a while? Your dad's on the tour in Augusta until tomorrow evening, so it's just me for now.'

My dad's role as an official on the pro-golf tour in the US meant that he was often away for long periods. Her implication rang clear in the brief pause, that whilst she only wanted my happiness, visiting home when Dad was away would mean avoiding his disappointment, the inevitable judgement. My career success was a source of huge pride to him, but it came at a cost. I often wondered whose ambition it actually was that'd landed me here, how what I wanted and what he demanded had somehow converged into the same thing. The thought of breaking the news about Kyle would be too much. My parents thought the sun was located directly up his ass.

Hesitating, I realized I should've thought this through before calling. But other than Hestia, who rarely got up before midday, who else did I have? I'd slid further away from my wider circle of friends in the last year, almost every waking hour occupied with work or Kyle and his mates.

'Okay, yeah, maybe. I mean, I need to look for something else pretty quickly – this place is expensive, so . . .'

'I know, I know,' she replied, the sound of the kettle boiling in the background muffling her words. 'But you can give yourself a few days to get over the shock and put a plan together. Why don't you come over? Archie will make you feel better.'

I wiped my eyes, almost smiling at the thought of their mildly insane spaniel, the way he would wriggle all over with excitement to see me, then spend the rest of the day trying to sleep in my lap.

'Okay, let me sort a few bits out and I'll check the train times,' I replied, listening to another few minutes of her pep talk before hanging up.

Groaning, realizing what I might've signed myself up for, I called Hestia.

'I thought you loved me,' she said, groggy and hoarse. 'This is just cruel.'

I checked the time, suddenly wondering if I'd somehow misread my phone before. No, it was 10.27.

'Kyle's been cheating,' I blurted, even though the sound of his name burnt my tongue as it left my mouth. 'He brought a woman home to his place last night; they were all over each other.'

'What the FUCK?' she suddenly roared as my eyes filled again. I laid my phone on the table and pressed my palms to them. 'Right. I'll go over to his work right now and tear him a fresh one—'

I hiccupped under the tears and she paused.

'Lottie Wright, you listen to me right now. Neither of these things are about you, okay? Kyle is a dickwad – always has been, always will be – and your job can and absolutely will be replaced. That's just business. This doesn't define you; they are NOT the sum of your existence. It's just the universe's way of clearing the path for you to find the things you actually need in your life. Okay?'

'Okay,' I repeated, voice on autopilot. 'It's just . . . I don't understand why? Kyle, I mean. Cressida just hated me. But he and this woman . . . they'd clearly been together a while – she had a key, for fuck's sake . . .'

My words trailed into incoherence and I let her rant in reply, the acerbic curses somehow forming a thin film over the wounds, a temporary patch.

'And now Mum's suggesting I come home and I just don't know if I can deal with the judgement on top of it all. She means well, they both do, but they're so invested in everything I've done.'

The sacrifices they'd made for me to go to a private sixth form college, to pay my uni fees and living costs so I didn't have to take on a student loan. The weight of it all, of their expectations, and now . . . my utter failure.

'They're invested because they care, Lots. They'll back you all the way, always have done – even your dad.'

'But I've let them down,' I replied, my voice withering under the pressure. 'The job, Kyle . . . they were so happy. It was everything they wanted for me.'

'And what about you?' she said, her anger dissolving every last shred of tiredness. Her eyes would be blazing through their smudged black surrounds, I knew. 'What do *you* want? What does success on *your* terms look like?' I couldn't answer. Instead, I took the last sip of my tea, now cold. 'Look, I think some time to think might be a good thing. Get out of London – you know how you feel different in the countryside. Some clean air and a change of scenery will clear your mind in no time. Just take Archie out for loads of walks, avoid your parents if it gets too much. Or you can come here anytime, you know that, but Cal has been on a three-day bender and this place looks like a black hole.'

I actually smiled.

'Jesus,' I replied, picturing the scene she was currently stumbling through, swearing as she tripped over something. For all their issues together, Cal was one of the nicest, but also messiest people I'd ever known. In every sense.

'He'll be fucking needing a saviour if he doesn't pull it together soon. I'm not built for domesticity and somehow he's forcing me to become some kind of fucking clean-freak mother hen.'

'Now you mention it, maybe the countryside is exactly what I need,' I said, biting my lip to stifle a laugh as she swore again. 'Thanks, Hes. I promise not to be a pathetic loser for too long.'

'Enough!' she barked. 'Leave the city now, you need some headspace. Call me when you're there. Okay? And no trash-talking yourself. I absolutely forbid it.'

I agreed, but as I hung up and the silence returned, the doubts immediately resurfaced. Was I just running away? Wouldn't it be better to stay here and face it? Try and talk to Kyle, maybe?

The thought of being face to face with him, the same hands

that'd grazed that woman's face last night being anywhere near me . . . A fresh wave of nausea rose up and I decided on a shower instead.

My phone screen lit up.

> Dad's actually going to be away for a while longer – he's dropping in to see Carrie on the way back home. It's her 60th, can you believe it? Not on the ranch, Lil's running that now. Carrie's in Denver. Anyway, more time for you, me and Archie. Love you, sweetie. It'll be okay. X

Feeling infinitesimally lighter, I climbed into the shower and attempted to scald the previous day away. The water engulfed me, a stark contrast to the feeling I'd had of being a dried-out husk, completely purged through tears and tequila.

I closed my eyes to it all, my mum's message suddenly bringing a memory to the surface. My cousin Lil and I, riding by a creek near the ranch she'd grown up on. In our grandma's family for a hundred years or so, the Diamond Back ranch was a few thousand acres on the edge of the Tetons, near Jackson Hole in Wyoming. My parents and I had been out there almost every summer when I was growing up, and Lil and I would spend our days riding for hours. One particular day by the creek, the sun beating down through the chill air to warm us, we almost rode straight into a grizzly bear, fishing further downstream.

My gasp had been swallowed by the sound of the water rushing past, frothy white waves rushing around boulders and rocks centre stream.

'Back up,' Lil said quietly. 'It hasn't seen us yet. We're upwind.'

In one lithe movement, she pulled out the shotgun from the holster on her saddle, swung it round into her right hand and pulled gently on Penny, her horse, to signal to her to walk backwards.

My heart thundered, wondering if my time was up. I was just eleven and Lil fifteen, but Lil just laughed quietly.

'What?' I hissed, incredulous.

'If you shit yourself on my new saddle, I'll feed you to the damn bear myself.'

Wide-eyed, I stared at her as we turned both horses in a smooth 180 and after a painful few seconds of walking until we'd rounded the corner, kicked them into a canter. As we approached the meadow beyond, Lil turned, first checking that the grizzly hadn't followed and then grinning at me as we slowed to a stop.

'You okay, cowgirl? Those pants dry?'

I was too full of adrenaline to scowl.

'Weren't you scared?' I asked, stroking my horse Jasper's neck, his black coat shining with health and, now, sweat. He pulled at the reins, wanting to keep going, clearly enjoying himself.

'Oh honey, that bear was just minding his business, he had no problem with us. C'mon now, you must've seen enough of the world to know that there's worse out there than a bear?'

Freckles dotted her tanned face and her hair was the colour of warm honey. She was only four years older than me, but had a lifetime's worth of wisdom already under her belt. The realities of helping her parents run a cattle ranch apparently taught more than my rural secondary school in England.

'Suppose so,' I replied, feeling embarrassment colour my cheeks.

'Hey,' she added, moving Penny over to me and reaching to squeeze my hand. 'I'm only messing. A summer here and we'll have those soft edges all roughened up, right?'

I smiled, trying to meet her eyes and squeezing back.

'You're a country girl, Lottie, I know it. You ride like you were born to it. You just need to get to know *this* country.' She gestured around at the snow-tipped, craggy peaks, the endless wilderness. 'She's the real main character here, you know? It ain't really about us.'

I nodded and, seemingly satisfied that I was no longer about to cry or ruin her saddle, Lil shifted Penny over to the left and raised an eyebrow.

'Race you back to the barn?'

Jasper's ears cocked, and he suddenly danced sideways as he saw Penny getting ready to leap forward, only Lil's expert skills preventing her from bolting.

'What do I win?' I laughed, now having to wage my own fight with Jasper's spirit.

'My eternal respect and maybe a trip into town to ride the rodeo bull at the Cowboy Bar?'

Before she had a chance to finish, I'd urged Jasper into a flat gallop, enjoying the flash of shock on her face before Penny followed. As I clutched my hat to my head with one hand and the reins in the other, we flew over the grass, the sun like a warm hand on my back.

The feeling was pure, unadulterated joy. The kind of freedom everyone dreamt of and few would ever really know.

And now, as I reached for my shampoo and started to scrub the last couple of days away, I couldn't remember the last time I'd felt that.

———

In a daze, I got busy with packing, rolling up what few casual clothes I had. Most of my wardrobe was corporate wear, a dismal selection of well-made suits in various shades of blue or grey, just one pair of overly white trainers amongst the heels. My stomach rumbled but I ignored it, not wholly trusting the contents to stay put just yet.

I checked train times, realizing that if I got my ass in gear, I could make it to Paddington to catch the 12.15. Suddenly, systematic, neat packing turned into chucking anything and everything into my small wheelie case, and as I calculated that one week might turn into two at my parents' place, I promptly emptied the sparse contents of my fridge into the bin, putting it outside. Eventually, my favourite Dior bag on my shoulder and my case at my feet, I stood at my front door. The silence was thick, broken only by the low hum of the fridge. Looking around, mentally checking off essentials I knew I couldn't forget, I was struck by the flat's emptiness. So few personal touches, so little life on display.

It was cold. A box, like many newbuild flats. But where others had made theirs home, mine was all hard surfaces, muted colours. Was this really me?

I shivered, quickly wheeling my case out into the hall and letting the deadlock click shut quietly. Calling the lift, I frowned at the carpet. Had they changed it? Since when had it been dark blue?

It wasn't until I'd emerged on the ground floor and made it outside that I realized. I rarely ever saw the carpet in the daylight. Leaving and returning in the dark in all but high summer meant I'd never really noticed its proper colour.

Shame crept over me as I walked slowly to the tube. Despite the trainers and a whole array of plasters, my feet stung and ached at every step. They were cut to ribbons, patched and cushioned but still in pain. Much like the rest of me.

My phone buzzed and I pulled it from my bag.

How about Saturday for dinner?
I'm still entertaining the American
clients for the next two days, but
free on the weekend. How was your
dinner last night? Hungover? x

Kyle.

Bile rose in my throat. If I'd had any doubts about leaving, wondering if I should stay and just carry on, maybe even try to talk to him and sort things out, they died in that moment.

Entertaining the American clients. Right.

Approaching the tube station, I did a quick mental calculation. These clients had become a feature of his life, what, three or four months ago? I'd met two of them, two men, at after-work drinks with Kyle's colleagues, but they'd mentioned there were another couple of people in the party.

The coincidence seemed too great. Whenever they came over, Kyle disappeared for days on end, was slow to respond to messages and dodged every attempt to arrange stayovers at his place.

Tears pricked under my eyelids again as I descended on the same escalator that'd carried me into a different life only yesterday.

I forced myself to breathe steadily, dabbing under my eyes at the make-up that *would* last for the whole damn day. Anger swelled and Hestia's words replayed in my head, her one long stream of profanities melding with my own thoughts. The platform was empty for once, and as the tube roared in, I yelled, opening a vent to the rage.

The carriage was mercifully empty too, and I spent the first few minutes forcing myself to do breathing exercises and trying to picture the fields surrounding my parents' home; the way the wind howled through the woods on top of the hill opposite. But somehow, the hill morphed into mountains. Huge, a thunderous grey against cerulean sky, pristine snow glimmering in the sunlight. The Rockies from my daydream, from my childhood.

Snapping my eyes open and leaning back in my seat, I focused on the tube map in front of me, next to the window opposite. I knew the route to Paddington without thinking, but just there, to the left of it, was Heathrow. Our trips to Wyoming had always started there, flying over to Denver first and then changing to a smaller plane for Jackson Hole.

As though conjured by my imagination, when the tube drew into the next station, three people stepped into my carriage, each hauling a large suitcase. A man, woman and teenage girl, all gratefully sitting down and chatting away with animated smiles.

The idea popped into my mind before I could even look away, London tube etiquette forgotten. In seconds my arms were covered in goosebumps, butterflies released in my stomach.

I should go. Back to Wyoming.

Stunned, I sat with the words clanging like a bell in the front of my mind.

The girl looked over, the intensity of my stare clearly making her uncomfortable. I gave a quick smile and looked away, back at the tube map again. Two more stops and I could change onto the Piccadilly and trundle all the way down to Heathrow.

Mind now racing, I reasoned I could afford the ticket; my carefully hoarded savings of the past year would barely be dented. I even had my passport in my bag, tucked into a travel case that I always took with me, alongside cash, railcards and various other travel necessities. But would Lil welcome me just turning up out of nowhere? I didn't even have her number. Mum would, but I wasn't sure if I could face a conversation with either of them.

'This is a do it first, apologize later thing.'

Kyle's well-used phrase arrived in my mind unbidden, and though it was possibly right in this case, the attitude behind them slotted in with last night with horrific ease.

I squeezed my eyes tight again, trying to force logical thought and reason. A week with my parents might help a little, but then, it might be stressful too. And after that week . . . well, I'd be heading straight back to London to pick up the pieces.

Maybe time away – truly away – would be better. Give me real time to think. Plus, I knew running a ranch was hard work – more hands were always better, and I could be free labour. My riding skills were a bit rusty, since I'd largely given it up ahead of uni, but they'd come back.

My heart leapt at the thought that Jasper might still be there, might still be able to enjoy me brushing his gleaming black coat, or scratching his neck in the place that made him doze off to sleep.

I was still hesitating as we reached the station where I'd need to change lines. The family got off instantly, wheels clattering down the platform.

Fuck it.

As the doors bleeped to warn of their closing, I leapt onto the platform and, filling up with adrenaline, followed the family down to the right platform and onto a Piccadilly line train. As always, now that the decision was made, I felt easier with myself. Now it was just a case of following through.

As the tube emerged overground, I was tempted to search for flights and get stuck into the logistics, but for once, I just let go. It would be what it was; there was no need to plan anything more just yet. Slipping on my headphones, I chose a random recent playlist and leant my head on the glass partition.

———

It wasn't until I stepped into the busy, voluminous space of Terminal 2 that reality dawned. I pulled my phone from my pocket and searched for flights, feeling a huge rush of satisfaction at finding two flights I could viably make this afternoon. The first was on Lufthansa, whose desks were almost opposite where I now stood.

Not quite believing I was going through with this, I approached the counter and just twenty minutes later, boarding pass in hand, I went through security. Walking out onto the other side, I felt as though I'd somehow shed my skin and was re-emerging as a slightly different version of myself, one I didn't know just yet.

Looking at my messages, I hovered over Hestia's name but stopped. She'd get a much bigger kick out of a call from the US. But Mum . . . I sighed. Like it or not, that needed to be a call right now.

'Slight change of plan,' I said sheepishly as she picked up. Hearing the change in my tone of voice, she waited for me to continue. 'I, umm . . . I'm not coming home today after all. I thought . . . well, I've decided to go on a bit of a trip. Please don't say anything to Carrie, or Lil, but . . .'

To my complete surprise, she chuckled.

'Oh baby girl, I wondered if you'd thought about it,' she replied, her Wyoming drawl suddenly ringing through loud and clear. My stunned silence prompted another soft laugh. 'Are you shocked that I'm not surprised? You might not be coming back to the home you grew up in, but it sounds like you've finally listened to your gut, huh? That ranch is as much your home, and your heart, as it was mine, Lottie. I saw how much you loved that place, how you opened up like one of those little summer meadow flowers when you were there.'

Mum sighed, the sound of life, of responsibilities and the past all bundled up in one sound.

'Yeah . . . I suppose,' I admitted. 'But I . . . I'm not that same person now. I don't know if it'll feel the same way as it did. But however it feels, it's a break from all the stuff here.' Mum hummed her agreement but added nothing else. 'And, if I'm honest, I'm not sure if I can handle Dad's . . . disappointment.'

'Oh honey.' Mum sighed again, deeper this time. 'I'm not gonna sugar-coat it, I can imagine his reaction too. But listen, this is about you, my darling. Not him. This is your life, not his, okay? Deep down he only wants the best for you, the same as I do. We've just got different ways of expressing it.'

I raised my eyebrows, glad we weren't having this chat in person, where it'd be impossible to hide my scepticism. I was no psychologist, but I was pretty sure there was a term to describe people that lived through their kids' achievements, a couple of toxic steps beyond being simply a 'pushy parent'.

'I'll let you know when I get there, okay?' I replied, not wanting to get into it now, aware of the fine line between conversation and argument lurking in the shadows. 'I've got to get to the gate pretty soon – you know how massive this place is.'

'Okay,' she relented, her voice soft. 'Take care of yourself, honey, and give all of my love to Lil. Oh – and one other thing.'

'Yeah?' I asked, suddenly wary.

'Mind you watch out for those cowboys. Most of them around Jackson are some of the finest men you'll ever meet – real salt of the earth, genuine types. You might just be in danger of having some fun.'

'Jesus Christ, Mum,' I muttered, repressing a smile despite myself.

'All I'm saying is, I know you have Kyle, but you're a Dean woman, through and through. And if there's one thing I do know, cowboys cannot resist a Dean woman . . .'

'Okay, gross – I'm going now, Mum. I love you.'

We hung up, the sound of her laughter held fast in my mind.

I realized that for the first time in the last twenty-four hours, I didn't feel like crying. Still reeling from my own spontaneity, I had no idea what to expect; but this time, for the first time, the reins were in my hands. I was in control.

CHAPTER 5

Jackson Hole was just as magical as I'd remembered. I was now on the second flight, fourteen hours after leaving London and aboard a much smaller plane, and the reconditioned oxygen and border-line edible food suddenly felt worth it.

The sight from the window was startling as the plane lowered and dipped, revealing a patchy blanket of snow across the endless craggy peaks. In the late-afternoon sun, the glistening white was almost unbearable in its brightness, but I drank it in greedily, closing my eyes for a moment, the image imprinted on the insides of my eyelids. There were so many happy memories lodged between these valleys and ridges, a postcard of unfiltered joy almost too idealistic to be believed. I'd listened to my gut instinct and whilst I had no idea where it would take me, I was grateful.

It still didn't stop the nerves as we stepped out of the plane to be immediately met by a blast of cool air, so fresh that it tasted sweet in the back of my throat. At ground level, the surrounding mountains were utterly dominating, coloured every shade of grey, purple and blue in the low sunlight.

I moved quickly through immigration, my American passport acting like a fast-pass at a theme park in a sea of tourists, and a lack of checked-in luggage meant I was first out at the taxi rank. Having had plenty of time to think about it on the plane, my plan was to head into Jackson itself, maybe buy an extra sweater or two and then call Lil. I'd found the ranch's number online easily enough, and had been surprised to see that they now even offered dude ranching, one of the old barns having been converted into three cabins for guests.

I just had to hope Lil wouldn't mind me arriving out of nowhere.

The valley passed by the taxi window, the vivid greens of the trees, vast rolling fields and lower hillsides blending into a collage of spring. The warmth from the heater belied the real story out there, of a season quite different to London. With no smoggy blanket to raise the temperature, Wyoming was only just out of winter, snow still a real possibility and thick jackets a must.

My thin city mac wasn't going to cut it here. Neither were these trainers. I sighed. Always the interloper.

Gradually the number of buildings increased on either side of the road, the traffic picking up from a handful of cars to a steady stream. As if in deference to the mountains beyond, everything was squat, the buildings made of wood or occasionally stone. The tallest features were the towering spruce trees, clumped together at intervals down the main street, a perpetual reminder of the winter season. A large family stood outside the Jackson Museum, a small blonde girl imitating the pose of the bronze cowboy statue, Slim, whilst someone took a picture. I'd done the same thing a lifetime ago, the photo now stored in the stack of oversized albums my mum treasured.

Memories slid over and around me at every turn until we arrived at the antler arch, just across the road from the Cowboy, Jackson's infamous honkytonk bar. Lil and I had once gone there and monopolized the rodeo bull for an entire afternoon. I could hardly stand the next day.

I'd loved it.

The taxi driver slowed to a stop and I stared out at the main square, sudden overwhelm hitting me squarely in the chest. 'Y'all set?' he asked as I paid the fare, then we said our goodbyes and I stepped out onto the sidewalk. As the taxi drove away, stirring the cold air around me, with just a small roll-on at my feet and my handbag on my shoulder, what I felt was entirely different to what I'd expected.

How the hell had I got myself into this? I wasn't free, I was alone. Had been alone for a long time, in fact. Swallowing back a sudden surge of emotion and shivering as my thin jacket failed to stand up to the mountain air, I opened my phone and tapped in the number I'd copied over from the ranch website. As it rang, butterflies stirred, fluttering madly in my gut. What if she said no?

'Howdy, you've reached the Diamond Back. We're likely roping some cows or out back somewhere, so just go ahead and leave a message. We'll call you back after sundown.'

The sound of her voice, the deep, warm Wyoming twang shaping each word, made me want to smile, even as guilt jabbed me in the gut. I should've made more space for Lil in my life, but thanks to my obsession with good grades at school, uni and then work, I'd made space for nothing but my own ambition. My words froze in my throat. I couldn't just announce my arrival on her voicemail. I hung up, unsure.

The Cowboy Bar beckoned, warmth and smiling faces visible inside even from where I was standing. But it was too full of tourists, who were likely to want to strike up a conversation, inevitably forcing me to explain why I was here and . . . I shook my head. A drink would be welcome, though; maybe I could stay one night here in town and then I'd pluck up the courage to call Lil or just turn up tomorrow. Not now. Not this full of jet lag and regret.

Practical brain taking over, I spent a short while checking in to the motel just up the main street, anticipating the need for sleep and requesting a late check-out. The room was surprisingly nice, with cosy touches and a vast, soft bed that part of me wanted to crawl right into. But the other part, the bigger part, felt too cold and alone to sit in a room by myself. So, back outside, I headed towards a smaller bar I'd seen just off the main street. There were no tourists outside, and as I took one of the only free seats at the bar, I realized I was one of the few people here not wearing a cowboy hat and shirt.

'Whiskey sour,' I ordered as the barman nodded at me, no friendly greeting, his tired eyes glancing over my clothes. Maybe it was the hard, London-honed look I gave him in response, but he made no comment and got to making the drink.

Rubbing my eyes, I glanced around. The vibe was understated but lively, all the tables in the main area taken, laughter and conversation buzzing, groups of people standing round the edges and the occasional glance at the stage where a band was setting up.

My drink appeared and I paid, the barman moving on without a word. The relief at avoiding small talk was almost as good as the first sip. The whiskey was deep and smoky, just how it should be. Swirling the contents for a moment, I employed the same fuck-it decision-making technique as I had on the tube – and downed it.

It burnt my throat, my eyes watering in response.

'Another?' the barman said, now eyeing me with interest as he dried a tumbler, both of us sensing where this was going.

'Neat this time. Ice.'

The guy on the stool to my right turned for a moment, eyes narrowed as though he couldn't quite make me out.

'Rough day?' he asked, his voice gravelled, his eyes beginning to glaze.

'Yep,' I replied, looking over to the barman and watching as he poured out a measure.

'New in town?'

'Nope,' I said, taking the glass from the barman as he passed it over.

The barman glanced at the guy and they shared a look.

I turned towards the stage, keeping my back to them, and nursed the drink, watching the band prep. A small group in the corner, closest to the stage, burst into fits of laughter. The ringleader was telling a story – a good one, judging by their reactions. Only one of them wasn't joining in, a small smile playing on his lips. Like everyone else, he was in standard-issue cowboy kit – bootcut blue jeans, a plaid button-down shirt and dark cowboy hat. But the way he wore them was . . . different. He was hot, model hot. Almost as though he'd heard my thoughts, he glanced up, revealing a face to match.

I looked away, refocusing on the band for a moment, but as I felt his eyes still on me, I knocked back the rest of the drink and turned to order another.

Out of nowhere, I was hit by thoughts of Kyle, replaying the moments he'd arrived home with that woman. The way my stomach had fallen away, a landslide of hopelessness giving way to a void. Hiding in the shadows whilst the truth blinded me, the intimate gestures between them, the key to his house already in her bag.

'You want anything to eat?' the barman said, raising his voice as the band started up. He pushed a glass of water next to my drink.

I shook my head, feeling the gentle spin of the room as I did so. Everything had become softened, edges removed from the sounds, my thoughts. As I listened to the music, people began to gather in front of the stage, and I tried as hard as I could to sink into a state of nothing.

Except, with every song about heartbreak and loss, which was most of them, a creeping anger began to grow. On the surface it was directed towards Kyle and every futile fucking feeling I'd had for him, but it grew to cover my job, even my dad for pushing me so hard to become the success he so desperately wanted me to be. But mainly it was directed at myself, for failing at all of it. So when the band took a break after their first set and a bunch of new people flooded the bar, I felt like a coiled cobra, ready to rip into the first thing that came close.

'Say, you new here? The Cowboy Bar's right round the corner.' A new guy had hopped onto the stool to my right, the one on my left still free.

'You don't say,' I replied, gripping my glass, my eyes fixed on the ice inside.

He chuckled.

'I'm only messin' with ya,' he added, ordering a round of drinks. 'How many more of those before you'll agree to a dance with me later?'

I turned to him, narrowing my eyes.

'There's not enough damn whiskey in this bar,' I hissed. 'Now leave me alone.'

'Woah there, we've got a live wire here!'

He laughed and nudged the guy next to him, who joined in with the amusement.

I clenched my teeth, my foggy brain deciding on the best response when a voice to my left cut in. It was deeper, smoother, an undercurrent of authority ringing loud and clear.

'Leave her alone, Jim.'

Great. Feeling distinctly like I was about to become centre-stage in some kind of pissing contest, I moved to hop off my stool. Time to call it a night.

'It's fine, you don't have to leave. Jim was just about to anyway.'

A hand touched my arm, the grip gentle but firm.

I looked up, right into the face of the hot guy from earlier. Up close, the whiskey haze allowing me to maintain fierce eye contact, he was even more gorgeous than I'd realized.

'Reckon Cole's found his entertainment for the night,' Jim laughed, although as the hot guy took another step closer, he shifted off the bar stool and stalked away.

'I don't need a damn bodyguard,' I said, shrugging off his

touch and sliding off the stool, standing for the first time since I'd arrived. The room spun at alarming speed and before I could work out what was happening, a strong arm had reached around my waist, holding me up.

'Maybe you don't,' he replied, his voice alarmingly close to my ear, one side of me pressed against his rock-hard chest. 'But the problem is, you look like you don't care what happens to you.'

I struggled back from him, his smell, a heady, musky cologne. He let me go, but kept a hand under my arm, steadying me as I held on to the bar instead.

'Why do you care?' I spat, hating myself for the state I was in and resisting the urge to press up close to him again. I staggered, trying to turn away.

'Because if you were my sister, cousin, friend – whatever – I'd want someone to do the same,' he answered, an angry edge to his tone. 'Listen, if you want to take whatever's going on with you out on someone, then take it out on me. That way you'll feel better and I'll know you're not going to end up with someone like Jim.'

I stared at him, watching as he adjusted his hat, strands of deep brown hair escaping at the back. His eyes were fierce but careful, his chiselled jaw set as firm as my own.

'You know what I want? I want people to stop telling me what to fucking do all the time,' I began, the remaining drops of my reserve draining away. 'Especially men. Assholes like Jim are nothing – it's the hot ones that cause the problems.'

The sounds from the bar filled the space between us as I heard my own words repeated in my head.

'You calling me hot?'

His lips twitched; the touch of his hand on my arm suddenly branded me like an iron.

'*Oh fuck off,*' I said, turning away fully this time, walking round the bar towards the restrooms, planning to hide in there instead.

'Wait, wait,' he called, but I reached the door and yanked it open, taking a left in the dark corridor. 'I'm sorry.' His hand touched my shoulder, using just enough force to stop me in my tracks, causing everything to spin again. 'Let me help you home. You're gonna hurt yourself like this – walk into the street and end up under a truck or something.'

The corridor was tight, and his considerable height and build were taking up most of the room as he towered over me. I should've felt scared, cautious at the very least, but instead, whiskey stirring the burning embers further, I took a step into him, placing a hand on his chest.

'Why do you care?' I repeated, searching his face. He was a stranger, a no one, but somehow my palm was splayed against him, my head tilted upwards to read his expression.

'I don't know.'

His voice was low, barely audible against the background noise from the other side of the door. I realized I could feel his heartbeat under my fingers, pounding at a rate that matched my own.

In the same moment, as his eyes moved to my lips, his hand dropping from my shoulder and grazing my back, I let my intuition make the decision for me. Reaching up on tiptoes, my hand moving to his jaw, I pulled his face towards me and kissed him, hard.

He stilled for a moment, surprised, but as I pulled back, locked into his gaze, it was him that leant into me instead, his other hand working into my hair as he kissed me right back. His lips were soft, but the need was hard.

Even through the whiskey, the jet lag – the swirling emotional mess of the past couple of days – I felt something I knew I'd never felt before. This man, *God, this man*, was like a flame on the edge of a taper, the edges black and smouldering as the fire caught hold. It grew, flaring brighter until it roared through me.

My fingers fisted his shirt and pulled him in closer still as I leant back and let myself become crushed between his body and the cold wall behind. The feeling dragged me under, both of our breathing between the kisses becoming ragged, a necessary frustration in the frenzy. His hand brushed the skin in the gap between my top and jeans, his fingers resting there briefly before inching upwards, grazing the band of my bra, my hand almost reaching to unhook it myself. His skin against mine had fire breaking out on the surface, just as it raged inside.

It was as though he was a fever, invading every cell in my body. My body reacted; goosebumps formed and I shivered.

'Cold?' he murmured, letting up for a moment, both of us trying to catch our breath.

I shook my head. 'Not that kind of shiver.'

He dipped his head, the most heart-achingly beautiful smile crossing his face.

I groaned, resting my head against the wall and shutting my eyes.

'I can't believe I'm saying this but I think I need to go.'

With my eyes still closed, I felt his lips brush my ear, his hand now fully on the bare skin of my waist.

'Maybe you should – we've both had a lot to drink . . .' he began, and although we were still standing in the restroom corridor for all to see, the fire roared in my ears and instead, I just . . . let go.

This time the kiss was fierce, surprise in his response at first, then it deepened. His mouth eventually left mine and travelled down my neck, his tongue leaving a trail of sparks across my skin. My hands reached his belt, pulling us together, evidence of his own feelings as rock hard as his abs, pressing against my thigh. I had never wanted anyone like this, not even in my wildest, romance-book-reading mind.

The door opened, music flooding the corridor and wrenching us apart.

The guy who'd opened it immediately veered away with a wry smile, tipping his hat to . . .

'Wait, I don't even know your name?' I said, pressing my fingers to my lips, now tingling from the force he'd applied.

He laughed, still holding my waist.

'I'm Cole. And you are?'

'Lottie. Nice to meet you.'

His smile was kind, but his eyes burnt with the need I'd just felt in his jeans.

'So, what's a British girl doing in a cowboy bar?' he asked, sudden curiosity taking over, his hand shifting off my skin.

I sighed. The moment was over. Time to escape the questions.

'Long story. I better go.'

He hesitated, then nodded, shifting aside to open the door for me.

We crossed the bar and made it outside, the chill night air forcing me to hug myself tightly.

'I'll walk you home,' he said, holding up his hands at my arched eyebrow. 'Believe it or not, I was raised to be a gentleman.'

I laughed and he gave a sheepish smile, half hidden as he looked down, the brim of his hat concealing his face.

'I'm at the motel,' I replied, pointing down the street. 'It's just one crossing and a short walk. I think I can make it.'

'If you're sure.'

Nodding, I hesitated, wanting to kiss him again but not trusting myself. He seemed to be having a similar battle, his body turned towards me but his hands rammed in his pockets as though he felt the same.

'Night, cowboy,' I said as the crosswalk turned green, the frigid air somehow sobering me up enough to turn without wobbling and walk across the road.

Arriving outside the motel, I made it up the steps and pushed open the door, turning to look back down the street. He was still there, hand moving to pinch the brim of his hat, then dipping it to me before he moved off, heading back towards the bar.

————

The night passed fitfully, sleep evading me despite the bone-crushing tiredness, my body clinging to UK time despite the whiskey, replaying the feel of the cowboy against me over and over.

So when I finally awoke the next day, bright sun streaming into the room, it was with no huge surprise that I saw it was almost 2 p.m. Groaning at my throbbing head, I took a moment before turning over and grabbing the phone to call reception. I booked the room out for a few more hours, wincing at the add-itional cost but grateful they weren't fully booked. The thought of having to get up, pack and check out in the next ten minutes was unbearable.

Slowly I pulled myself together, careful to think of nothing except the mundane tasks ahead. A long shower, several pain-killers, and a large coffee and sandwich delivered to the room eventually gave me the courage to call Lil again.

The answerphone picked up once more and I sighed. Nothing for it.

Eventually checking out, I dragged my roll-on bag down the street and headed into the first clothes shop I could find, emer-ging some time later with boots, jeans, shirts and a warm coat. The only thing I couldn't decide on was a hat, but I reasoned that if Lil wasn't keen on me staying, there might not be any point in getting one anyway.

The jeans hugged my ass and thighs, flaring in a subtle bootcut, the tan boots poking out from underneath. A deep blue plaid shirt, tucked in, with a tan belt and low-key silver buckle finished it all off. Somehow it didn't look stupid. In fact, it made my previous outfit seem like the imposter.

I called a taxi and waited in the town square for it to arrive, wondering if Lil and I still looked alike. Despite our hair-colour difference, Lil and I shared our mums' freckles, wide blue eyes and heart-shaped face. We'd always been mistaken for sisters when I'd visited and as an only child, it'd been a nice fantasy to live, if only for a few weeks a year.

Finally, butterflies building and scattering as the taxi took us out of town, the vast expanse of sky opened up, with low wisps of cloud burnt orange by the waning sun. The vast Teton Range towered in every direction, surrounded on all sides by grass and trees and space.

Pulling off the main road, the side road growing rougher and steeper with every second, we passed under a tall wooden arch, the 'Diamond Back' name carved into a plank at the top. As we wound up and up, the spruce trees thickened on both sides until they suddenly stopped on the right, revealing a view over the valley, the main ranch house straight ahead.

Two people stood near the main door, both turning towards us. Even at this distance I could see the confusion, their faces shielded under cowboy hats, one dark brown, one black.

'Here's fine,' I said as the driver pulled to a stop a short distance from them. I knew Lil was on the left, but I couldn't quite bring myself to look yet, though the heavy tint of the windows concealed my identity from her.

I took one last steadying breath and opened the taxi door, swinging my bags down first and following with a thud in my new boots. As I looked up, Lil's eyes found mine, forming wide blue saucers, her hand lifting to cover her mouth. The blond cowboy next to her looked between us from under the brim of his black hat.

'Lottie?' she whispered, her voice hoarse. 'Is that—'

Not trusting my voice to hold, I launched myself into her instead, receiving a hug that threatened to crush every bone in my body.

'Hey, Lil,' I whispered as the taxi backed away.

Right as I turned into a sobbing wreck.

CHAPTER 6

I was thirteen again. Summer stretched far, far ahead, responsibility and exams in the same category as the horizon. Visible, but out of reach. Just a concept in the back of my mind, nothing to worry about, not yet.

But Lil . . . I worried about her. The atmosphere was strange this time – I'd noticed it as soon as we arrived: clear strain on Aunt Carrie's face, Uncle John nowhere in sight.

'There's something going on,' Lil had whispered as we snuck into her room and closed the door, my heart leaping despite the concern. The exposed logs of the ranch house, a rich conker-brown, dominated the room. Despite the touches applied by any teenager – posters, clothes strewn haphazardly, make-up and jewellery randomly dotting most surfaces – it was undeniably western. From the carved wooden bedframe to the intricate, colourful patterns on the Shoshone-made quilt and the building collection of cowboy hats, in my mind, we could only be in Wyoming. 'They've been arguing non-stop. I think they're getting a divorce.'

It was the only time I'd really seen her cry. There was a pinched tiredness around her eyes, and her freckles were dulled in her wan complexion. We held each other on the edge of her bed, me trying to find any words to make a salve. None came.

Instead, all I could think of was how it might affect our trips out here, realizing just how much I needed and looked forward to them. Lil was my de facto older sister, and this ranch a safe place, away from the demands of home.

Now, the selfish nature of those long-ago thoughts curdled in my gut. My conscience forced me awake, rapping on the side of my head for attention.

Groaning, I blinked at the sunlight streaming through the thin curtains, a few confused seconds of trying to figure out where the hell I was. Then, like a dam lifting, the events of yesterday rushed through my mind.

There had been a lot of crying, mine this time, with Lil holding my hand throughout as we sat at the heirloom kitchen table together, knees bumping. I gripped steaming coffee in my free hand as my stilted explanations and recounted events of the last few days pooled in the space between us.

Lil had sworn on my behalf, cursed Kyle to the pits of hell and back and most importantly, thankfully, had absolutely backed my spur-of-the-moment decision to visit.

Still, my conscience pricked, guilt needling me at Lil being there for me in a way I hadn't been for her. At us losing touch at the worst time of her life.

Wait . . . was someone knocking on my door?

Startled, I sat up. The knocking sound filtering through the edges of my reverie wasn't just my guilty conscience. Someone was making a total racket, near my window.

I checked my phone, now adjusted to US time. 7 a.m.

Seriously?

Falling back onto my pillow, I shut my eyes. A reprieve in the noise meant silence fell over the ranch again and I tried to quiet my mind.

Knock. Knock, Knock.

I shot up again, tiredness turning to irritation. Didn't they know it was early? As well as me, weren't there guests here, paying ones, that wouldn't appreciate this?

Unable to stifle my curiosity, I pulled back the curtain and peered out, but the spruce beyond was the only thing in view. As I turned back to the room, the sound echoed again and this time, irritation now pulling on my temper, I marched out of the room and down the hall towards the back door. There was no sign of Lil anywhere, but the boots she'd been wearing yesterday were gone from the rack.

I yanked open the door, a blast of mountain air taking my breath away. Crossing my arms over my thin T-shirt, suddenly very aware of my short-shorts PJs, I stepped out, committed to my indignation.

Striding barefoot over the wide deck curving around the back corner of the house, heading straight for the source of the noise, as I emerged into the bright morning sun, I stopped in my tracks.

Ahead of me was the small red barn, logs stacked against the side in neat piles. But in front of that was a sight I didn't quite have words for. Where the cold air had taken my breath, what stood before me just about stilled my heart itself.

Just a few metres away was a man with his back to me, a topless man, swinging a large axe round in an arc, his long, muscled arms bringing it down onto the log in front of him.

The wood cracked in two, falling either side of the tree stump it had been resting on. Before I could turn and run, mouth half open like a gawping fish, he turned to me.

He was covered in a sheen of sweat, and lean, hard muscle flexed as he leant on the axe. Standard-issue blue jeans, black boots and a chestnut brown hat failed to distract attention from his broad chest and shoulders, and arms that'd lift someone like me without any effort. To my horror, I felt a blush creeping across my face and as I tried to gather myself and refrain from outright ogling, he turned.

We locked eyes.

HOLY FUCK.

Cole.

The cowboy from the bar.

His eyes widened, mirroring my own as we just stared, neither of us able to make a sound.

'But . . . I . . . you,' was all he managed, but it was enough.

Goosebumps broke out across my arms and legs, but once again, I knew it wasn't the cold air.

'You always do that this early?' I blurted, my initial irritation tempered by shock.

His face remained still, other than the ghost of a smile and a fraction of movement from one eyebrow as it rose.

'Well now, only when I need to top up my tan in the morning sun.' Any other words gathered in my mouth dried up. He lowered his gaze slowly, briefly resting on my chest, before inching slowly down my legs. 'Seems we had the same idea.'

I glanced down, realizing that both my tee and shorts were fairly transparent in the bright sunlight, and more than that, despite my crossed arms, my chest was standing fully to attention in the chill air.

Fuuuck.

'Oh, hey Lottie, you're awake! And you've met Cole? He's my ranch manager.'

Lil emerged from the direction of the barn, brushing straw from her jeans. As the silence stretched between us, she glanced more closely at me.

'Oh, sweetie, you're going to catch your death in that! Help yourself to anything in my room. It might be a bit big for you, but it's better than freezing to death out here.'

Cole dipped his head and turned to Lil, seemingly recovering himself.

'Friend of yours?' he drawled, the picture of casual innocence, tucking a thumb into the waistband of his jeans. I tried and failed not to watch as it inched below his belt.

'My cousin, from London,' she replied, shaking her head. 'Did he wake you? I'm sorry, darling, we start early most days. But you go on back to bed if you like, I know you must be dog-tired. I'm gonna start on breakfast, though, if you want some? Pancakes and such?'

She carried on walking around to the front of the house, leaving the two of us in the same charged silence as before.

Before I could embarrass myself further, I turned to walk away, but not before catching a last look from under his hat. His eyes seemed to burn into mine, as if asking a question. Before he could vocalize it, I disappeared inside.

Dignity in shreds, back in my room I started pulling my clothes on with unnecessary aggression. Embarrassment coursed through me, my heart still thudding, as the feel of his eyes on my body replayed in my mind.

I pulled out one of the new sweaters, a deep blue with a cream tribal print across the front and back, tucking the front into the jeans and doing up my belt. I scraped my chaos of curls back into a low bun and settled my expression into corporate blankness. I might have to face him again, but I would do it with clothes on and a poker face even Cressida would approve of.

As I groaned at the sheer cringe of it all, my bruised ego also reminded me of the mess the last hot guy had caused.

I hesitated, seized by a sudden urge to call Hestia and fill her in, relive the last ten minutes and listen to her reaction. No doubt she'd tell me to jump him and be done with it, but even if he hadn't worked for Lil, there was still the small matter of dumping Kyle. There were no messages on my phone, but that was bang on trend for when the US 'client' was in town. I made the time difference calculation: just after 2 p.m. He'd be in the middle of work. It'd have to wait until later.

As I wound my way down to the kitchen-diner, contemplating just how to deal with Kyle, I heard the sound of voices and laughter.

'There she is,' Lil exclaimed, holding a spatula up in the air, hair tucked into her shirt collar as she leant over the big steel stove. 'Take a seat over there – Jesse, scooch over, will you? Lottie – you met Jesse last night, and that's Bailey.'

Both smiled, Bailey shooting up and holding out her hand.

'Well, howdy – it sure is nice to meet some of Lil's family at last!'

She was my height, 5'5" at a push, but stocky where I was willowy. She had the build of a gymnast and the handshake of a bodybuilder, and her smile was as white as her eyes were green. A thick auburn braid hung over her shoulder.

'Hey,' I said shyly. Then to Jesse, who was watching with a mischievous smile in the background, 'I promise I'm not normally a crier. Yesterday was a bitch.'

Bailey laughed, clapping me on the back and guiding me to Jesse's side of the table, a long bench in front of a vast dresser, full of family trinkets.

'It ain't nothing I haven't seen before.' He smiled, his face lighting up as he considered me. I silently resolved to ask Lil how she'd managed to employ not one, but two guys who looked like they'd take on a grizzly and win, before posing for a high-fashion photo shoot. Even without the cowboy hat, with his sandy hair swept back and stormy grey eyes fixed on mine, I had to look away at the table to keep from staring. 'I've got two sisters,' he continued, as if my stare was nothing out of the ordinary. 'I've seen just about every emotion on the damn scale – sometimes all at the very same time, if I'm real lucky.'

He winked, stretching over to steal a piece of bacon just as Lil reached the table and offloaded a short stack of pancakes onto each plate. There were two empty spaces – one for her and one for . . .

'There you are,' Lil said, swatting away Jesse's hand as he reached out for more bacon.

Cole.

This time, shirt firmly in place and buttons done right up to the neck – just as I'd done with mine – he carried his hat over to the pegs on the wall and placed it next to three others.

'Who wants eggs?' Lil asked, juggling another two pans on the stove.

'Yep,' Jesse and Bailey said, now fighting over the coffee and cream.

'Can I give you a hand?' Cole asked in a voice low, approaching Lil, his eyes averted from the table.

My traitorous heart began to pound, but I held my neutral expression in place. Even if my eyes did slide down to his ass, hugged pretty perfectly by the Wranglers wrapped around it.

Lil threw him a grateful look but shook her head. I noticed again the deep furrows under her eyes, the manic flyaway hairs around her hairline. Although never polished, Lil had always been put together, scrubbed and made up, pretty enough to turn heads without a whisper of make-up. But now . . . it was as though her seams were exposed, ragged and worn at the edges.

I pretended to listen as Bailey messed with Jesse, but I poured myself a coffee and took a sip, resolving to help. Really help. I'd combine straightening out my life, job hunting, Kyle, all of it – but Lil would take equal priority. I owed her.

'Nice to meet you again. Almost didn't recognize you with your clothes on.'

The room suddenly went quiet, just the crackle of eggs frying on the stove as I looked up from my mug into Cole's eyes. He held his own poker face, just a hint of amusement tugging at the corner of his mouth as he sat down, reaching for the orange juice.

'Likewise,' I replied quietly, a suffocating mix of embarrassment, annoyance and pure, feral attraction merging into one word.

At Jesse and Bailey's shock, Lil laughed.

'Cole was chopping logs by the store, woke Lottie up in her tiny little city pyjamas.'

Jesse snorted.

'I like her,' Bailey said to Lil, shaking her head. 'That same whip-crack style as you.'

Lil's eyebrow lifted, her keen eyes moving between Cole and me.

'Oh she sure does, don't be fooled by the British accent. Ain't nothing stuck up or uptight about that one.' She laughed at my incredulous expression. 'We're just the same as our moms. Pair of them could tear down every wise-cracking asshole in town.'

Cole ventured nothing else, just a brief, curious glance back to me as he slowly helped himself to the contents of the table.

'So, you're a city girl?' Bailey asked, mouth half open as she made light work of her pancakes. 'London, right?'

'Yeah, sort of,' I replied, not missing a second glance from Cole, but this time, it was colder. A flicker of fear ran through me. Maybe I was wrong, maybe it was about something else. I added, 'I mean, I'm not *from* the city, I just moved there for work.'

Lil sat down, Jesse and Bailey nodded, too engrossed in their breakfast to speak.

'Country not enough for you?' Cole asked quietly, his voice soft, but the words had an edge.

It hurt. More than it should. His warm, bright brown eyes were suddenly dark. The man that'd lit my entire being on fire just two nights earlier had gone.

I frowned, watching as the others looked between us, seemingly unsure of his reaction, of what mine would be in response.

'No, that's not it. Just more opportunities, that's all.'

He shrugged and my stomach dropped. Whatever had taken

place the night before last . . . had I imagined it all? Had I just been so starved of any depth of feeling with Kyle that the first gorgeous guy to kiss me with any passion had turned into something else in my head?

After a pause, Lil launched into a list of jobs and chores for the morning and I ate as much as I could, realizing how unused I was to real food, or certainly any large quantity of it. Nutrition had been fairly low on the list of priorities in the past year.

'Okay, time to fly,' Bailey said eventually. 'See you sometime at the barn, Lottie?'

'Sure.' I nodded, giving her a brief smile, carefully avoiding looking at Cole.

'Hold up,' said Jesse, swinging himself off the bench at the same time as Cole and swiping his hat off the pegs. 'Look forward to showing you the ropes, Lottie.'

He winked again, smiling as I nodded and tried very hard not to imagine him helping lift me into a saddle. Cole said nothing, disappearing under his hat and striding out into the hall.

'Come out back with me.' Lil grabbed her coffee. 'Let's take five minutes to ourselves before the day really gets going.'

Feeling numb, I followed her out onto the same deck I'd stalked across earlier, and we each took a rocking chair.

Lil sighed, clutching her mug like it was a lifeline, looking out over the view. The ridge we were on fell away steeply, the tops of the spruce trees below just visible over the edge, nothing to block the panoramic view of the valley floor below and the knife-edged Tetons in the far distance, the sky as blue and clear as sapphire.

'In some ways this place hasn't changed at all, has it?' I murmured, lifting my legs up onto the chair and hugging my knees. 'The trees are a little taller maybe, but the mountains, the house, the town . . . it's like I never left.'

'I can see that,' Lil replied, rubbing at her eyes for a moment. 'From your point of view. It's a different place for me now, in lots of ways. Ever since Mom left for Colorado; maybe even before that when Dad left. Sometimes . . .' She shifted, wincing almost. 'I feel like an ungrateful asshole for saying it, but sometimes I just wish I'd let her sell it. Maybe then I could go get myself one of those city jobs, have a social life and some pretty clothes.'

Smiling, I shook my head.

'Come on, you've got living proof sitting right here that that life isn't all it's sold as being. You're even less of a city person than me. Besides, this place can't be all bad, right?'

Lil shook her head, looking back out at the mountains, as if to anchor herself.

'No . . . of course not. I love this place, to its bones, like you do,' she said, glancing at me as she sipped her coffee. 'It's just, the financial side of running a ranch is complicated. Having guests helps, keeps things ticking over, but managing this much land is hard. Even with help.'

It dawned on me just how small my worries were in comparison to hers. How my life was just about me, my job, my relationship – whereas Lil's were about a legacy, a family name and the livelihoods of three other people, not to mention the other services and small businesses that relied on ranches like the Diamond Back.

'Anyone . . . special out there, to share the load?' I asked, curious about the absence of any talk of boyfriends.

She gave a wry chuckle, raising her eyebrows.

'Oh honey, even if I didn't know every last man in town either from high school or through running this place, I'd need an extra day in the week to do anything about it.'

'Bullshit,' I teased, watching her indignation turn to amusement as I grinned at her. 'You telling me there's no time for a night out? Some whiskey and live music? There's got to be someone to have some fun with?'

Laughing now, she put her head back against the chair. It

felt good to see a glimpse of the old Lil, the one I remembered. Silently, I vowed to use this trip to bring her more of that, a small relief from the heavy duty across her shoulders.

'Maybe, honey, maybe.' She considered me for a moment. 'We always had a lot of fun, didn't we?'

I nodded, flooded with memories.

'But everyone here is really great. I mean, I know I only just met them but they seem like a good team,' I said quietly, just in case any of them suddenly appeared from around the side of the house. 'Although . . . what's with Cole? He seemed a bit . . . off with me?'

She studied me for a moment, expression shifting from the thoughts that creased her forehead to something else I couldn't quite define.

'Oh, pay no attention to him. It's just his way, he doesn't mean anything by it. Or if he does, it's all his own shit.' She paused, taking a sip of her coffee. 'He's been a lifeline to me these last few years. He's not perfect, but I'd have lost the ranch a long time ago without his help.'

'I had no idea things were so tough,' I replied, my voice quiet. 'I want to help. I mean, I need to figure out a job and straighten my life out too, but I'm here because I want to help you, however I can.'

'I've missed you, Princess.' Her smile was sad.

I returned it, remembering the nickname her parents had given me one summer, when they'd declared I could pass for a younger version of Kate Middleton.

'Princess? I thought you said Lottie was just a regular girl,' Jesse announced, approaching the deck and leaning a foot against it.

'She lied,' I jumped in, trying to save Lil from explaining the origins, from making her think too much about her parents, about the way things used to be here. 'I'm actually an undercover princess escaping the paparazzi in the mountains.'

He chuckled.

'Well, Princess, if it's not too much trouble for a royal such as yourself, I could use a pair of hands saddling up the horses for a ride. Got a few guests going out and Bailey's had to run down to the river meadow with Cole to patch up a fence.'

Lil groaned.

'What happened this time?'

Jesse shrugged. 'Think it's just old. There's no real damage, the wood's rotten is all.' Lil made a sound as though this was a well-trodden conversation. 'Lil said you're good with horses,' he added. 'You in?'

CHAPTER 7

I barely contained a squeal as within minutes of arriving at the stalls, Jesse led out a tall, rangy black horse, distinctive white socks on his back legs.

'Jasper!'

Taken aback, Jesse stood aside as I walked towards the horse that'd become as precious to me as family, as the ranch itself, on my visits. I extended my hand towards his nose, letting him make up the distance. He lowered his head and stepped towards me, passing his velvety soft muzzle over my skin as he fixed his wide liquid chocolate eyes on my face.

'Well hell,' Jesse said, his voice soft as Jasper came to stand right by my side and I ran one hand across his neck, the other scratching right behind his cheek. The hours I'd spent grooming this sleek coat, the scratches I'd given him as he'd fallen half asleep, head resting on my shoulder. 'This grumpy old mule barely keeps it civil most days; almost took a chunk outta Domino just last night.'

'He's not grumpy,' I said, voice almost a whisper as I smiled at the big animal's groans. 'He just knows what and who he likes, that's all. I had no idea he was still here.'

Jesse chuckled. 'Well, he sure likes you. Why don't you take him out and get him started, then? I need to get the other three.'

'Three guests then?' I asked, noticing the fine white hairs now sprinkled across Jasper's face.

'Yep,' he replied. 'I could get another out if you want to come along?'

I hesitated, tempted. Fear won out.

'It's okay, another day maybe. I need to ease in slowly, haven't ridden for years.'

He shrugged, handing me Jasper's lead rope and pointing towards the tack room as he headed to the back of the stalls. 'His name's above the pegs.'

I nodded, leading Jasper out and tying him up, my hand still grazing his neck. A strange sense of wonder passed through me as somehow, eight years concertinaed into nothing, as though it hadn't passed at all.

Picking up a brush, I began working over Jasper's coat, muscle memory taking over, slowly warming up to the point that I had to stop to roll up my sleeves. I'd barely noticed the three other horses now brought out, Jesse working round them. He glanced at me from under his hat.

'Why did you stop riding?' he asked as he brought out two saddles at once.

I hesitated, waiting to guess the motive for his question, brace myself for the judgement.

'My family – well, my dad – thought that riding would take up too much time, interfere with school. I used to spend all my free time doing it back then, so, you know, it made sense. I guess.'

'Hmph,' he replied, still fixed on the job in hand. 'So, you got the grades? Was it worth it?'

Still, the question was open. No malice. I realized how conditioned I was to it, how guarded I'd become.

'Yeah, I got them,' I replied, but couldn't quite bring myself to answer the second half of his question.

He seemed to notice, thoughtful eyes watching me. I pretended to focus on Jasper, finishing the brushing and pacing into the tack room to grab his saddle, Jesse following.

'Here, let me,' he said, waiting politely for me to move to the side in the small space before leaning right over to take the saddle off the high peg. His arm brushed mine, his shirt tightening around his bicep as he reached up. 'I forgot how high up Jasper's was and you're only an itty-bitty thing . . .'

'Itty-bitty?' I said, imitating his accent, unable to help myself. I was rewarded by a megawatt smile, and a blush threatened to break out again.

'All right, Princess pint-sized.'

He swept out of the room, chuckling to himself.

I paused. I liked him – he was friendly, easy to be around. But I had to be careful. After everything with Kyle, it was almost as though I was waiting for a delayed reaction to hit. And Cole . . . well, I had no idea about him either.

Back outside, Jesse was pulling the cinch tight, muttering something at Jasper, who looked like he might take a chunk out of his arm if he pulled any tighter.

'When did you start working here?' I asked, determined to keep things neutral.

'Me? Or all of us?'

'Well, you . . . but yeah, all of you. I don't think I remember you from when Aunt Carrie and Uncle John ran things, but it was all cattle then.'

He nodded, face suddenly serious.

'I got here just last year, used to be a bull rider. Ever been to a rodeo?'

My mouth fell open.

'Seriously? You did that? Riding those crazy fucking bulls? Yeah, I went to a few. Saw someone get stomped on one year, blood everywhere.'

Jesse tipped his head to one side, pursing his lips.

'You do it long enough and it'll happen, that's for sure. I just got one injury too many – broke my back twice, my collarbone, ribs, you name it. Figured I'd stop before my head was next. I stick to roping now. Plus, being on the circuit is hard on your relationships; living in hotels is only fun for so long.'

'But you did have fun, I imagine?' I asked, unable to help myself, instantly rewarded with a quick grin.

'Oh sugar, it was six, seven years of a good time.' He shook his head, clearly running through some of it in his mind. 'I mean, outside of the hospital visits. More parties and buckle bunnies than I could possibly handle.'

'Buckle bunnies?' I asked, thoroughly regretting the question when his smile became positively rakish.

'You fit in real well here, I forget you might not know some of the basics.' He chuckled. 'Buckle bunnies are . . . how do I say this without sounding like an asshole . . . Well, I guess they're mostly ladies that hang around the rodeo circuit, hoping to hook up with some of the guys competing. Especially the bull riders that usually win.'

He gave me a suggestive sideways glance, moving over to one of the other horses and preparing it, fixing the saddle. I stroked Jasper's face, smiling as his eyelids began to droop with relaxation.

'And what now?' I asked, wanting to steer back to neutral ground, despite knowing just how easy it would be to take this conversation further. 'You all settled down now? No more bunnies?'

He laughed, half hidden as he dipped down to grab the cinch.

'Never say never, right?' he replied. 'But we've been so busy up here in the last year, trying to get things working for Lil, there hasn't been a whole lot of time. But rodeo season starts again real soon, so I'll be roping, and who knows, maybe I'll meet someone.'

He shrugged, but there was an undertone there that was quite the opposite to the flirty, light quality of his earlier words.

'Someone a little more permanent?' I asked, then, realizing that I sounded like I was volunteering myself, added, 'I mean, I'm not suggesting it's the best solution – I can definitely see the benefits of staying single.'

Jesse glanced at me more intently. I felt a real curiosity growing.

'I'd like to, one day. It can take me a while to get to know someone, you know?' he admitted. 'Parties, girls, rodeo . . . it's a surface thing, fun. The other stuff, the stuff you need for a real relationship? That's something to work on.'

His honesty was like a gut punch, worded without ceremony. I was struck by just how lucky someone might be one day, to be with this man.

I nodded, inspired to share my own thoughts in the same way, but knowing it would take a little more time to process what I was feeling.

'What about the others? Did you know them before this place?' I asked, hoping he would take the cue and move on.

As if he could read my thoughts perfectly, after a brief hesitation he gave a quick nod.

'Yeah, I knew of Bailey, but Cole and I had been buddies for years on the circuit. He was the one that told me about a job up here.'

I nodded, my mind snagging on his friend's name.

'What did Cole do?' I asked lightly, moving to put Jasper's bridle on, waking him up a little, realizing how long Jesse and I had been chatting.

'Bronc riding and roping – best in the whole damn state,' Jesse replied, finishing up the two other horses.

'Why'd he stop?' I asked, unable to help myself.

Silence. Jesse walked around Jasper, looking round the side of the barn down towards the guest accommodation.

'That's not my story to tell,' he replied finally, satisfied that no one was arriving imminently. 'Now Bailey, well she's a barrel racer. Still does it. She and her horse, Dunkin, move at the kinda speed that cricks my neck just to watch.'

'Dunkin?' I asked, trying not to smile again. 'As in . . .'

'Donuts, yeah. No idea why. Listen, I've got an idea – why don't you take Jasper around the corral for a minute or two? Get yourself used to it all again. We're driving some of the cows down this weekend – we could use extra hands if you'd be willing?'

I hesitated again, recognizing the loss of control I was stepping into, how uncomfortable it felt.

'Sure,' I said, trying to sound more confident than I felt. I needed to help Lil, and getting used to riding again would be a start.

Jasper followed me willingly into the soft dirt ring, and before Jesse could come over to offer me a hand into the saddle, I'd hooked my new boot into the stirrup and, grateful for all the hours I'd put in on the StairMaster at the gym, pushed myself up and into the saddle.

'Seems like you remember just fine,' Jesse called from the fence, leaning against it with one leg up on the lower bar and his arms crossed.

From way up on Jasper's back, the ground seemed a long way off, but he stood and waited patiently.

'I've missed you, old boy,' I whispered, gathering the reins and smoothing his neck again. 'Will you show me the ropes again?'

I nudged him gently into a walk and trot, then, as I found my balance easily enough, one further nudge took us into a canter. His ears perked up as he listened to both my voice and my body. From nowhere, tears threatened and I blinked hard, touching my hand to my eyes to stop any falling.

'How it's feeling? He's behaving himself at least.'

'Good,' I replied, slowing Jasper back down to a walk and wandering over to Jesse. 'Just like I remember.'

Voices sounded from our right, and Jesse turned to the three people approaching, two adults and a boy.

'Howdy! Y'all ready for a ride out? Beautiful morning!'

They fell into easy conversation as I dismounted, bringing Jasper around to the yard and handing him over to Jesse.

'Sure you won't come with us?' he asked as the family all approached the horses. 'We're meeting up with Bailey on the way, heading up to the ridge by the pools.'

I shook my head.

'Not this time, but I'll be there for the cattle drive, I promise.'

He nodded, guiding the guests out of the yard and mounting everyone up. Footsteps sounded from the barn just as Jesse swung up into his saddle.

Cole.

Instinctively I turned, my stomach tightening as he headed straight for me.

'You going out for a ride?' he called, forcing me to look back at him.

'Not this time, no,' I replied, with less force than I wanted in my voice, which was somehow weakened by the sight of him, already towering over me at six feet away.

Jesse walked his horse over.

'Want to do something useful then?' Cole asked, the same edge to the question as there'd been in his statement at breakfast. 'Lil says you're hot shit on a horse, so reckon it's time you proved it.' Incredulous, I stared back at him, my reserve beginning to evaporate. The contrast with Jesse's easy, flirty manner gave me whiplash. What the hell was with this guy?

Jesse interrupted, a half-smile on his face as he glanced at his friend.

'Don't rise to it, Princess,' he said, shaking his head. 'Cole loves to get his kicks this way—'

'Fine, I'll prove it,' I replied, ignoring Jesse, unable to bury my growing irritation. 'What do you want?' I said to Cole.

Eyebrows raised and suppressing a smile, Jesse turned his horse and began to move off.

'See y'all later – try not to rip too many chunks outta each other.'

'Princess?' Cole repeated, clearly fighting back amusement.

I took a deep breath, hating the way he got under my skin like this after years of successfully curbing my reactions, keeping things neutral and professional.

Just treat him like a lawyer. *A really fucking hot lawyer.*

At my lack of response he shrugged, walking over to the stalls.

'We've got a young horse, broken last year but she's as green as they come. Reckon you can handle her? Need to get some supplies and run them down to Bailey, take over for a while.'

'Fine.'

My voice was as clipped and British as it was possible to be as I marched behind him, trying to catch up.

He opened the stall door and led out the horse. She was a beautiful pinto, with large chestnut brown patches on a snowy white coat, skittering to the side on the hard surface, her hooves clattering.

'Hey, hey,' I said, moving slowly towards her, watching as her small ears bent forwards and her neck arched. 'It's okay, sweetie, you just ignore him and come hang out with me.'

Cole's mouth twitched and he watched with interest as the horse and I slowly met in the middle.

'What's your name, good girl?'

'This is Bambi,' Cole murmured and without even glancing at him, I took the lead rope from his grip.

'Who came up with that then?' I said, still using the same soft, quiet tone, gently stroking her neck, shushing her nervous breaths on my shirt.

'It's one of Bailey's,' he answered, a new gentle tone to his voice as Bambi rubbed her head on my arm.

I couldn't help a low laugh, but my eyes stayed fixed on Bambi's face, not daring to look at his.

'Well, I guess it's better than Dunkin,' I said to her. 'At least you didn't become Dairy Queen.'

Leading her out, still talking nonsense in a low voice, I brought us to the corral.

'Can I get used to her for a few minutes in here?' I asked, half turning back to Cole, noting the way he considered me, his stance casual but his face hard.

'If you need it, I guess so. I'm gonna get Domino.'

I rolled my eyes to myself.

'What's his beef, huh?' I asked Bambi, tucking the rope around the pommel and tightening her cinch. 'I think your cowboy has a stick up his ass about something.'

She grunted in a way that almost sounded like agreement, and as I swung on, she immediately started moving off.

'Hey there,' I said, guiding her into the corral, a thread of fear winding through me. Could I actually handle this? 'Let's take it easy, okay?'

We circled the corral, her gait much bouncier than Jasper's, youth and energy flowing through each step. After a few minutes I felt her relax and as I began to ask her to slow down, speed up, change leg, she was really listening.

'Good girl,' I said, leaning down to pat her neck, unable to keep from smiling.

'It's all well and good in there,' Cole's voice floated across from the yard, 'but this isn't a dressage competition. You want to do some real riding?'

I paused, deciding to rise above.

'By all means,' I replied, guiding Bambi back to the gate. 'I'd love to see your definition of real—'

A gust of wind caught the gate, still ajar from when I'd entered, and slammed it shut with an almighty CLANG.

I grabbed the pommel with my free hand, but I was too slow. Ears back and terrified, Bambi leapt backwards, and despite sitting down low, heels pushed down hard, with one almighty buck, I found myself on the ground. Ass first.

'Lottie? Shit! Cole, get in there, goddamn it!'

I watched as Lil ran down the path from the house, hat almost lifting clean off her head. With my dignity in tatters for the second time in one day, I didn't dare look up, just concentrated on moving slowly and bringing my legs round so I could stand. Bambi stood on the other side of the corral, fidgeting and snorting, thoroughly wary of the gate.

'I warned you – she's just as green as the damn horse,' Cole said in a low voice as Lil approached. Then, as he climbed the fence into the corral, heading towards me, he added, 'Guess this is what dude ranching is all about, huh? Picking city folk out of the dirt.'

Pure, unbridled temper stirred in my gut.

I rushed to stand up by myself, brushing dirt off my new jeans and taking a step back as he offered a hand.

'Are you okay, Lottie?' Lil asked, reaching the fence and vaulting over, heading for Bambi.

I looked up into his face, ignoring his hand, my cousin and the damn butterflies that immediately took flight.

'First of all,' I hissed, braving a step forward, 'I'm not *city folk*. And second of all, you don't know the first fucking thing about me. Anyone could've come off at that. I wouldn't make assumptions – you come across like an asshole.'

Lil slowed and I felt her hesitation at catching Bambi or getting in the middle of whatever this was.

But Cole's eyes burnt into mine as he crossed his arms, the huge bulk of his body casting a shadow between us.

'I know one thing,' he said, taking a half-step into my space, his eyes slowly shifting to my lips. 'You're definitely no princess with that filthy mouth.'

My breathing almost stopped, the tension between our bodies shimmering in the air. Neither one of us moved, as though we were locked in place. Grasping at any shred of self-control, my back and ass now throbbing, I leant into the pain and narrowed my eyes.

'It's okay, Lil, I'll get Bambi. I know you must be busy.'

Keeping my head high, I turned from Cole and waved Lil away, despite her concern.

'You sure, honey? You landed pretty hard there,' she said, then as I levelled my side-eye at her, she backed off, hands up. 'Okay, okay. Nice to see the Dean stubbornness is still alive and kicking.'

Ignoring Cole's soft chuckle, as Lil leapt back over the fence, I approached Bambi slowly. Her eyes and nostrils were still wide, and I muttered soothing nothings to her until she lowered her head a little, allowing me to gently scoop up her reins.

'There you go, sweetie. You're a good girl, aren't you?' I said, keeping my focus on her as I led her back over to the gate, determined not to look at Cole. 'It was just the noise of the gate, nothing to worry about.'

As we neared it, I heard Cole approaching.

'Hey . . . Listen, I'm sorry,' he said, reaching for the gate and opening it wide enough for us both. Bambi skittered sideways, throwing her head up.

I shushed her gently, stroking her neck, letting her calm herself for a moment. I braced myself, expecting Cole to intervene, and when he didn't, I risked a quick glance to where he stood.

He was watching carefully, his eyes alight, but any sense of hostility had seemingly abated.

'Come on,' I murmured to Bambi, feeling her resistance but keeping firm. 'Let's brush you down instead, okay?'

I heard the gate close behind us, just a gentle click as the latch was secured this time. As I tied Bambi up and loosened her cinch, working my way round and taking off her saddle, Cole suddenly appeared in front of me. I stopped, and in silence, as I dared to look up at him, he stepped closer, the saddle the only thing keeping his body apart from mine.

The anger I'd felt before still simmered, but as he reached out and gently took it from me, our hands brushed each other. Sparks shot up my arms, my heart responding instantly, even as I shoved the thought away.

'I can handle that, you know,' I blurted, gesturing at the saddle.

'Oh, I get the feeling you can handle a whole lot more than that,' he replied, barely breaking his stride as he carried it away towards the barn.

Closing my eyes for a moment, resting my hand on Bambi's shoulder, I willed away the feeling it left me with, one that sat right next to the anger, that threatened to boil right over.

'Who the hell *is* this man, eh, girl?' I whispered to Bambi, reaching down to the tray full of brushes I'd spotted by the barn wall.

I started gently on her back, throwing my focus into her response, any sensitive points where the brush might feel too much. But in seconds she had relaxed, her head lowering as I applied more pressure, taking out some of the frustration of the last half an hour.

'You understand them, don't you?'

Cole's voice was low as he leant against the barn, watching.

I bit back the sharper response that formed in my mind. He had apologized. He was making an effort. The version of him I'd met in the bar flashed in my mind, the feel of his lips on mine.

'Yeah, as much as a city girl can,' I said, not pausing to look at him.

There was a silence, broken only by the sound of the brush working through Bambi's beautiful coat, and the other horses moving around in the barn.

'Right,' he replied. 'Lottie, I—'

'I'm not interested,' I lied, working my way around Bambi to her other side, letting her body shield me from him. 'I've got other things to do today once this is done. So I just need to concentrate on finishing this up and go.'

'Other things?' he asked, after another pause.

'Applying for jobs at home. In the city – you know, the real world.'

The words came out harder than I'd intended and, unable to resist, I looked up, catching his expression. That same hint of amusement was there, the infuriating gleam in his eyes that meant he knew just how far under my skin he was.

'Okay, I won't hold you up. And I'm guessing you don't need help taking her back to her stall after? I'm going out on Domino for a while.'

I shook my head, not trusting myself to speak again. And as Cole walked away, I made a resolution.

It was time to reassess and deal with the mess at home, I decided, before a whole new one emerged here.

CHAPTER 8

'I'll give you this much,' Lil said, holding back a yawn. 'You got here just in time. We need every pair of hands this weekend to move the cows. You sure you'll be okay riding again? I'll make sure Jesse gives you Jasper.'

'Yeah, fine,' I replied, knowing that my two-day stint of avoiding Cole would be coming to an abrupt end.

'You got a bathing suit with you?' she asked, a half-smile on her lips as she stood, stretching. 'We'll be going up to the pools.'

When I shook my head, she eyed me critically.

'Well, you could borrow one of mine, but I reckon we'll need to feed you up for another month before you fill it out. Wait a sec – when are you leaving? You didn't just book a week, did you?'

'Nah, two,' I replied, but at her crestfallen expression I added, 'I guess it depends on any job interviews coming up. I applied for a whole bunch of them, so I'm not sure how long it'll take.'

My avoiding Cole had involved endless searching and applying for jobs online, trawling through LinkedIn until my eyes felt like they were bleeding. When I couldn't face that any more, I'd started the mammoth task of tidying Lil's office, itching to re-organize her own haphazard 'filing' into something neat and tidy.

'I don't think it's ever looked like this,' she'd breathed, genuine wonder in her eyes as she gazed around the room. 'Dad was just as messy as me. Mom was always poking at him for it.'

I squeezed her arm.

'How they doing now?'

She rolled her eyes.

'I mean, they're speaking again, which is something, I guess. Couldn't make it to Mom's party this week, though – not with the guests and the ranch. Suggested she come over here instead, see some of her old friends but, yeah . . .' Lil paused, biting her lip. 'Still too painful, I think. It was real bad at the end, Lottie. I'm glad you never saw that.'

I hugged her tight then, and she returned it.

'I'm so sorry you had to do all that alone,' I whispered.

'I had Cole,' she said, giving me a last squeeze. 'He held me together.'

Even though it had no right to, my heart dropped like a stone.

'Wait – you and Cole . . . you knew him back then? Were you together?'

She giggled then, her face lighting up, looking suddenly younger. 'Oh, hell no! I mean, I thought about it at the very beginning – who wouldn't, right? But he's just been a good friend. The best, actually. I know he comes across different sometimes.' She cocked her head at me, arching an eyebrow. 'But he's not an asshole. The opposite. If anything, he's overprotective, takes on too much to save me worrying about it. Dude ranching is hard work and keeping the bookings coming in is even harder. There are things in Cole's past that complicate stuff. I don't want to speak for him, but honestly, the way he is – it's not about you, Lottie. I swear it.'

I nodded, keeping my face blank. Clearly Cole hadn't said anything to her about our drunken kiss, and strangely, I didn't know whether to feel relieved or disappointed.

'I'm glad he's been good to you,' I replied, trying to smile and placate her a little. 'You deserve nothing less.'

———

We'd left it there, with things unsaid on both sides. Now the weekend was finally here, and with the fine May weather continuing, there was one more thing to do before we left.

'You did WHAT?' Hestia had bellowed, the sound distorting on my phone as she screamed and laughed in the background. 'YES LOTTIE! Fucking epic – tell me everything, ohmygod – I can't believe you did that!'

I'd filled her in, but strangely the closer I came to telling her about Cole, the further I pushed it away. I wasn't sure what I felt about any of it, especially after talking to Lil. Her picture of Cole, the best friend, the kind, hot guy in the bar whose mouth and hands had made me feel more than I ever had before . . . and then the provocative asshole here on the ranch.

'Do not come home until you've had a good, long break, okay? Ride some cowboys. What is it they say? Save a horse, ride a cowboy?'

'I miss you,' I laughed, tucking in the edges of my shirt.

'Me too,' she added. 'I could go for a cowboy – or girl – myself. Cal's being a total dick.'

We'd talked about him for a while and I'd ended the call wanting to invite her here for a break of her own, thinking how well she'd fit in. Then I'd realized that on second thoughts, she'd take one look at Cole and me, and know. Plus, he'd be receiving a roasting if the asshole side re-emerged. I smiled, imagining it. He wouldn't stand a chance.

And now there was the last, most difficult message to deliver.

Chickening out of a phone call and not wanting to replicate his own dick behaviour by stooping to a WhatsApp message, I decided on an email. It took about half an hour to write, and I tried to sound matter-of-fact rather than angry. I wanted him to know that I'd seen him with that woman, that it left no room for argument or further conversation about us. I left out the part about leaving London, not wanting to give him the satisfaction of knowing it'd devastated me enough to make me retreat to another country.

Having ignored his two messages from the previous day – You're very quiet, all okay? and What about Claridge's next Friday? x – I knew it couldn't be put off much longer. Grabbing the small bag Lil had loaned me for my overnight things and finger hesitating over the send button, I closed my eyes and tapped it. Done.

Leaving my phone on the bed, I headed out to the yard, shielding my eyes from the sun. New people chatted with Jesse and Lil as horses were taken out of two large trailers nearby. The drive was a big operation, meaning cowboys from other ranches came to help. Bailey was tacking up the horses and with Cole thankfully not present, I made a beeline for her.

'Oh hey, glad you're coming along, bunking with me tonight.' She winked at me as I approached Jasper, checking his cinch and giving him a quick scratch.

'You snore?' I asked, receiving a resolute head shake in return.

'Course not,' she replied, mock insulted as she swung up and onto her horse.

I did the same, noting with a jolt that Cole had now joined the party down by the trailers, seemingly orchestrating the whole thing. He led a tall, broad-backed horse with a grey coat and dappled black spots, mounting in seconds.

'Is that an Appaloosa?' I asked Bailey, trying to focus on the horse and failing. I saw Cole's face light up as someone made him smile, his powerful thighs gripping the horse as he urged her forward.

'Sure is – she's a beauty, ain't she?'

Something clicked.

'Wait – is that Domino? Jesse mentioned her before. Jasper doesn't like her much.'

Bailey laughed. 'Something like that. She's a little full of herself and Jasper's got no time for it. Dunkin gets on with everyone though, don't ya, sugar?'

She patted her neck, then swung around towards the field.

'I need to ask you about how you name horses,' I said, following.

'Hold that thought, honey – we're up front. Come on, Dunkin, *git*!' she yelled and before I could answer, added, 'Keep up, cowpoke!'

Jasper didn't need telling twice. In seconds we were flying, the field ahead long, flat and seemingly endless. His gait was as smooth as ever, but as I kept in line with Bailey's streaming red hair in front, I realized he was slower than he used to be, not able to extend himself in quite the same way.

Eventually, mixing slower and faster periods of riding, the other cowboys joining us along the way, we approached the elbow of the river. The cows were spread out across the two vast pastures beyond, their calves romping around as steam rose from two pools in the gathering twilight. The pools came from the natural hot springs underground, dotted all over the state around Yellowstone. These particular pools had always been well used by our family, one of them big enough to fit six people at a push, while the other was much smaller, perfect for one or two.

We made camp, and I studiously ignored Cole, focusing on Bailey's instructions to get the tent up and ready. As night flooded the sky, I caught a glimpse of him out of the corner of my eye, looking over at us both before someone called him away.

'Got something for you,' Lil said a little later, emerging from the darkness between the trees. 'Meant to give it to you earlier, but Bailey had you racing off so quick I thought it best to wait.' Her tent was set back a little, next to Cole and Jesse's. They sat out the front, deep in conversation. Beyond that, uphill a few feet were a couple of campfires where the rest of the cowboys gathered, the flickering light spitting sparks into the inky blackness beyond. In Lil's outstretched hand was a cowboy hat, a pale camel colour, with a deeper brown leather band around the crown.

'Really?' I breathed, loving it instantly. 'Are you sure?'

She just smiled and gestured for me to put it on. I let my hair down, dark curls spilling out, and placed the hat over them. It fitted perfectly, just snugly enough to stay put and keep my hair still.

'Damn, Lottie girl, you're too pretty, you know that?'

I nudged her away, feeling the soft felt brim between my fingers.

'I love it – thanks, Lil.'

She tipped her own hat to me and started walking back up towards the campfire. 'You eaten?' she tossed back over her shoulder. 'Come get something, we'll be bunking down soon. Crazy early start.'

'I'll be there in a minute,' I called out, taking my hat off and putting it back on again, twirling round once to see if it would come off.

'She's right, you sure do pass for a fine cowgirl.' Startled, I glanced to the left. Jesse and Cole were both watching me, Jesse smiling wide. 'Just be careful no one else takes it and puts it on, y'hear?'

I risked a few steps towards them, Cole's face unmoving, his features shadowed. My heart sped up.

'I'm sure you're going to tell me why?' I asked, watching as Cole shifted, finally looking up, his lips curving.

'Wear the hat, ride the cowboy – or cowgirl, Princess.'

He held my eyes as though willing a response. The darkness

covered the redness I knew was spreading across my cheeks. Jesse grinned.

'Best be careful then,' I answered, slowly turning towards the campfire.

———

Eventually, after the camp had settled down, I discovered that Bailey was a liar. Despite me poking her to roll over at least three or four times, her snoring all but lifted the canvas off the ground.

I lay still, looking up into the darkness, thoughts drifting to Kyle, to his response. Would he be sorry? Promise to change? I'd have to face him eventually, when I went home. Sighing, I pushed deeper into the sleeping bag to find more warmth, adjusting the rolled-up towel I'd put under my head as a pillow. My legs and back were still sore from my fall, today's riding adding to it. Tomorrow was going to hurt.

Suddenly, an idea hit.

The pools.

Before I could talk myself out of it, I crept out of the tent, shining the small torch Bailey had brought to navigate through the trees. The fires had been carefully extinguished earlier to prevent any chance of causing wildfire, which meant that the moon was the only source of light. Luckily it was almost full, casting a silvery sheen across the river as the wisps and whorls of steam from the pools danced.

I climbed the bank to reach them, clutching my towel under my arm.

And froze.

'This your way of saying you're sorry?'

I almost choked. Cole.

Leaning back against the smooth rocks at the side of the smaller pool, exposed arms and broad chest reflected in the moonlight, he looked like he owned this space. As though he was one and the same as the untamed landscape.

'Sorry? For what?' I hissed, only just resisting the urge to rest my hands on my hips as I said it.

'For calling me an asshole?' he said, raising an eyebrow as he ran his fingers through the hair that fell across his face, chasing it back.

'But you . . . I didn't actually call you an asshole. I said your assumptions about me made you come across *like* an asshole.'

If my year of working alongside lawyers had taught me anything, it was to be careful about the words you used, how to skirt the lines between different meanings.

'Right,' he replied. 'Same thing. So, you getting in, or you going to freeze yourself half to death out there?'

I hesitated. Technically it was my family that owned this ranch; these were not his pools to monopolize. But . . . I risked another glance at him and saw the open curiosity in his face, the hard planes of muscle in his chest, and under the surface of the water . . . well, that I could only imagine.

'Well, I can't,' I replied, stepping back. 'I'm not just stripping off in front of you. If you were any kind of gentleman you'd get out and leave me be.'

I turned and began to walk away.

'Wait up, wait up,' he called, keeping his voice low. 'I'm sorry, I'm only teasing. How's about I turn around and keep my eyes to myself, then you let me know when you're safely in and tucked away?'

The deep aching in my legs begged me to return, the sincerity in his eyes egging it on.

Narrowing my eyes in response, I walked over, drawing closer before making a motion with my hand for him to turn around. He did so immediately, presenting me with a back so toned and sculpted that I simply stared at it for a solid few seconds before shaking myself and stripping off. I hesitated at my underwear, but figuring I didn't want wet clothes in my bag, they followed.

'Why are you awake anyway?' I asked, clutching my towel to my front and stepping over to the larger pool, separated from his smaller one by a few rocks.

'Jesse snores,' he replied as I dropped the towel and stepped in, the warm water sending goosebumps across my cold skin. It was the temperature of a perfect bath. I lowered myself under the surface, twisting my hair back to keep most of it out of the water. 'And I like sitting out here like this, it's . . . peaceful. Usually.'

'I'm in,' I said, rolling my eyes at his comment and mirroring his initial position, arms out of the water on the rocks beside me, but carefully keeping my chest under the surface.

He turned back around, his eyes lingering a few seconds longer than I knew how to handle across my face, my neck and where my skin disappeared into the water. A silence fell, even the soft sounds of the river, the horses and cows around us fading out, and a feeling crept through me, my thighs aching in a whole new way as I watched him right back.

Clearing his throat a little, he broke eye contact, leaning his head back on the rocks and looking right up at the moon. My pulse thudded in my ears as I wondered if he could see below the waterline, and about what might happen if he climbed in here. Once again my mind took me back to the night I'd arrived, to his hands on my body. Imagining how they would feel now on my bare skin, where they might wander, unrestricted by clothes.

'So given that you're not a city girl,' he said, gradually turning his head back to me, moonlight reflected in his eyes, 'then what's a country girl doing in the city?'

I arched my eyebrows at his admission of his previous misconception, a handful of sarcastic responses landing alongside the more straightforward answers I could give. But, if I was being honest, with him and myself, none of them fitted.

'Trying to make something of myself.' I shrugged. 'Honestly, I don't know.'

Admitting it out loud felt painful, especially to someone who I couldn't get a read on and whose reaction I couldn't guess.

I closed my eyes and leant back, waiting for the provocation to begin again. Would he try for a reaction? Maybe try and get me to stand up in the water if I was angry enough and forgot myself? Could I goad him into doing the same? Did I want to?

'My mom was a country girl in the city,' he said, his voice lower than before, jolting me from my thoughts. 'She . . . felt the same thing, I think.'

Confused, I turned back to him, noting the tightness in his jaw. This was hard for him to admit too, I could see – painful, even.

'And how did it work out for her?' I asked, keeping my voice gentle, wanting to repay his honesty in return, the rush of empathy I felt deep down.

He paused, finding my eyes again. We stared at each other for a moment, goosebumps building across my arms, forcing me to lower them into the water.

'I don't know,' he said, ducking his head a little as a raw under-tone crept into his words. 'She rarely visited me, my brother or my dad after she left us. Last I heard she was running some tech company in San Francisco, found herself a whole new family over there.'

I swallowed as the pain now openly seeped into his expression. It was all I could do not to reach over and offer a hand, a touch on his arm to express the ache of sadness I suddenly felt on his behalf. The city girl jibes now made perfect sense, expressing the hurt that was clearly still so close to the surface.

'Shit,' I replied, 'I'm sorry. No wonder you're not keen on city people. I had no idea.'

His half-smile was sad, the accompanying shrug not quite casual enough to be convincing.

'How would you know? It's okay. I mean, it's not, but I'm a grown-ass man.' He sighed, shaking his head. 'I need to let this shit go, you know?'

I kept still, aware of just how vulnerable he was being with me. It felt like a real apology somehow for the past few days; not a few words at the surface, but pulling the truth from the deep, painful though it was. It reminded me somehow of how Hestia was, a genuine generosity of spirit shining through.

'Or, live with it, recognize it for what it is. You don't have to be defined by her actions.' I paused, considering him in a new light. 'From what Lil tells me, you're defining yourself in the opposite way. She told me what you've done for her, for the ranch. I get the impression you're about as far from selfish as it gets.'

My voice was quiet, but the words found their mark. He stayed quiet a moment, eyes on mine, softened.

'So what do you want to make of yourself?' he asked, shifting slightly in the water and disturbing the surface. I caught a glimpse of his abs, and fought to look away.

'I just want to be good at what I do, whatever that is. If I could do that away from the city, then . . . that would be the dream. But that's where all the opportunities are.' I stopped, suddenly hearing my dad's voice, somehow melded with mine. 'Maybe it's just a temporary thing,' I added, my voice dropping to a whisper. 'I'm not sure I can live surrounded by concrete my whole life.'

I felt his eyes on me, searching.

'You and Lil kinda look alike, you know?' he said, a new edge to his tone. He shifted across the pool, drawing closer to the edge that bordered mine. 'Makes it difficult.'

My heart stuttered as I glanced up to see the change in his expression, the look he was giving me melting me right down to my core.

'Makes what difficult?' I asked, cursing myself for how breathy and ridiculous I sounded, the same way I had after he'd kissed me back in the bar. The way his lips had dragged against my neck, the feel of them as they'd brushed against my ear.

He smiled, eyes dipping.

'I think of Lil as family,' he began, his hands emerging from the water, gripping the side. 'But the thoughts I've had about you, well, they're not things you ever want to be thinking about family.'

I blinked, my eyes widening.

He chuckled and without warning, suddenly launched himself up by his hands and pulled himself out of the water. I turned my head away, but not before I'd caught sight of . . . everything.

'Holy shit, Cole,' I muttered, the image of his perfect, round ass, strong, long legs and package now branded onto my mind, filling my whole damn body with fire.

'That's what they all say,' he laughed, and before I could retort, added, 'What I mean to say is, no hard feelings, Princess. I've got no problem with you, never have.' He paused, and I heard the sound of a towel over skin. 'It's just what to *do* with you.'

Speechless, I gripped the rock in front of me, still listening as he started to walk away. 'Don't stay out long – the other cowboys will be up soon and I don't fancy starting my day knocking skulls together.'

Still stunned, I turned, watching him slowly disappear into the darkness like a figment from my imagination.

CHAPTER 9

Lil was right. It was a crazy early start.

After pulling on my boots and wandering over to the campfires, now re-lit to heat some drinking water, I realized just how far I was from home. With my hands jammed in my jeans pockets to keep them warm, I looked across to the river, the first slivers of coral bleeding into the clouds at the horizon, the towering Tetons backlit with the first hints of dawn.

'Ma'am.'

A voice at my side made me jump.

Cole. He was holding out a coffee cup, the contents throwing a haze of steam across his face.

'What a gentleman,' I replied, returning a small smile.

'Milk and sugar over there,' he added, acknowledging my words with a nod.

'I like it as it is,' I replied, watching as his mouth twitched. He appeared to fight back a reply, settling for a nod before wandering back over to the campfire.

Something had shifted between us.

I drank my coffee alone, keeping my eyes on the view ahead, not trusting myself to turn to the one behind, the one that would probably stare right back. It felt like the precipice of a whole other level of trouble, trouble that I couldn't afford to get into. There was only a week or so left before my return flight home, and there was too much to fix there without making more problems for myself here.

Once we'd all packed up, the real work started. Lil and I kept to the left of the herd as Cole and three of the other cowboys drove from the back; Bailey stayed near the front, with Jesse and another two cowboys hanging right.

It was slow, steady progress, sometimes hard work when a calf got separated, but after a few hours, Jasper felt like an extension of my legs, my thoughts, as I guided him into a flat gallop to bring a breakaway group of cows back in. Several times we had to change direction on a dime, and by the time we trotted back to the main herd, Lil was whooping, a broad smile lighting up her face.

'Goddamn, that horse loves you!' she yelled over the noise of the herd, shaking her head. 'Sure you can't make it over every time we drive them?'

'Maybe,' I called back, slowing Jasper as we reached a steeper incline, leaning back in the saddle as he picked his way down the slope. I couldn't quite bring myself to admit how much I'd like that.

By the end of the day, legs aching in protest, dust covering every inch of our bodies, we emerged from the trees, the flat pasture next to the ranch ahead of us.

'Why did you start the dude ranching?' I asked Lil, deep in thought as the end of the ride beckoned.

'Money,' she replied, pursing her lips. 'Making a living from ranching is hard. Costs are going up and profits are difficult to make. It's why Mom left – she wanted to sell up, had a good offer, too. But I couldn't. It just wasn't right.'

The thought of the ranch gone, Jasper sold, Jesse, Bailey . . . Cole, all scattered. It felt wrong.

'But dude ranching helps?' I offered, wanting her to confirm it wholeheartedly.

She shrugged. 'It keeps me out of the red, just. But you know how it is, the Hole has so many ranches, hotels, motels . . . competition is tough. Guests are demanding and you know I'm no good with any of that stuff. Give me a herd of cows to brand and I'm your girl. But choosing bedding and making welcome baskets . . . that's way out of my comfort zone.'

I smiled, imagining Lil trying to choose between bedcovers in Bed Bath & Beyond.

'Why don't you let me help?' I replied, urging Jasper ahead to draw level with her. 'Whilst I'm here. Marketing's my thing, remember? Branding, aesthetic – all that.'

She smiled back, reaching out a hand. I did the same and we squeezed each other for a moment.

'I wish you didn't have to leave.'

'I've got time still,' I reassured her, not wanting to think about leaving, not yet. 'But first, we need to honour an old tradition.'

She frowned, clearly about to ask what the hell I meant when I touched my heels to Jasper's sides, letting out my reins. Ears forward, rested after a long walking stint, he leapt forth with the same sweet enthusiasm as he'd always had, his long legs eating up the ground.

'Fifty bucks says I can still beat you,' I yelled back, watching as she grinned, Penny skittering to the side then bursting forward in pursuit.

I heard the cowboys on the right holler, and some whistling and laughs from the back. And just like we had all those years earlier, before dude ranching, before money and men and every other complication, I grabbed onto my hat with one hand and let Jasper fly. Wind whistling in my ears, cold air making my eyes stream, I finally felt it. A gut punch, a reminder.

I felt free.

––––

A couple of quiet days followed, the additional cowboys gradually heading home after showering me and Lil with praise and suggestions, including entering me for the barrel racing at the upcoming rodeo. Bailey had offered some coaching, but I'd retreated, barely able to stand after so long in the saddle, my legs unused to the physical onslaught.

In the quiet of my room in the house, gently stretching to ease the pain, I knew it was only part of the story. The other part was right there on my phone, the screen littered with notifications, my life on the other side of the Atlantic tapping my shoulder.

With a sigh, I opened it up. Other than one from Hestia, checking in on whether I'd ridden any cowboys yet, all the messages were from Kyle.

> Lottie, we need to talk. I'm coming over after work.

> Where are you? It's 9 p.m. – are you still at the office?

> This is ridiculous, you've got the wrong end of the stick. Please don't be childish about this. We need to talk.

I closed my messages, rage building up.
Fucking bastard.
The emails from him were no better – four of them in total, all along the same lines, all feeble attempts at gaslighting me. But there were two others, both invitations to job interviews after the applications I'd shot off earlier in the week. I scanned them, noting that both were online – one just before I was due to leave the ranch,

the other a day after I was due back. Both were similar roles to my old job, marketing in banking and law.

I blew out the tension I was holding, mind racing with everything I needed to prepare, trying to digest everything I'd just read.

A knock sounded at my door and seconds later, Bailey's head was hanging round it.

'Lil's sent me to get you rodeo ready. Now I'm no girl's girl, but you can come raid my wardrobe if you need? I'm assuming you only got a handful of things before coming up here from town, right?'

I thought about the majority of my clothes, hastily loaded into the washer the previous day and re-washed again this morning, the dust here somehow ingraining itself into every fibre. I only had my city clothes left to wear, but from what I remembered of the rodeos I'd been to as a kid, they wouldn't cut it.

'I'm all yours,' I said, letting out a sigh as I chucked my phone back on the bed, tucking the dressing gown around me. The weight remained in my hand, in my head.

'You okay?' she asked, opening the door wide as I came out.

'Yeah,' I lied. 'Stuff at home, nothing interesting.'

She eyed me, missing nothing.

'If you say so, sugar,' she replied. 'If you want my advice, best thing to do is get good and drunk, find yourself a nice cowboy to pass the time.'

I snorted, a pang of emotion hitting me square on.

'You'd really love my friend Hestia,' I replied, missing her more than ever. 'And yes, maybe you're right.'

We reached Bailey's room, a surprisingly tidy space with her closet doors already wide open.

'The weather's staying fine, so think it's time to mix it up,' she said, glancing back at me, eyeing my legs with a smile.

Some thirty minutes later, somewhat overheated from trying on half Bailey's wardrobe, we'd landed on a cornflower blue sundress, almost the exact shade as my eyes. It was shorter than anything I'd worn since uni, showing off my legs and chest in a way I wasn't used to after a year of buttoning up in the city.

'You sure this isn't too much? I feel like I'm hardly wearing anything?' I asked, torn between self-consciousness and objectively liking what I saw.

Bailey just chuckled.

'You look just right to me. I mean, I reckon half the rodeo will be queueing up to pass the time with you,' she said, ushering me out and guiding me to the back of the house, hurriedly putting on her boots. 'I've got to get Dunkin ready – come on over if you like, give me a hand?'

Down at the yard, despite the hat, boots and a cropped denim jacket over the top from Lil, I still felt exposed. Especially when Jesse wolf-whistled, standing in the corral with Cole, rope in hand, a plastic cow head attached to some hay bales in front of them.

'I told you,' Bailey said, glancing back at me before splitting off towards the stalls. 'Eyes on the prize, Jesse. Ain't no one paying out for roping cowgirls.'

'Told him what?' I shouted after her, not quite brave enough to look towards Cole.

'That you'd look way hotter in a sundress than any of those buckle bunnies,' she called back, her voice muffled as she turned into the stalls. 'Better watch your back!'

Unsure whether she was joking or not, I gave Jesse an apprehensive smile.

'Ever tried roping, Lottie?' Jesse asked, an expression of pure mischief on his face as he approached the fence. He was dressed in full rodeo gear, from the leather chaps to the Diamond Back-branded jacket.

'As a kid,' I admitted, careful to give only a quick glance back at Cole, who remained near the hay bales. His face was neutral, but his arms were folded, his body rigid.

'C'mon then, give it a try. If it's anything like your riding, you'll be a natural.'

He beckoned me over the fence, but when I gave him a dead-eyed expression, glancing down at the short dress and heading for the gate, they both cracked a smile.

'Worth a try,' Jesse said as I approached, gathering together rope in his hands. Cole remained a few feet away, present but distant, his eyes following every movement Jesse made.

My first attempt was awful, missing the cow's head by a mile.

'Your movement was nice, just need that aim,' Jesse encouraged, beaming at my attempt. 'Oh dang it, I need to load up – Cole can take over. Ex-state champion, used to be better than me, if you can believe it.'

Cole raised an eyebrow at his friend, arms still folded.

'It's okay, you don't have to,' I said, gathering the rope in a clumsy imitation of Jesse as he strode off towards the stalls.

Cole approached slowly, unfolding his arms as he drew closer.

'Sure I can,' he replied, voice gentle as he reached for the rope. I handed it over without a word, our hands touching as I did so. Shock registered as he didn't attempt to move his hand away, seeming to pause instead, brushing my finger with his. I was rendered mute by the same look he'd given me the previous night, the one that had promised a reprise of our first meeting, given the chance.

'You're aiming a little too low,' he said eventually, breaking my trance. 'Try for the space above the horns instead.'

He stood back from me, lifting the rope up, swinging it briefly over his head before flicking it out and over the cow's head in one smooth motion. Except I didn't move my eyes off him the whole time, remembering what I'd seen as he'd left the water the night before. The same vision that'd played over and over in my mind since, along with what might've happened if I'd pulled him into my pool, or I'd got out with him.

'Lottie?' he said, stepping back, closer than before. I had to lift my head to meet his eyes. 'It definitely won't work if you're not going to at least look at the target.'

Busted.

'Right. The rope. Aim higher,' I repeated, feeling like a total pervert and taking it back from him, ignoring the smile under his hat. He knew what was in my mind, just as I could guess the contents of his.

I changed my stance, trying to copy his, trying not to look as awkward as I felt.

'That's right,' he guided, 'now give it a wider loop and keep your eyes on the horns. Up a little higher . . . yeah, that's it. That looks good.'

Taking a breath, desperate not to make a total ass of myself, I threw out the rope and hoped for the best. By some small miracle it caught one of the cow horns, before slipping off.

'Perfect.'

His voice alone threatened to push me over the edge as I thought of being around him for the whole evening ahead. I wasn't sure how I would cope.

'Not perfect,' I replied, shrugging as he walked over to the cow's head to unhook the rope. 'Better, though. Probably beginner's luck.'

He tilted his head, waited for me to brave another look at him.

'No, I meant . . .' He gestured at me, my outfit. 'Perfect. Your roping's not bad either.'

Now a familiar feature, I blushed again, looking down at my boots in the dirt. Unsure what to do with myself, I chose to keep him talking, keep us talking.

'Why did you get into roping?' I asked as he walked back with slow, measured steps.

'Always done it, since I was a boy. My dad taught me and my brother as soon as we were old enough to hold a rope.' He came to a stop, his distance from me as deliberate as my attempt to hold back whatever it was between us. 'My family has a small ranch on the other side of Jackson, right on the state border. It's nothing like this place, but still plenty to manage. My brother's in the process of taking over, now that he's getting married soon.'

'And bronc riding? Did you get into that young too?' The atmosphere changed as he frowned, his fist clenched around the rope. I kicked myself, remembering what Jesse had said, that this was likely to be a touchy subject. 'I'm sorry,' I started, walking towards him, then stopping. 'I'm being nosy. You don't have to answer.'

He stared at me, close up now, the same clear honesty as he'd shown back in the pools shining through again.

'It's okay,' he answered, rubbing the back of his neck. 'I don't talk about it much, and maybe that makes it worse.' He seemed to gather himself and before I could apologize again, added, 'I started bronc riding young and competed from when I was fifteen or sixteen. I watched Seth, my best friend, die doing it though, three years ago now, so I decided to quit.'

My stomach fell away, a violent stab of empathy almost taking my breath as I held my hand to my mouth. The thought of it, of that happening to Hestia . . .

'Oh fuck,' I breathed, hating myself for the pain in his eyes. 'That's . . . awful. I'm sorry for making you bring that up. I can't imagine . . .'

He shook his head, dismissing my apology.

'You didn't know,' he replied, eyeing my distress carefully. 'Besides, it feels good to think of him sometimes, you know? Away from what happened, back to all the good shit before it. He had a hell of a sense of humour, smartest mouth I'd ever heard, always cracking jokes at my expense.'

I smiled, not able to help myself at that description.

I was relieved when he returned it. 'He sounds great,' I said gently.

'He would've liked you, I know it. Would've had a lot to say about something like this outfit right here.'

At this shift in the conversation, I looked down, startled as he took one last step towards me, his fingers lifting my chin. Looking up into his beautiful face, close enough to see the dark stubble across his jaw, I saw a very different emotion in his eyes now.

'Cole, I—'

He let the rope go and it fell at my feet.

'Tell me you don't want to pick up where we left off at the bar,' he breathed, cutting me off, his free hand now trailing across my chest, just above the neckline. 'This damn dress is here to fucking torture me, ain't it?'

I was stunned into silence yet again, the very last slither of my self-control dissolving as he moved his fingers up to trace my lips, parting under the pressure, and I willed him to close the gap between us.

'Cole?' Bailey's voice rang out across the yard. 'Can you give me a hand with this ramp? Damn thing's stuck.'

We sprang apart, Cole immediately walking away towards the stalls, leaving me to recalibrate my breathing. Needing to do something with my trembling hands, I reached down for the rope on the ground, gathering it up into some kind of loop. Jesse led his horse past the corral, heading for the trailer attached to a huge red Dodge Ram truck.

'Lottie, bring that with you – you're riding with me, honey.'

CHAPTER 10

The rodeo was everything I remembered from all that time ago.

Tendrils of gold and apricot slid across the snow-tipped mountain peaks beyond the banked seating, and as day bled into night, the atmosphere under the floodlights changed. The whole town seemed to have arrived, locals and tourists blending into a noisy mass of conversation, music, and announcements over the tannoy.

'First one of the season,' Lil announced as we made our way in. 'Let's get some drinks before it gets going. Bailey's up first, I think, so we need to get some good seats at the front.'

We cut through the growing crowd, Lil leading me through towards the covered stand and the less busy food stalls around the back. I'd lost sight of Jesse after he'd dropped me at the front entrance, Bailey and Cole also swallowed up in the masses, prepping Dunkin somewhere. I tried to convince myself that I wasn't looking for Cole, watching out for his tall, broad shoulders amongst the crowd.

'So I know it's fun,' I started, distracting myself from the memory of his fingers on my chest. 'But is there any other reason that everyone competes? I know there's prize money, but surely that's not enough incentive to risk getting your head cracked open by a bull?'

Lil smiled as we reached the stall, ordering her drink and letting me do mine.

'From a business point of view, it gets our name out there,' she said, gesturing to the ranch name embroidered on the back of her jacket. 'But it's more than that. Bailey, Jesse – all cowboys work damn hard. They can let off steam, get recognized for their skills and make some extra money. Above all, though, it's just tradition – it's what we do here.'

She tilted her drink towards the seats she was aiming for.

'There are so many tourists,' I said, seeing enthralled expressions, selfie after selfie being taken against the JACKSON HOLE RODEO sign. 'Is the ranch on social media?'

'Come on now,' Lil laughed, shaking her head as we slid between the seats and found two near the front. 'You've seen a week at the ranch already – when do you reckon we would've had time for that?'

I shrugged. 'It's not that hard once you've got the basics set up. There's almost too much to film and capture.'

My mind immediately led back to Cole, to think of the storm it would cause to film him in the hot springs pool and post it on socials. The way his eyes had held mine through the steam, the water sluicing from his bare torso, running down his abs towards his—

'You okay? You seem a little distracted since the drive,' Lil said, forcing me to take a breath, then a deep drink from my beer.

I shrugged, filling her in on the job interview requests and Kyle's tirade of gaslighting.

'That man sounds like a real snake,' Lil said, shaking her head as the stands filled around us, the anticipation for the events now a physical thrumming energy.

'Bailey told me to just get drunk and find myself a cowboy,' I said, throwing her a speculative look.

Eyes narrowing for a moment, she cocked her head.

'You asking for permission or something, honey?'

I swallowed. *Less permission, more forgiveness.*

The announcer cut in, saving me from answering. The show started, a rider kicking off the evening by riding around the arena, a huge, rippling US flag catching the lights, obnoxiously loud music pounding through the stands. The barrel racers were up first, Bailey third in the line-up of a dozen or so.

I watched, mouth half open as she belted across the dirt, Dunkin at full stretch, her golden coat shimmering in the lights, Bailey's hair loose for once. Like a streak of fire they shot towards the barrels, turning as tight as possible to make a turn, the laws of physics half denied by the angles they made.

'Holy shit,' I hissed. 'How is she doing that?'

Lil laughed, knocking her beer back.

'Those two are magic,' she said. 'Like you and Jasper. But ain't no one getting those long legs round a bunch of barrels.'

I laughed, imagining Jasper trying it. He was too tall, his long, elegant stride a million miles from Dunkin's greedy thrusts forward, her compact size and immaculate balance making something difficult look ridiculously easy.

'You impressed Cole, you know,' Lil said after a moment, almost making me choke on my beer. 'On the drive. No complaining with the camping, you and Jasper making light work of the left side back down to the ranch. I barely did a thing, felt like a day off.'

'I guess,' I replied, barely daring to venture anything else.

'He's not a big fan of city girls, so you must've done something right.'

I nodded slowly. 'Yeah, he seems . . . like a good guy,' I finished, freezing as Lil turned to me with a raised eyebrow. 'I mean, he's . . . he probably said it because I'm your cousin.'

My words were lame and Lil knew it.

'He's the best,' she said slowly, her gaze suddenly intent on my face.

I dipped my head, hiding under the brim of my hat.

Shit.

'I like him but that's it,' I said, slowly looking back at her. 'My life at home is too complicated for anything else. I don't even know how I feel about Kyle . . . Everything turned upside down last week.'

Her searching look softened.

'But you're not going back to him, right? Not after all that. And a new job . . . well, that's still up in the air, right?' Unsure how to answer, I frowned as the last barrel riders shot across the ring. 'I'm just saying, give yourself a break,' Lil continued. 'Maybe just see where things take you, rather than trying to force it.'

There was undeniable logic in her words, the sense ringing true as the tannoy announcement came that Bailey was in first place with one more rider to go.

Gripping each other's hands, Lil and I craned to follow the last rider's progress, her impressive turns kicking up dust and drawing shouts and whoops from the crowd before crossing the line.

Her time was just under a second slower than Bailey's.

Lil and I shot up together, screaming like lunatics and hugging, beer spraying. People around us started calling up to Lil, a group of men and women to our left hugging her and whistling down to the arena where Bailey and Dunkin now circled, triumphant.

———

In between events we walked around to the roping chute, watching Jesse prepare. Cole stood nearby, talking to a bunch of other cowboys, foot resting on one of the bars and an easy smile on his face.

My insides turned liquid and I sipped my beer, not quite looking away quickly enough. His eyes caught mine, mid-conversation. Pausing, the cowboy he spoke to turned around, but this time I turned towards the arena.

'Goddamn it,' Lil murmured, watching a group of guys approach. Jesse straightened, his relaxed, golden smile straightening out. Somehow, he became imposing, walking ahead of us towards them.

'What's up?' I asked, knowing it couldn't be anything good if gentle, teasing Jesse bristled like that.

'Elk Creek assholes,' Lil replied. 'C'mon, let's go. Cole and Jesse will take care of it.'

As I looked behind, Cole was striding towards Jesse, two other cowboys at his back. Reaching the Elk Creek group, Cole towered over them all, stance spread wide.

'Should we tell someone? Security or something?' I said, a stab of fear for them making me hesitate.

'Honey, they are the security.' Lil laughed, but her eyes were hard. She knocked back the rest of her beer. 'This is Wyoming, Lottie, remember? Law enforcement don't feature real big around here. We deal with things ourselves.'

———

The rest of the rodeo passed quickly, with Jesse's roping event towards the end. He was immaculate, flying out of the gate in pursuit of the cow, taking it down in what felt like the blink of an eye.

Lil's jaw remained tight, her gaze focused on some of the Elk Creek cowboys below.

'What's the beef between you and them?' I asked, keeping my voice low in case someone they knew sat nearby.

'They're the ones that tried to buy the ranch from Mom,' she replied. 'Pulled every trick in the book to make her do it. Their land joins ours, down near the highway. We've got the better pasture, more scenic routes, sunsets, thermal pools . . . they want it all. Been dude ranching about five years now, starting to really draw 'em all in.'

I bit my lip, hating the way this clearly affected her.

'Are they still trying to buy it?' I asked, my stomach dropping as she nodded.

We watched the rest of the competitors in silence, letting the crowd fill the space. My thoughts were in overdrive, turning over everything Lil had said and everything she hadn't. It had to be tempting, to get rid of the worry and stress of running the ranch, and gain the freedom to live a more normal life. Lil was only twenty-eight, forced to act like someone with at least another decade of responsibility on her shoulders.

I was suddenly horribly aware of how pathetic my problems were in comparison; how immature my behaviour had been. Running away at the first stumbling block.

'Yes, Jesse!' Lil yelled, jumping to her feet. 'Holy cow, he did it, Lottie!'

We hugged again and I followed Lil as she bounded down through the stand to find him. I hung back a little, too caught up in my head to match her energy.

_____

Just an hour later, I found myself back in town. Having dropped the horses back, Bailey staying on the ranch and settling Dunkin after their win, Lil all but dragged me with her, Jesse and Cole already there at a bar on the far west side of town.

'First drink's on me,' she announced as we walked in. It was full of rodeo-goers, the music and voices an assault on my ears after the sleepy calm of the street outside. 'C'mon, quit brooding on whatever it is, it's been a while since we had a reason to party.' She stared me down until I rolled my eyes, breaking into a grin.

'You need something stronger than beer,' she announced. Before I could protest, she'd already yelled our order across the bar, the staff recognizing her and offering up their congratulations, some of the regulars leaning against it doing the same. I received a number of inquisitive looks, but whether it was because I looked like Lil or whether it was this dress, it was hard to say.

A small glass was pressed into my hand.

'Shots?' I groaned as Lil clinked hers against mine and gestured to me to knock it back.

I put the glass to my lips and closed my eyes, grimacing as it slid down.

Tequila.

All of a sudden I was back in London, the same sour warmth coursing through me, numbing the sting of betrayal.

'Now this,' she said, handing me a whiskey over ice.

I stared at it; that stirred a very different memory.

'Hold up, hold up! You getting drunk without us, boss?'

Jesse sidled up to Lil and I glanced around, automatically looking for Cole.

A brush of lips against my ear made me jump, but I couldn't turn. A gentle hand pressed against my waist, arm keeping me pressed to a very firm, very warm body.

'Right here, Princess.'

Before either Lil or Jesse could notice, Cole had moved to the side, nodding his thanks to Lil for the drink. He caught my eye again as Jesse led us all over to the area by the stage, the band already stirring up plenty of dancing, the drinking at the rodeo clearly starting the party early.

In that moment, I knew I had to make a choice. Either let go and have some fun, stay in the moment for now, or be sensible and keep the mess on just one side of the Atlantic.

Lil made the choice for me.

'C'mon, Lottie, some Brit you are – I've got drinks backing up here,' she yelled over the music, bringing over another four drinks.

Glancing over at Cole again, I realized how little I knew about him. I'd barely known Kyle either, before we'd got together . . . perhaps that was my problem, maybe I jumped in too fast. Or, maybe I'd met Kyle at a time when I hadn't known any better. Cole was different; his support for Lil showed that.

I knocked back the whiskey in one, taking the glass from Lil before she dragged me into the dancing fray. The band were good – fast, rock-infused country and clearly right up her street. Her enthusiasm was infectious, her smile the biggest I'd seen it since I'd arrived, so I dropped all my worries and just went with it.

We were still going some five or six songs later, the second whiskey chasing the first, a hand pressed on my hip.

'You two are creating quite the impression,' a voice said, forcing me to spin to my right to find its owner.

His face was hard, a scruffy dark beard under a dark hat.

'I'm Eli, from over at Elk Creek,' he added, in response to my confusion.

I drew back, finding Lil's hand and squeezing it.

'What do you want?' I asked, bracing myself as I felt Lil stiffen.

'I see she's already filled you in on the state of things.' He smiled. 'I'm not here to talk about that, though – that's just business. I'm here for myself right now, and myself would like to buy you a drink.'

I shook my head.

'No thanks.'

'Ah come on, sugar, you look like you need someone to show you around a little.'

His hands crept up on my hips.

'Eli, you ever want to use those hands again, you're gonna need to take them off her.'

Cole's now familiar warmth bloomed across my back as he stood behind me, his shadow falling across the smaller man. I had to resist the urge in every cell to close my eyes and lean into it.

'Okay, okay, cool it,' Eli said, backing up a half-step and releasing me.

'Cole, it's fine, don't start nothing in here,' Lil said, her hand catching his arm.

'I'm not starting it,' Cole growled, still staring at Eli, one of his own hands drifting around to my front, fingers resting on my waist. 'But I'll finish it if he doesn't quit looking at your cousin like that.'

I could hardly breathe. Enveloped in his body, his smell, the touch of his fingers . . . even through the dress it felt as it had that first night in the other bar. Overwhelming. Completely intoxicating.

Kyle had never made me feel like this. No one had. A sudden moment of passion in a bar and almost two weeks of flirting had affected me more than almost a year with someone I'd thought I loved.

The realization hit me square between the eyes and I put my hand to my throat, as though it would choke me. How could I have loved Kyle? How could that be possible when one touch from this man was enough to make me forget myself, to live a whole new level of feelings?

As Eli backed off into the crowd, Lil shot Cole a warning look and went back over to the bar, leaving us together. Alone. Slowly, he turned me to face him. Anger burnt in his expression, his eyes searching mine.

'You okay?' he asked, his voice gruff.

I nodded, unable to trust myself to speak, my eyes drifting to his mouth, then back to the warmth of his eyes.

'He's still looking over here,' he said, pinching the bridge of his nose, distracted. 'Lil's gonna kill me if I beat the shit out of him.'

'Then don't,' I replied as he blinked, trying to read my expression. 'There's more than one way to make your point.'

This time, my left hand pressed on his hip, the right brushing his fingers. They responded instantly, curling around mine.

'What did you have in mind, Princess?' he said, leaning down as I tilted my head up.

'Give him a reason not to touch me again,' I whispered.

With a barely stifled moan, he reached down and cupped my cheek, our mouths meeting in a rush, soft and crushing at the same time. Our hands, now intertwined, were bumped and jostled by the other dancers as we became our own moment, consumed by every surging feeling. His chest against mine was almost too much, and I felt an overwhelming urge to find a quieter place and rip everything separating my skin from his straight off.

We kissed as though searching for, and finding something, simultaneously. His hand eventually escaped mine and traced the outline of my breasts as I pulled him closer still. Our touches became too much for others to see, our breathing quickening. Finally, someone wolf-whistled and we paused, catching our breath, faces still almost touching.

'I've been imagining that all day,' he breathed, lips against mine again, tongue tracing my mouth as he held our bodies pressed tight. 'All fucking week, actually. I can imagine a whole lot more, but we'd need somewhere more private than here – more private than a corridor, even.'

I moved back slightly, smiling.

'I'd like that, but . . .'

He shook his head, arms still locked around me.

'I know,' he sighed, taking a reluctant step back. Hesitating, he looked down before he asked, 'When do you head home?'

It felt as though I'd been doused in ice water.

'What happened?' Jesse said, suddenly appearing to my left, carrying drinks as Lil followed. 'Was Eli making trouble?'

'Trying to,' Cole replied, taking his drink with his eyes still on me, frowning at the change in my face.

'Tell me you didn't fight,' Lil groaned. 'I just swore to Bill over there that we wouldn't make trouble and I definitely don't have the money to fix anything we break.'

'It's fine,' I jumped in as they both stared Cole down. 'Cole pretended to be with me instead, so Eli just gave up and left.' Jesse's mouth fell open and I shrugged. 'It worked.'

As Jesse high-fived Cole, a sheepish grin overtaking his surprise, Lil gave me a small, suspicious smile. I shrugged, but her face remained tight.

'I don't trust them,' she said, glancing back over at the bar where the Elk Creek cowboys were gathered in a large circle. 'I want to get us out of here – those assholes are hunting for trouble, I just know it.'

Cole nodded, holding back for Jesse and Lil to take the lead out of the bar. I moved to follow them, but as I did, he caught my hand.

'Just so you know,' he said, lifting the brim of his hat. 'I wasn't pretending back there. And I know you're leaving soon, and maybe this is more than you wanted from a trip out here to see your cousin . . . but a kiss like that doesn't happen very often. I've never met anyone like you before, Lottie.'

I searched his face, wanting to remember it all, memorize every feature as he stared back.

'Neither have I.' My voice was sad, and I was unable, unwilling to hide it. 'I . . . I don't want to leave. I . . . don't want to never feel that again.'

He took my hand again at that, his thumb brushing over my palm.

'Then don't. Fuck London.'

'And what?' I laughed, shaking my head like it wasn't as easy as all that. The whiskey dared me to say the words that formed immediately in my mind. 'Fuck you instead?'

He bit his lip, shaking his head.

'That mouth,' he murmured, urging me to walk forwards and follow the others. He kept hold of my hand, easily hidden by the crowd. 'You can't imagine what I've thought of it doing.'

I turned back, ready to tell him that I most definitely had, but his face had changed. His eyes were hard, fixed on the doorway.

'Stay behind me,' he pleaded, letting go of my hand with a gentle squeeze and striding past me, right towards the Elk Creek cowboys, who were now gathered around Lil.

'. . . can't put it off for ever, Lil. Not with our new investor. He's got pockets deeper than the valley out there and a whole team of people behind us. You'll be off that ranch by Christmas, you watch.'

'I swear to the almighty, Eli, get the fuck away from her – from all of us. How many beatings do you need?'

Cole stood within two feet of the other man, towering over him, Jesse at his side.

'Don't worry, Miller, I'm just the messenger. You can kiss all the pretty girls you want – you'll still be a drifter come spring.'

Cole paused and I froze, bracing myself for him to swing at Eli. Instead, with Lil on one arm and Jesse on the other, he left, with me right behind, opening the doors to the cold darkness beyond.

CHAPTER 11

The guest cabins were the definition of rustic chic. I opened the windows to air them out, following the instructions Lil had given me, reeled off in a rush the previous day when I'd agreed to help out. The guests weren't due until tomorrow, but I needed a distraction. Badly.

I'd left Lil, Jesse and Cole at the kitchen table, still playing cards at 1 a.m. In the wake of the Elk Creek threat, Cole and I had fallen back into the roles of ranch manager and cousin, comforting Lil and trying to offer solutions.

Doing our best not to catch each other's eyes.

Sighing, then sneezing as I beat out some of the cushions on the large couch, my hungover brain tried to fire up again. There had to be a way to really help her, to get the Elk Creek bastards off her back. Then there was the not-so-small issue of whatever this was with Cole.

I sat on the couch for a moment, bed sheets still folded over my arm. Dust motes swirled in the shaft of sunlight that struck the tribal-style rug, right in front of the wood-burning stove in the corner. I pictured us in here, locked away together, the warmth of a fire removing the need for clothes . . .

I knew I had to snap out of this, to think of all the practical implications before launching ahead into what – a rebound fling?

I had five days left here. Three days to prepare for a job interview. I didn't have time for this.

'I've never met anyone like you . . . Fuck London.' His words echoed in my mind and I felt the frustration rise. Why did I have to meet someone like him now, at the messiest time of my life? For once I knew calling Hestia wouldn't solve anything. She'd tell me to follow my heart and . . . that just wouldn't work. Would it?

Forcing myself up, I took a couple of deep breaths and got back to work, stretching fresh sheets across the bed and scrubbing the bathroom as though the royal family was on its way. I noted the few little touches Lil had made here and there: a couple of antique vases on the mantle, a beautiful driftwood mirror above a sideboard. But it felt . . . sparse somehow. As though someone had grabbed things at random, as opposed to trying to curate a real feel for this place.

To me, this place represented family – both the blood and the chosen variety – fun and sanctuary. But it was also the cowboy state, with its stunning sweeping landscapes and its vast, endless skies. The cabins didn't reflect that at all.

I stopped, suddenly inspired.

The throw cushions in my room would match the rug beautifully and make the bed look even more cosy. There was also a set of old Wyoming postcards in an interconnected pewter frame that would match the colours in the bathroom just right.

Finished with the cleaning, I peeled off the gloves and stepped outside, heading up the path towards the entrance of the second cabin on the left. A small patch of delicate yellow flowers danced in the breeze, right next to the long, feathered grasses behind them. Picking a small bunch and trying not to ruin the wild meadow vibe, I headed back into the first cabin and arranged it in one of the antique vases, filling that with water and setting it under the mirror on the sideboard. There. A bright, live snapshot of the real ranch, right as you walked in.

Satisfied and encouraged, I jogged over to the house, scanning down the slope towards the barn and corral for signs of life. I'd yet to see Cole today, yet to figure out how we'd pick up after last night. Whatever the others thought, whether or not they'd bought the excuse of us pretending to kiss to get Eli away from me, we needed to work out what we were – if we were anything at all.

Inside, not bothering to slip off my boots, I headed straight for my room. As I reached the door, the phone rang from Lil's office down the hall and I hesitated, listening out to hear if she was in there, ready to pick up.

Instead, the answerphone clicked on, the beep sounding before a pause.

'Hi there, my name's Jenna.' I crept closer to listen. 'I was at the rodeo yesterday with my family. We've been looking for a ranch to stay at later this summer for a family get-together. Our usual place is booked and, well, we umm . . . noticed your cowboy in the roping competition – Jesse, is it?' Her voice became lighter and she giggled. 'Well, we noticed the ranch name on the back of his jacket and googled you. I had no idea you were there – the cabins look nice and you're so close to town . . . so, anyway, we wanted to know if you had any days free this July . . .'

Opening the door, I strode over and picked the phone up.

'Hi there,' I started, slightly startled by myself. 'I'm Lottie, part of the Diamond Back team, thank you so much for your message. I heard a little of it – was it a week you were looking for in July? I'm sure we can help.'

My mind whirred as we spoke, and as I scrambled to find the booking system on Lil's computer, I realized that she did it all from a paper diary, scrawled reservations in barely legible hand-writing. The summer months were worryingly free.

As I hung up, having secured a week's booking from Jenna at the end of July for all three cabins, my mind kept going in the silence. That family was taking the cabins here for a week, spending thousands of dollars for three reasons.

Two of those had nothing to do with us: Jackson Hole was beautiful, and it was a favourite destination for a ton of people, which meant that often places were booked out months in advance. But the third, most important reason – a reason we had control over – was Jesse had caught a potential client's eye and captured her attention long enough to sell the ranch as a whole.

What if this was the way to help Lil? Really help her? As in, beat back Elk Creek for good and make the Diamond Back a destination in itself?

Just as a depth of feeling had unfurled as I'd kissed Cole last night, a feeling of knowing rather than guessing, so an idea grew and grew in my mind, green flags and bells making a symphony.

I took off, leaving the house again, cushions be damned for now.
'Lil?'

Swearing I'd heard her voice from outside the barn, I ran over, hair flying out behind me in the breeze. I knew it likely looked chaotic, but I didn't care. This felt important.

Rounding the corner, I walked into the stalls, stopping abruptly.

Lil and Cole stood in the corner, Cole's arm around her shoulder as she leant on his chest, tears streaming down her face. They looked up simultaneously, Lil immediately wiping her cheeks and taking a step back.

A hollow sensation opened up in my chest as Cole removed his arm from her shoulder, his eyes creasing in concern at my expression.

I tried to speak, but the vision of Kyle returning home with the blonde woman flashed through my mind; the way his arm had draped across her shoulder in a similar way, a gesture of familiarity and closeness that I realized I'd never known from him – or from any other man.

'Are you okay, Lil?' I asked, not able to bear the sight of her upset, whatever else was going on.

'Hey, uh, yeah,' she croaked, moving forwards, but stopping as I stepped back. 'Sorry, I just . . . the whole Elk Creek situation got a bit—'

'It's fine,' I replied, my voice suddenly robotic. Maybe I'd read this whole situation wrong? Maybe Lil did have feelings for Cole, but was just unwilling to admit them to me or even herself? What if me and Cole kissing last night had forced it all to the surface?'

'Lottie,' Cole began, but I shook my head.

'I just wanted to tell you that I picked up a message from someone wanting to make a booking in July,' I said, keeping my eyes fixed on Lil. 'She noticed Jesse at the rodeo, took a look at the website and booked out all three cabins for a week in July.'

Lil's eyes widened and she glanced at Cole for a moment. He remained fixed on my face, but I didn't look back.

'Well, that's . . . Wow, really? All three of them?' she asked, her voice clearing.

I nodded. 'I've had an idea. If you'll let me, I'll set up some social media stuff for you. I just thought . . .' I paused, a lump threatening to rise in my throat. 'I thought I might be able to extend my trip to help get it off the ground for you. Maybe. I think the key to making this place a success is letting people really see it, get to know the people behind the business, see it the way that we do.'

I couldn't help a glance at Cole. His jaw was clenched tight, but his eyes were soft. Pleading.

'Oh honey, I'd love you to stay,' Lil said, striding over, giving me an all-encompassing hug. 'You really think the social media stuff would help? Isn't it a lot of work? I thought you had some interviews in London?'

I returned her embrace, relief at seeing her happy, temporarily overcoming my anxiety about the truth of whatever was between her and Cole. We squeezed each other hard and I focused on the plan of action I'd had before coming down here.

'Yeah, I do. They're both online, though, so I can do them from here. And I can do the social stuff, no problem.'

She studied my face, frowning.

'If you're sure,' she said slowly. 'You feeling okay? You look kinda pale?'

I nodded, risking a glance at Cole. The tension between us was instant, our gazes connecting in the way they always seemed to, like magnets pulling towards each other. Desperate to touch, to lock together.

'Just hungover,' I reassured her, smiling, forcing myself to concentrate on her relief. 'If you're okay with it, then, I need to find Jesse. He'll be my first victim, given he's proven himself already.'

Lil rolled her eyes, wiping underneath them one last time, but still leaving a small smudge.

'He'll love that,' she said, waiting as I reached out to finish the job, taking off the last bit from her cheek. 'Thank you for this, sweetie. It means the world.'

I nodded, looking down to prevent myself from catching Cole's eye again. If Lil did have feelings for him, whatever was between us would have to stop. Not that it'd really had a chance to start. But I couldn't hurt her. The way Cole made me feel was unlike anything else, but my loyalty, my family, was Lil.

Squeezing her arm, I turned.

'How long you gonna stay?' Cole's voice was steady, but I could hear the undertone. The same as last night, underlaid with need and thick with implication.

'However long this takes.' I shrugged. 'Or until I have to go. Whichever comes first.'

I smiled at Lil as I left, watched her trying to read Cole's expression. Out of the stalls I let out a jagged breath, heading back up towards the ranch house. I resolved to leave my feelings for Cole back in the bar in Jackson. I refused to become another source of worry for Lil, and I needed all my brain cells firing to make this marketing idea for the ranch work.

Thankfully, Jesse was still humming along to the radio up by the wood store, just as he had been when I left.

'Heyyyy, Jesse,' I said tentatively, watching as he leant over a makeshift workbench, a measuring tape in one hand and a pencil held in his teeth as he shifted things around.

'Oh hey, Princess,' he replied, glancing up with his trademark open smile. 'How can I help the new talk of the town?'

Startled, I came to an abrupt stop.

'The what?'

He chuckled, tilting his head to one side.

'It don't take long for word to travel. Turning down Eli in the bar and then showing him what he was missing was a bit of a statement in a gossipy town like this.'

'I . . . Oh, well, I just didn't want Cole getting into a fight. It seemed like a more, umm . . . peaceful option.'

He laughed, setting down his tools and leaning on the bench, turning to face me.

'I sure do like you, Lottie,' he said, adjusting his hat, his brilliant white smile giving him the perfect model pose. 'I'm pretty sure Cole was just fine with the arrangement.'

I tried to hide an almost instant smile, and failed.

'As long as it pissed Eli off,' I replied, shrugging. 'But listen, I've got something to ask, something I need your help with.'

He raised his eyebrows, a suggestive expression taking over.

'Hold on now, wait a minute – is it my turn to distract Eli?'

I blushed despite myself, giving into Jesse's irrepressible charm. There was a reason the woman had called earlier to book a stay after seeing him at the rodeo. He was classically handsome, yes, the epitome of a gentleman cowboy, with his gravelled voice, strong jaw and beautiful grey eyes. But it was his natural warmth, his unguarded joy that really shone through. I could imagine it being all too easy to love Jesse, and receiving this kind of genuine, unfiltered love in return.

'Quit it,' I replied, mimicking his accent, making his smile even more broad. 'No, I want to film you for social media.'

His eyebrows rose and eventually, in the pause, he removed his hat, running his hand through his hair.

'Film me? Sounds like stepping up a gear from fake kissing in a bar?'

This time I laughed.

'I'm going to promote the ranch across social media, try and boost our bookings. Once people get to know you and the others, I just know we're going to get booked up. We just need something . . . compelling to get them interested.'

He shook his head, smiling.

'I'm all yours, ma'am – use me however you like.' His voice was light, casual, but the tone was suggestive. 'I just need one favour in return.'

I folded my arms as though bracing myself against his charm.

'Okay,' I replied, eyes narrowed.

'Elk Creek are having some kinda open day at their ranch this afternoon – something to do with their new backer. I reckon we can sneak in, have a nosy around and report back. If I go with you, no one's going to try and start a fight, and if we need to distract Eli again, I'm sure I can help.'

'Does Lil know?' I asked, seeing the logic of snooping on the rivals, but wondering how Cole would react. Then reminding myself it didn't matter.

He nodded, replacing his hat and turning back to the bench.

'It starts at two, so I'll just finish this up and we'll head over, right?'

I agreed, and began walking back to the ranch.

The next hour was spent planning, quickly securing usernames for the ranch on various social channels, making notes and planning things out on my phone. It wasn't until a horn beeped from outside that I suddenly realized the time, grabbing my hat and running out towards Jesse's truck.

I climbed in and as we headed down the drive, passing the barn, Jesse raised his hand in greeting.

Looking up from my phone, I caught the edge of Cole's stare but looked away, knowing that if I kept it up for long enough, he'd stop.

CHAPTER 12

> Umm . . . so Kyle turned up at my studio?

Hestia's message flashed on my screen as Jesse and I walked through Elk Creek Ranch.

> He is PISSED. Naturally I told him to fuck off before I could tattoo 'cheating twat' on his forehead, but not before he said he wasn't going to take no for an answer when it comes to getting you back. Something about a big mistake . . . the usual cheater bullshit.

My jaw dropped; I couldn't physically imagine Kyle in Shoreditch, face to face with Hestia. They'd met before, of course, but on his terms, in places he knew where he could lead proceedings. She was the antithesis of everything about him. I should've known then.

'Y'all okay?' Jesse said, glancing over as we walked.

'Sort of,' I replied, stopping. 'I need to reply to a message from home – could we maybe stop for a drink for a minute?'

Jesse tipped his hat.

'Course, ma'am. What'll it be? There're all kinds of fancy drinks here. A cocktail? Glass of wine?'

I looked up at the food and drink stalls gathered on the manicured grass, hundreds of people milling around in front of the large, newly built ranch house. Elk Creek was a completely different operation to Diamond Back – one with big pockets.

'Just a water, since I'm working,' I replied with a quick smile, noting his inquisitive look as he nodded and wandered over to the stalls. Gaggles of women watched as he approached, their eyes and mouths working overtime.

Shit, so sorry, I replied, hating that my mess had impinged on her life.

It was kind of funny tbh, she replied. Especially when Cal offered to show him out of the studio.

I smiled, imagining Cal – more ink than skin – escorting Kyle back onto the street.

Just be careful, though, she added. He threatened to get in touch with your parents and find out where you were. I didn't tell him, of course, but please God tell me you've found a beefy cowboy to pummel the shit out of him?

Biting my lip, I considered telling her everything. It wouldn't fit in a message.

Maybe. But it's complicated.

The thought of Kyle besieging my parents pissed me off.

> WHAT THE FUCK! I need every detail!

> I'll call you – too much for messages. So sorry about Kyle, hopefully he won't be back. Prick.

Too much for messages? A photo
will do?!

I laughed, looking up and seeing Jesse walking back over, two
beers in hand.

I'll see what I can do. Love you,
Hes xxx

UGH. I hate you being so far
away. But love you too. London
sucks without you xxx

'One water for the pretty lady in the tan hat,' Jesse announced,
handing over a bottle and standing next to me. 'Free bar, too –
they're really putting their money where their mouth is, I guess.'

'I had no idea it was such a big place,' I said, looking up and
tucking my phone back into my jeans pocket. 'Sorry about that –
just catching up with Hestia, my best friend at home.'

He nodded, studying me for a moment.

'She anything like you?' he asked, sitting down next to me.

I laughed, imagining his reaction if Hestia and I had been
standing next to each other right now.

'On the outside, no. But under the surface, yeah. She's about as
sassy as they come, as you guys would say.'

In the same moment, we watched as a much older woman,
straight-backed and elegant, walked across the bottom of the field,
next to a tall man. His suit was conspicuous, clearly expensive, his
grey cowboy hat clearly never worn for the purpose of anything
other than show.

'I think I recognize her.' I squinted against the sun, holding my
hand above my eyes. 'Who is she?'

'That's just about the queen of sass in this state, second only to your grandma. That's Dotty Sinclair – she owns this place. And the piece of shit with her is her eldest son, Zach.'

I remembered her now, as she had been, hair a little longer and a warmer shade of blonde, now replaced with white.

'Oh man, me and Lil were fucking terrified of her. I remember when she gave my dad a piece of her mind about something. I've never seen him intimidated in his whole life, but she razed him to the ground in less than a minute.'

Jesse chuckled, swigging his beer.

'Yep, that's about right, I'd say. About as close to celebrity in Jackson as anyone will get. It's always been the Sinclairs and the Deans here, a hundred years of it.' He shook his head, smirking at me again. 'Guess that's not very old to a Brit, huh?'

I snorted. 'The town I grew up in is over a thousand years old,' I said. He let out a low whistle. 'But a hundred years is still a long time to live alongside the same people. I wonder what my grandma would've made of all this, of dude ranching and the Sinclairs trying to take over Diamond Back.'

Jesse nodded, contemplative for a moment.

'I reckon she'd have more to say about you cosying up to a cowboy.'

Side-eyeing him, I laughed, shaking my head. His own laugh was irrepressible. 'Listen, what's the deal with you and Cole?' said Jesse when I didn't respond, his voice suddenly gentle. 'Maybe it's not my place to ask but . . . I like you, Lottie. We could have fun, but Cole's my brother, you know? I can't fuck that up. But if you and he were just messing around . . .'

I sighed, wanting to keep it light but feeling the heaviness creep back across my shoulders.

'I don't know,' I said, trying to be honest but not sure how to voice the situation. I also didn't want to out Lil's possible feelings, unsure if Jesse had any idea. 'It's more that I don't know how long I'm here for, and things at home are . . . complicated.'

He pursed his lips, considering me.

'Boyfriend complicated?'

I raised my eyebrows.

'Ex-boyfriend. He's an asshole. I found out he cheated on me, so I left.'

Jesse shook his head, taking a drink.

'What a bastard. Some guys just don't know what they've got.' I nodded, watching as some ranch cowboys walked nearby, Eli amongst them. 'We're not all like that, you know.'

I turned to him then and was met by a full stare, as intense as it was warm.

'I know,' I murmured. 'I'm sure you'd be the total opposite.'

He kept his eyes on mine, his hand reaching forward to brush my cheek.

'You just say the word, Princess, and maybe we can see.'

My heart picked up a beat, knowing, feeling how easy it would be. But he wasn't . . . Cole.

'You're sweet,' I replied, giving him a soft smile. 'But I need to figure this whole thing out with Cole first before it becomes any messier.'

He nodded, hands back on his beer, staring out at the people milling around in front.

'I get it,' he said, then, bumping against my shoulder, 'but if y'all change your mind, you know where to find me.'

'I know. But in the meantime, there is something you can do,' I said, giving a slow smile at his surprise and holding up my phone. 'Let me film you walking down there, maybe even take your shirt off. We need our introduction to social media to really make an impact.'

He raised his eyebrows, pure mischief in his expression.

'I will if you will?' he replied, smirking at my mock frown.

'Although I'm not sure the good folk of Elk Creek are going to be impressed. It might even get us kicked out.'

'Sounds like fun to me,' I said, setting up the video. 'Maybe Dotty will get involved . . . now that would make for a good watch.'

He laughed, setting his beer down on a nearby table. I gave him directions: to walk down along the fence, look moody and hot, then towards the end, take his shirt off. The sun was casting long shafts of golden light right across the pasture in front and would catch him perfectly.

'Sure you want me to wait until the end to take this off?' he asked. 'If we're going to get kicked out, may as well do it right.'

Smiling and more than a bit awed by his confidence, I shrugged, watching as he unbuttoned his shirt, the deep blue fabric giving way to . . . quite a sight. I tried not to openly gawp at his toned abs and broad shoulders.

'Changed your mind?' he asked, watching my reaction with amusement as I took the shirt from him.

'Focus on the task, cowboy,' I replied, lining up the shot, already filming him standing near the fence, adjusting his hat. 'Okay, take it steady . . . More of a stroll. Keep going to the flagpole at the end of the fence.'

He tipped his hat to me, cocky smile on his face as he set off, sun highlighting the definition on his abs, the hint of his smile visible. I quickly panned out to the people around us, hoping to capture reactions, and I wasn't disappointed. A group of older women openly gawped, one almost spilling her drink across their boots, while another pair of younger girls next to them were clutching each other in shock.

I came back to Jesse, now approaching the flagpole, then coming to a stop by leaning on the fence. The light across his face was perfect, and even when he went against orders and turned towards me, breaking into a small smile, I knew it was perfect.

That was Jesse, right there. Confident, unafraid of who he was and willing to show it off with a smile that could melt the snow right off the mountains.

I stopped filming and almost skipped towards him.

'That was fucking perfect!' I cried, replaying the footage as I approached him, showing him the screen.

'And you think this will get people to come to our ranch?' he asked, looking over to the women that'd been staring, giving them a wink as he shrugged his shirt back on, doing the buttons up slowly.

I shrugged.

'It'll grab attention, that's for sure. It might take a while to build up a following and get enough people interested, but yeah, with some editing and using the right hashtags . . . plus with videos showing off the ranch itself – a sunset wouldn't be quite as effective as you, I imagine, but y'know, it would be close.'

He chuckled. 'Let's get out of here, seeing as we've made it this far without being sprung. We've seen enough anyhow. Money's what they've got, that's all we need to know.'

I nodded, barely listening, still looking at my phone and already playing with the edit.

'You enjoy this stuff, don't you?' he said, a light hold on my shoulder as he guided me back to the truck, then opened the door for me.

'It's not bad, especially when your subject's easy on the eyes.'

He shut the door and walked round to his side, getting in and watching as I cut up the clips, put them in order and added some easy country music – a trending Riley Green song – with the caption 'POV – cowboy forgets his shirt'. Replaying it before I posted it, Jesse shook his head.

'I mean, I'm biased but that looks . . . good,' he said, shaking his head.

'And . . . posted!' I replied, waiting a few seconds for it to upload. Clearly Elk Creek also had the resources to ensure perfect phone signal even halfway up a mountain.

Clicking my phone off, I turned to him.

'Thanks, and I'm sorry. Think I'm just about the only person here that would turn you down.'

'You're welcome. Maybe you could invite some of your friends out here instead? What about your girl, Hestia?'

I laughed as we swung out of the ranch and headed back onto the interstate. I imagined her here, actually picturing her in a black felt cowboy hat, ripped jeans . . . Yeah. It'd work – and she would LOVE Jesse.

'That's not a bad idea, actually,' I said. 'Maybe I'll invite her out sometime.'

He glanced at me as we roared down the road, a knowing smile on his lips.

'That mean you're staying?'

I shrugged.

'For a little bit. See if I can make this work,' I said, holding up my phone. 'But I need to get a job again – living in London is expensive.'

He nodded, slipping into thought.

———

We arrived back and pulled in to see Cole and Bailey standing by the corral as Lil rode Bambi. The sound of the truck made her skitter sideways, but Lil easily corrected her.

Cole turned, continuing his conversation with Bailey but glancing over as we got out. Jesse and I began walking over to them.

'Could we do a bit more filming before we lose the sun?' I asked as we approached. 'The sky over there looks heavy; we might lose the light soon.'

'Need me to change, or we not bothering with clothes again?' he asked, winking, right as we reached Cole and Bailey.

'Goddamn, what *was* that party at Elk Creek?' Bailey asked, breaking off from her conversation with Cole, eyebrows raised. She had dirt smudges across her cheek, and more dirt on her chaps and jeans.

'Lottie just getting frisky is all,' Jesse teased, elbowing me as Bailey grinned.

'I'm filming him for social media,' I clarified, braving a glance at Cole, but he'd already turned back to the corral. 'Maybe some roping?'

He nodded.

'I'll get set up.'

'Okay – I just need to go up and grab my charger. Meet you back here in ten?'

Back up at the ranch house, I dived into my room for the portable charger and plugged it in. My phone suddenly lit up, a dozen or more notifications on the screen.

As I tapped into them, then opened the social apps, my mouth fell open. The video of Jesse had somehow already been viewed almost 500 times, a bunch of comments ranging from emojis to exclamations already there. Quickly checking the link in the ranch profile was correct, I turned the screen off and walked out of my room at speed – right into Cole.

'Hey, sorry,' I said, stepping back. 'I was just—'

'I'm not sure about all this filming stuff,' he announced, folding his arms. His face was impassive, but his body language screamed at me.

I raised an eyebrow, standing just as firm.

'Filming generally, or filming Jesse?'

His jaw tensed and his eyes hardened. A silence developed, and the space between us suddenly felt small, charged.

'Is there anything going on with you two?'

The words were abrupt and as I opened my mouth to tell him to mind his own business, his expression stopped me. There was a sadness to it.

'No, of course not.' I slumped, shrugging. 'I'm just trying to help the business, help Lil. But why does it matter?'

He studied me, nodded. Mentioning Lil stirred the same feelings in me as it had earlier – the complications that arose from even standing here like this with him.

'I need to go,' I said, moving to the side, trying to walk around him.

'Lottie, wait.' He moved to block me, gentle hands on my arms. The feel of his touch sent my heart into overdrive. 'We can't keep dancing around each other, it's—'

'It's too complicated, Cole,' I replied. 'It doesn't matter what we feel, there are other people to think about.'

'Who?' he asked, moving closer, forcing me to step back against the wall. I couldn't answer. His proximity was setting off every instinct, every deep-seated desire rising to the surface. The door to my room was open, the huge bed beyond it like a beacon. 'Because from where I stand it's just you and me, right now.'

'I like you,' I whispered, biting back a groan as his fingers found mine, his face perilously close. 'But I'm in the middle of a mess at home . . . and Lil, I don't want to hurt her.'

His forehead creased as he studied me. 'Lil? This isn't about her right now. And whatever's across the pond isn't here. I am.'

I gasped as he tilted his head down, his lips grazing my ear, moving down my neck.

'Cole . . .' I started, my breathing hitching as his hands grazed my waist, moving up. 'Not here.'

He stopped, glancing at my room. I bit my lip.

'I know that kiss yesterday was real,' he began, slowly moving me backwards and through the doorway. 'And I'm generally a very patient man, but I can't get it out of my head – can't get *you* out of my head.' I stopped any pretence of resisting, letting my hands grip his shirt.

'You barely know me,' was all I could say, shivering as his fingers began popping open my shirt buttons.

'Then let me get to know you,' he whispered, moving me back further still until I hit the bed, sitting on the edge as in one smooth motion he knelt down right in front of me. 'What's your favourite colour?'

I smiled despite the intensity of his gaze, his cowboy hat still in place.

'My favourite colour? That's your most pressing question in getting to know me?'

He smiled back and I reached over to touch his lips, tracing the curve of his mouth, not missing how his eyes darkened, a feral quality taking over.

'All right,' he growled, reaching up and slowly taking off his hat, running his fingers through his long dark hair. Gently, reverently, he placed it on my head. I felt the rush of blood to my cheeks. 'What's your favourite way to ride?'

Before I could stop myself, I pulled his face closer.

'Slowly,' I began, feeling him peeling back one side of my shirt, my bra strap falling. 'With the door locked and a guarantee of no interruptions for hours.'

'Hours, huh?' he murmured, smiling as he reached over to kiss my shoulder, lips tracing lower and lower. 'I'm not sure it would be enough.'

I closed my eyes, committing the feeling to memory, but they were startled open again as I felt his lips on mine, teasing them open with his tongue. Unable to stifle it, I moaned as he kissed me, his fingers brushing my nipple as he moved into my bra.

Everything began to move quickly with the urgency of his lips, the pure, burning heat between us. He removed his hat from my head, cupping my face in his hands as I moved to his shirt buttons, then made way for his fingers as he undid them more quickly than I could. Just as I reached for his belt buckle, pulling it back to loosen it, the front door of the ranch slammed shut.

'Lottie?'

Lil's voice echoed down the hall and Cole leapt off me, moving up and wedging himself behind the door with surprising agility for a man of his size. His shirt hung open and my eyes lingered for a few seconds too long.

'Yeah, hold up, just getting changed,' I lied, taking off my shirt and ignoring the pointed look from Cole at my entirely exposed bra. Grabbing a fresh shirt from the closet, I swung it on and started doing up the buttons, walking over to the doorway to prevent Lil from walking in.

'You're not gonna believe this,' she said, finally appearing, holding up her phone to show me. 'An email – someone asking about availability for the cabins this winter! They said they saw us on social media.'

Focusing on my buttons, I hoped her own excitement would distract her from my own, feeling it stamped across my cheeks like a blazing trail.

'Told you!' I smiled, tucking my shirt in and turning back to my bed to look for my hat, then realizing with horror that Cole's was still lying there instead, right by the scrunched-up mess of my bedcover, all but revealing the imprint of our bodies from moments before. 'I'll be out in a moment, just need the bathroom, okay?'

'Oh – sure, sure,' she muttered, reading through the email and heading back towards her office. 'I'll call them back now, check for any other messages.'

With a sigh, I closed the door behind her, watching as Cole finished buttoning his own shirt.

'That was . . . umm . . . close,' I said, smiling, scuffing my boot against the floor.

He surveyed me for a moment as he tucked in his shirt, his eyes on my mouth as I bit my lip. There definitely wasn't enough room in his jeans.

'We've got this the wrong way round,' he started, keeping his voice quiet. 'Lottie, would you go out with me, on a date?'

'A date?' I repeated, eyes widening. 'After *that*, you just want a date?'

He stifled a laugh, moving forward to stand in front of me, very consciously keeping his hands to himself.

'No,' he said, voice soft. 'I want you on that bed, wearing nothing but my hat and doing everything I've imagined and then some.' He paused, grinning at my embarrassment. 'But you're right. I'd love to know more about you, and you about me. So come out with me, somewhere without any interruptions. A well-behaved, good ol'-fashioned date.'

I raised an eyebrow, desperate to say yes but knowing I'd have to speak to Lil first, get whatever was or wasn't between them straight.

'Even if I'm not staying?' I whispered, watching as his face fell.

'Even then. I'll take whatever time I've got.'

I felt it then, a jolt, deep down. As though a fissure had appeared, threatening to tear me open. Stepping to him, I reached up on tiptoes and kissed him again. This time it was gentle, a question and answer twining together. His response was sweet, slow and full of the promise we'd almost made on my bed.

'Okay, a date,' I said as I drew back eventually. 'Just one condition.' He raised his eyebrows. 'No whiskey. Slippery slope.'

CHAPTER 13

Jesse enjoyed roping for the camera so much that it even encouraged Cole into the ring. The sight of the two of them at work was more than I could bear, even with their shirts on. To the sound of their knowing laughter, I'd taken myself back up to the ranch to grab some more shots of the house and the view from the back porch, and film some room tours of the cabins. Then, after a break and a cold shower, I started the editing process, mixing the cowboy and ranch content, satisfied that the blend of the two would set the rapidly growing number of followers on fire.

The last two days had been a flurry of cautious excitement as a steady stream of enquiries came in, along with another booking for the winter season and me setting up an online booking system for the ranch's website. Two more posts – another of Jesse, roping in slow motion, then one of the view across the long meadow, now coming alive with wildflowers – had only accelerated the response, bringing the kind of numbers that would've set jaws dropping in my old job.

It was all a distraction from my date with Cole, which was set for this evening, on what would've been my last day at the Diamond Back. I'd yet to talk to Lil about it, needing to find the words to explain how rapidly my feelings were growing for her ranch manager. Even though Cole had promised the date would be well behaved, I wasn't sure I could put it off until afterwards, given the way things always seemed to escalate between us.

Ignoring the judgy pokes from my own conscience, I'd moved my flights home, giving myself another two weeks to get things going for Lil. My savings would cover my rent and bills for a few months yet, but I didn't want to run them down quite that far if I could help it. The online interview for job one had been somewhat underwhelming — a disconcerting lack of nerves on my part had made it easier to answer their questions, but the disconnection I felt from that world was far greater than I'd expected. The other interview was scheduled for tomorrow, but right now, other than the date, there was only one thing on my mind.

'Lil, you busy?' I knocked on her office door, opening it to see her staring at the computer screen intently.

'Yeah, but come in. Hell, I'm only busy because of you . . .' She stopped, her smile dropping at my expression. 'What? What's wrong?'

I steeled myself, wondering if this was the moment it might all come crashing down.

'Can I talk to you about Cole?'

Lil's mouth opened a little as she frowned, leaning back on her chair.

'Shoot.'

I tried to read her, but she was clearly keeping her feelings well below the surface. Fuck. Maybe I'd been right, maybe she did feel something for him, which, given what Cole and I had almost done a couple of days earlier, would make me a total bitch.

'Umm, so . . . well, you know how we kind of got off to a rocky start,' I began, twining my fingers together, not quite able to meet her eyes. 'Well, it's kind of changed a bit since then, but, when I saw you guys by the barn the other day I wondered if . . . I mean, I just don't want to get in the way if there's something already between you.'

In the silence that followed, I chanced a look up, hoping, begging, for her not to be upset.

'Oh honey,' she started, a warm, thoroughly amused tone to both her voice and her smile. 'Is that what you thought was going on? Oh shit.' She laughed and I held my breath, not quite daring to believe it. I watched as she got up and strode around the desk, approaching me and reaching out, resting her hands on my shoulders.

'Lottie, I do love that man. But as a brother, as a friend I'd lie in the damn road for. Nothing else, y'hear? It's never been like that for us. Whatever's happening for you two makes me so happy I could burst. I mean that.'

Fighting tears of relief, I grabbed her into a bear hug, laughing at her surprise.

'Oh thank fuck,' I sighed, pulling back after she complained about not being able to breathe, but chuckling as she did so.

'You really like him, huh?' She grinned, watching as I tried to calm the hectic excitement bubbling up inside me.

'Maybe,' I offered, trying and failing to act coy as she snorted.

'Okay, well, you take that maybe and go raid Bailey's wardrobe. Mine sucks – but she's had to wear some fancy stuff for parties on the circuit. I've got to get back to all these enquiries – never had so many emails in my damn life.'

We grinned at each other as I left, trying not to appear like a total lunatic as I ventured out to find Bailey. True to form, she was with the horses.

'Can I borrow something to wear?' I asked her, finally tracking her down in the tack room, rubbing down Dunkin's bridle. Her cheeks were flushed, hair escaping into feathery curls at her temples after an hour of hard training. 'I'm going out, so I need something a little dressier.'

She raised her eyebrows, a crooked smile on one side.

'Sure thing, honey. Where you going?'

I tried to maintain an air of innocence.

'Umm . . . The Kitchen, I think?'

She let out a low whistle.

'So, a *date-date*, then? That place is fancy.'

I smiled, remembering the pictures from the website. She wasn't wrong, but it had been Cole's choice.

'Well, sort of – but as friends.'

She focused on the cheek strap of the bridle, concentrating on one particularly stubborn piece of dirt.

'Well, you help yourself to my closet. If I were you, I'd try the black dress right at the back. I've only worn it once when I won at Cheyenne last year and I could hardly breathe all night. It'll fit you just right.'

'But still with cowboy boots, right?' I checked, smiling as she laughed.

'I'm pretty sure Cole would combust if you wore it with high heels, sugar.'

I blushed but didn't deny it. Thanking her as she chuckled to herself, I ran back to the house and got myself ready. Reaching into my make-up bag, hair freshly washed and already curling at the ends, I stopped myself. The automatic instinct to plaster on a full face of make-up suddenly felt ridiculous after two weeks of concealer and mascara at most.

Instead, I applied the minimum and gently combed through the length of my hair, allowing the natural waves and tighter curls to do their thing. It fell right to the middle of my back now, to just where the zip ended on Bailey's dress, which was strapless, tight and pushed my breasts into a fairly compromising position. But she was right – the fit was perfect, and with my boots, loose hair and cowboy hat, it felt right.

And that made me pause. Everything about me, about this moment, was the antithesis of my life in London. The stress, the loneliness, my lack of choice in anything – pushed from pillar to post by work or Kyle. And now, here, I was making the call to go on a date with someone I could never dream of meeting there, on my own terms, supported by my cousin and in clothes loaned by a new friend.

As I left my room, I wondered when it'd switched over. When I'd stopped running from my life and started living it. The change had been subtle, but it was obvious now I'd noticed it.

Lil was still in her office, so when I walked into the kitchen to find Cole waiting, hat in his hand, black shirt tucked into indigo jeans, we were alone.

'Ready?' I asked, trying to hold it together as I took him in, the way he stared at me, eyes lingering on my chest.

'You look . . .' He stopped, gathering himself before letting out a long breath. 'How the hell am I supposed to behave when you look that fucking good?'

I swallowed, feeling the tension begin to gather, knowing there was a very good chance we wouldn't leave the house unless I stopped it. I raised a stern eyebrow.

'Because that's the deal,' I reminded him. 'A platonic date to get to know each other first.'

The implication of what came second was loud and clear in the silence.

'Okay, let's go then,' he said, almost shaking himself, sliding his hat on. 'Afraid I haven't got a fancy ride, just the truck.'

———

Thirty minutes and a very charged, quiet drive in the dark later, we found the restaurant. Cole held the door open, trying so hard not to openly stare at my body that I laughed as we removed our hats.

'What?' he asked, a sheepish smile appearing as the waiter took our drinks orders.

'It's okay, you can look – just no touching,' I replied, thankful for the busy, low hum of other diners around us, our conversation blending in.

He smiled back as I looked around, the low ceiling and clever lighting making it feel cosy and intimate. It could've passed for a London restaurant, with modern and expensive-looking tables and chairs, flawless white linen and polished wood floors.

'What do you think?' he asked, settling back in his chair and taking his drink from the waiter. I did the same, swirling mine around the glass, realizing how odd it felt to hold a wine glass.

'Gorgeous,' I said, holding his gaze for a moment. 'But unnecessary. You didn't need to bring me somewhere fancy – you know I'm down for a regular bar and some live music.'

He huffed a laugh, taking a drink.

'I wanted to go somewhere nice. It's been a while since I've had someone I wanted to go with.'

We stared at each other, slowly getting lost before the waiter arriving to take our order broke it up.

'So, you first,' I said, matching his pose and leaning back in my chair. 'Did you grow up here? How do you know Lil?'

He told his story well, his deep, whiskey-smooth voice almost distracting me from the words, but as he talked about meeting Lil as a teenager, not long after we'd stopped visiting the ranch, I was rapt. He smirked as he told me about their initial flirtation, telling me easily in a way that made it clear that those feelings were long gone. His life had become about rodeos – riding broncs, the injuries and wins, competing at ever higher levels, becoming state champion.

'No time for women?' I asked as he paused, watching as I smiled.

'A little,' he admitted. 'But it's hard to settle down on the circuit. A lot of buckle bunnies too, more interested in your wins than you.'

My stomach fell at the thought of the attention he would've

received, the inevitable hook-ups. The thought of seeing him with someone else filled me with a sudden, burning jealousy.

'You ever thought about going back to it?' I asked softly, aware that we were moving into sensitive territory.

Cole's face changed, but his eyes remained warm. Trusting.

'I think about it every now and then. I think Seth would be pissed that I stopped because of his death. But . . . I don't know. Bronc riding is still a crazy-ass thing to do. Money's okay if you get it right, though.'

I nodded.

'If it makes you happy, you should do it,' I said. 'The rodeo last week was awesome. I'd be there to watch,' I added, giving him a shy smile. 'I could even learn to scream and holler like all the regulars do.'

His answering smile was breathtaking.

'Oh I bet you could, Princess,' he murmured, biting his lip for a moment. Leaning back in his chair, as though forcing the distance between us, he considered me.

'Enough of me, I wanna know all about you. Where you grew up, right up to now.'

I raised my eyebrows, letting out a breath as I figured out how to sum up twenty-four years without boring him. But, as he held his wine glass, almost bracing his arms to himself, I told him about growing up in the English countryside, the pressure from my dad to make something of myself. The striving to get into uni, then meeting Hestia and letting go for a while, embracing her sense of adventure.

'She sounds fun,' he said, smile widening.

'Hestia's the best,' I replied, smiling back but feeling sad. 'I hope you meet her someday – I think you'd like her,' I added, lost in the fantasy of getting her out here, imagining her fitting in with the ranch. 'My boyfriend – I mean, ex-boyfriend,' I stumbled, internally kicking myself, 'never understood her. But, turns out I should've listened to her instincts about him. He turned out to be a complete prick.'

Cole's expression had become deep, brooding.

'What happened?' he asked, not quite managing to conceal the feelings that I could see simmering under the surface.

As I told him, slowly working over the events that had led up to me getting on the plane, he gradually leant forward, reaching out for my hand over the table.

'It was shit, all of it,' I finished, finding his hand. 'And I've been waiting for the weight of it to hit, you know? To really feel heart-broken or whatever, like a delayed reaction to arrive.'

He frowned, his thumb slowly stroking the back of my hand.

'And? Are you heartbroken?'

Holding his eyes with mine, I shook my head, the words almost drying up.

'I can't have been,' I said, noticing how his thumb had stopped moving, his hand now completely still. 'Because thinking of him doesn't make me feel anything. It's all coming from somewhere else right now.'

He glanced down for a moment, seemingly trying to decide something.

'I'll admit, I've never been in love before,' he said softly, looking back up at me. 'But I've heard folks say that when it happens, you know. Deep down.'

My heart hammered; I couldn't look away from him, from the way he held my eyes.

'I've heard that too.'

I smiled as he squeezed my hand. Before either of us could say anything else, reality arrived in the form of the waiter with our food.

'You going to film this too for social media?' he teased, break-ing the intensity between us.

I laughed, shaking my head. 'No chance! It's cowboys and sunsets that people want, not food.'

'Dude ranching sure is different to the old way of doing things,' he said, his expression becoming thoughtful again. 'I remember going out to help Dad and Jay, my brother, in the dark, before school, all weathers.'

I grimaced, remembering one of the winters we'd visited Jackson and experienced what minus 20 degrees felt like, realizing just how tough the locals actually were to live through it.

'Must've been hard,' I ventured. 'I remember bitching and moaning about going up to the stables at home when it was one or two degrees – that's mid-thirties to you.'

He scoffed.

'Nah, it wasn't that bad. Took my mind off all the shit with Mom, you know? My dad's not great with emotional stuff and Wyatt's just like him. It actually wasn't until I met Lil that I had anyone to talk to.'

My heart broke for him, and I reached my hand out again immediately. He took it.

'Were you young, when she left?' I asked, just hoping that he hadn't been alone for long. But as he nodded, I pressed my lips together, not able to prevent the prickle of tears that welled up. I could picture it so easily, a young version of this beautiful man, coping with something that no one should have to go through, never mind with no one to talk to.

'I was seven,' he admitted, squeezing my hand, still watching as I processed his pain. 'It was the worst time of my life. But . . . I don't know. Somehow, in a fucked-up way, it's made me love the people I've chosen to be in my life even more? Maybe if it'd been laid out on a plate I wouldn't appreciate it so much.'

I couldn't speak for a moment, turning to take a sip of my drink instead.

'You've got a big ol' heart, haven't you, honey?'

His voice was soft, matched by his eyes.

'I can't stand the thought of anyone I care about being hurt,' I whispered, the words simple but the meaning clear.

The rest of the meal passed in a blur of more questions and answers about life, our points of view aligning on almost everything, to my surprise. Somehow I'd imagined the difference in our backgrounds would create more of a gap in our thinking, but it turned out the opposite was true.

'Hey, hey – none of that,' he said, waving me away as I opened my bag to reach for my wallet when the bill arrived. 'It might be old-fashioned compared to the way you do things back home, but out here, a guy pays on the first date and there's no argument.'

I raised my hands in mock surrender, a little worried about the bill in such a nice place. I had no idea what being a ranch manager paid, but I didn't want to assume.

'Listen,' he said, as though he could hear my thoughts. 'I'm no investment banker with a rich daddy, but I did well enough from competing – had a couple of sponsors, too.'

'And now you're a social media star,' I added, making him chuckle. But as we walked out, the lights catching his sun-kissed skin and highlighting the bright warmth of his deep brown eyes, I realized how much he looked the part.

Leaving the restaurant, we fell into step, his right hand catching my left as we crossed the street.

I caught his eye.

'Friends hold hands sometimes,' he said, shrugging, but the grip changed, my fingers sliding between his, locking together with an ease that made me wonder how I'd only known him for a couple of weeks.

'I feel like I've known you for so much longer,' I admitted as we reached his truck.

He paused, his hand on the handle. 'I was just thinking the same. That and it's real difficult staying well behaved.'

I nodded, smiling, and he opened the door and waited for me to climb in.

He flipped the radio on low before we set off, catching the beginning of a song I knew.

'I like this one,' I said, smiling as he turned it up a little and gave me a quick grin as we set off.

'You know it?' he asked quizzically.

'Sure, I like a bit of country.' I shrugged. 'Mom still listens to it, and I grew up on Dolly and John Denver, Johnny Cash . . . I'm more of a Riley Green, Lainey, kinda gal, though.'

He shook his head, then reached over with his right hand and grasped my left, squeezing it.

'Well, looks like we've got the same taste in music too, Princess.'

The rest of the drive back to the ranch was spent humming and singing along to song after song, Cole eventually switching to Spotify to play some of his other favourites. Our hands remained clasped, and as the turn-off to the ranch approached, I didn't want our date to end.

'Thank you for tonight,' I said as we turned off the interstate, up the beginning of the drive. 'A perfect gentleman and a perfect date.'

As Cole slowed the truck to a stop, I turned, but before I could say another word, his hand was on my cheek and he leant closer, coming right in to brush his lips over mine.

'No, Princess, the perfect is all you. From these lips to singing in that cute accent,' he said.

I drew a shaky breath, my body suddenly lit on fire at his touch.

'Cole, you have no idea what you do to me,' I admitted, closing my eyes as he kissed my jaw.

'Honey, I get turned on just hearing your voice, especially when you say my name,' he whispered.

And this time, in the darkness, it all clicked together so quickly that my head spun as he began to kiss me, gently at first, then pressing harder. There was beginning to be something familiar about his touch, the way we responded to each other, the way his tongue felt on mine and the rapid sense of need that built and built inside. My hands wandered down his shirt, further, down to his jeans.

He pulled away too quickly, leaving me gasping.

'I can't have you thinking it's easy holding back on you,' he said, breathing hard himself. 'I try to be a gentleman, but I'm really not perfect.'

'You don't have to stop,' I whispered, still trying to catch my breath.

But he chuckled, shifting the truck into gear and pulling off, roaring up the steep track to the ranch.

'I don't want to,' he replied, his voice rough. 'But not in my truck, in the middle of the drive. You deserve more than that. I've got bigger plans for you than that.'

I gritted my teeth at the thought of it, hands clenching the strap of my bag.

'Hold up,' he said suddenly, the truck racing forward as a car came into view, parked up outside the ranch. 'Who the hell is that at this time of night?'

'A guest?' I replied, noting the Colorado plates. 'The ones that booked are already here though, right?'

He nodded as we got out, both of us striding to the front of the ranch house. As we opened the door, the sound of voices reached us, coming from the back.

'You recognize the voice?' I asked, hanging back a little as we walked through the house and out to the back porch. The voices stopped.

'Oh, there you are,' Lil said, a thread of relief in her words. 'Is Lottie with you?'

Cole stopped abruptly, moving to the side so I could come through. Confused, I walked forward slowly, stopping next to him.

Just as a figure stood up from the rocking chair to the right of the back door, turning to face me with an expression like thunder.

My dad.

CHAPTER 14

'What are you doing here?' I asked, confused. 'I thought Mum said you were in Georgia?'

Dad glared at me, the combined weight of every one of my childhood and teenage fuck-ups delivered in one look.

'Would you both mind giving us a moment?' he asked Lil and Cole, his eyes lingering on the cowboy, a calculating look at the proximity of our stance, my dress.

I felt Cole's hand on my lower back.

'I'll be right inside,' he murmured as he turned, his and Lil's footsteps loud against the vast quiet outside. 'Just say the word and I'll be right back here.'

As the door swung shut, Dad shook his head, hands balled up on his hips.

'What am *I* doing here?' he hissed, his face darkening by the second. 'What are *you* doing here? And saying nothing to Kyle either? It wasn't until he called a few days ago and spoke to your mum that he realized you'd even left the country!'

My gut reaction was to take it, let his angry outburst flow over me. Placate and agree until it's over. Dad's temper had been an ever-present threat growing up, one that had pushed me to take up hobbies that involved staying out of the house or tucked away in my room, and had pushed me into a more academic route at university than I otherwise would've chosen.

'It's none of his business,' I said, trying to keep my voice even as the anger built, rising steadily. 'I told him it was over and that should be enough.'

'Of course it's his business, you're his bloody girlfriend! You can't just up and leave people like that – it's cruel, Lottie. We raised you better than that. What must his parents think, for God's sake?'

The anger stirred further. Of course, he was only interested in appearances, in making sure the sodding Montgomerys had the best possible impression of me, of our family. I resisted the urge to tell him just how far down her nose Marina looked at us, how a middle-class no one like me – with an American mother, no less – couldn't matter less to someone who didn't give a flying fuck about anyone outside of her own circle of wealth.

'I'm not doing this,' I said, fighting with myself to keep it civil and stepping back, placing my hand on the door handle. 'You don't know anything about the situation. Honestly, Dad, it's none of your business and you have no right to come here and yell at me like I'm still a child you can bully.'

His face changed, blanching white with rage. He knew the truth of my words, felt it at his core. I braced myself, knowing this conversation had been a long time coming.

'I'll speak to you however I like,' he hissed, stepping forwards. 'You will get yourself home on the next flight and stop behaving like a child. You have responsibilities at home, not least that of owing Kyle a damn good explanation for your behaviour—'

'MY behaviour?' I gripped the handle, rage breaking through, self-restraint be fucking damned. 'MY behaviour? Really? I suppose he conveniently forgot to mention that he's been fucking some woman he's working with? No? No mention of her?'

His silence said it all.

'I don't owe Kyle the shit on the bottom of my fucking boot,' I spat. 'He's a liar, a cheat and an all-round condescending asshole.

Hestia was right about him all along, all while you worshipped the ground he walked on.'

My father shook his head.

'First of all, your language is disgusting – no doubt a product of hanging around with that misfit,' he began, his voice shaking, fist turning into an index finger that pointed right in my face. 'Second of all, it might all just be a misunderstanding and something you two can work through. You don't just run off at the first sign of trouble and come here, to the middle of godforsaken nowhere with a bunch of hillbillies.'

I gave a laugh as sharp and bitter as his words.

'Oh my God, you snob,' I sneered. 'Where do you get this bullshit from? You've used it on Mum her whole life too, Jesus. Why are you so obsessed with status? With what people have and haven't got?'

'Because it matters!' he roared. 'And because I broke my back working to put you through university without debt. And this is how you repay me? By running away and shacking up here? There is not a chance in hell I'm letting you throw your life away. I got your mother out of this place, but your aunt wasn't so lucky. Look at the mess she made.' He shook his head, eyes wide with rage. 'I noticed that cowboy, I saw how you looked at each other—'

'Don't you fucking dare say another word,' I hissed. 'Keep him out of this. And yes, I ran here for a break, to get some distance. But you know what? The longer I stay, the more I see of GOOD people, in this amazing place, the more I see I was running to something, even if I didn't know it to begin with – to something way better than corporate bullshit and entitled, cheating bastards.'

Dad paused, his expression turning to disgust.

'Oh God,' he said, hand rubbing at his forehead. 'You've run off over here and shacked up with a filthy bloody cowboy—'

'How DARE YOU!' I yelled with every ounce of force I could

muster, every fibre of my body thrumming with frustration. 'You don't know the first thing about him, or anything here – and it's none of your damn business anyway!'

'You are my *daughter*, of course it's my business!' he yelled back, taking another step forward. 'He's not good enough for you, and that's the bottom line.'

I forced myself to breathe, to calm down enough not to lash out in a way I knew would finally tip us over the line and take us beyond repair.

'That man is worth a hundred of Kyle,' I said slowly, my voice loud but even. 'Two hundred. And you have absolutely no right to be here. Get out.'

He laughed.

'I will not. Not until you promise to come home and sort out whatever this mess is between you and Kyle. And what about getting another job? I'm not paying for your rent in London, you know.'

I let out a long breath, staring down at the decking under my boots.

'I'm not asking you to,' I said. 'I don't need your money. I made enough of my own, thanks. And I am applying for jobs. I had an interview yesterday – again, not that it's any of your business.'

'And Kyle?' he cut in, finger wagging in my face once again. A memory hit me, of him doing the same to Mum once, in front of her friends. Belittling her. I wondered how many times he'd done that before she'd stopped fighting back. Whether living in a foreign country, reliant on her marriage to him in order to stay, in order to not be forced to leave me, had played into it. Guilt struck immediately, followed closely by more rage.

'Kyle can go *fuck* himself,' I spat, enunciating every word clearly, watching as he began to boil over too.

'Right, so you're throwing away a perfectly good relationship with someone that can offer you the world, for this shithole?' he countered as he gestured towards the house.

I tried to stop it; thought I had a handle on it. But the floodgates opened.

'Yes, Dad, I am!' I yelled. 'And for your fucking information, I'm not actually in a relationship with Cole, but even if I was, I would be really goddamned happy. Being here, with him, is a massive life upgrade. And you know what?' I paused, revelling in the shock on his face. 'If he asked me to marry him tomorrow, shack up with him and have a whole bunch of babies, I'd be fucking delighted to do it. That's how much better even *the potential* of a relationship with him is compared to the absolute fucking NOTHING I had with Kyle.'

Dad's face was thunderstruck, as though the person he knew had died.

'I don't know who you are,' he said, shaking his head. 'This is not the girl I raised—'

'You didn't raise me, you BULLIED ME,' I shouted. 'Now get out! Just leave!'

A sob built up, exploding as he opened his mouth to retaliate.

'JUST GO!' I screamed, folding in on myself, nothing else to give. 'Leave me alone!'

The handle moved under my hand, the door opened and suddenly arms were circling me. Cole. I took in his intoxicating smell, the sheer size of his body next to mine.

'I've got you,' he said, propping me up as I turned into him, pressing myself into his body. 'It's okay. Let's go inside.'

'Get off this property right now,' Lil said, her voice calm but anger underpinning each word.

Cole began to guide me through the doorway.

'Don't be ridiculous, Elizabeth,' Dad scoffed. 'That was between me and Lottie.'

'As if,' Lil said, shaking her head. 'You made it real personal, real fast. And even if you hadn't, you don't get to speak to her that way. Now get off this ranch before I fetch my shotgun and have to persuade you that way.'

'What a disgrace,' he hissed.

I tried to turn then, rage boiling up and over again, trying to fight against Cole to get back outside and defend her.

'It's okay, honey, Lil's got it. She's seen worse off this ranch.' Cole's voice rumbled through his chest as he guided me back to my room.

'Fucking bastard.' I shuddered, desperately trying not to cry. 'How could he . . . how dare he . . .'

Finally, through the door to my bedroom, he closed it behind us, leaning on it and pulling me into him as I gave in and cried. His hand stroked my hair, his other arm firmly around my back. At several points I felt his lips on my head, pressing down, trying to soothe away what felt like a lifetime of jagged edges.

As the sobs slowed, he moved us over to the bed, setting me down and taking off my boots to lay me down, peeling the cover back and then pulling it up over me.

'I'm going to get some water, okay?' he said, his voice almost unbearably gentle compared to the abuse I'd just taken – and thrown back.

In the quiet that followed, more tears flowed, as I imagined with embarrassment how Cole and Lil had likely heard everything. Shame scorched through me at having anything to do with someone who thought like that, and at having gone along with his bullshit for so long and never having fought back before now.

The door opened, but this time it was Lil that stepped inside, her face pale but determined.

'He's gone now, honey,' she said, coming over to the bed and leaning down.

'I'm so sorry, Lil,' I croaked. 'I can't believe he said those things about you and your mum.'

She hugged me tight.

'It's water off my back, darlin', don't worry about that. Your daddy's not much different to mine, in a lot of ways. I've already been through this shit once before, remember?'

I nodded, looking up as Cole came back in, a glass of water in his hand.

He and Lil shared a look.

'Get some rest, okay? It'll feel better in the morning.'

Kissing my forehead and squeezing Cole's arm, she left, closing the door behind her.

He placed the water on my side table, switching on my lamp and turning off the main light before perching on the side of the bed.

The weight of the words that had been spoken outside settled across both of us.

'I appreciate everything you said out there,' he said, hands placed on his legs as though he couldn't risk them being elsewhere.

'I'm so sorry you had to hear that,' I whispered. 'He's . . . I hate him for saying such awful shit.'

Cole nodded.

'It's people like him I feel sorry for. They'll never know what it's like to be happy, you know? But I can't believe he spoke to you like that.' He shook his head. 'I know he's your dad, but I swear . . . I might not be able to hold back next time if he ever treats you like that again in front of me. Breaks my damn heart watching you cry.'

I stared up at him, watching as he stared back, searching my face. This wasn't how I'd pictured the best date of my life ending, and I felt anger mixed with sadness at how our happy evening had been ruined.

'You need to get some rest, I'll—' he began, as though warding off the inevitable.

'Don't go,' I blurted, reaching out and holding his arm before he could get up. 'I mean, you don't have to go, unless you want to.'

The smallest smile flickered as he looked down.

'I'm not sure . . .'

'I don't mean . . . Just . . . stay,' I said. 'I just . . . don't want to be alone.'

He nodded, getting up to walk around to the other side of the bed, and I heard the sound of boots hitting the floor and the creak of the bedframe as he moved in close behind me without actually touching. I hesitated, then closed the gap between us, my eyelids fluttering shut as his arm wound around my waist, fingers weaving through mine.

We said nothing, my body reacting as it always did to him, but I resisted the temptation to turn over and start something quite different. I knew it would happen in an instant, the flame just inches from the fuse, but I knew better than to let that happen tonight, after everything that had taken place. Eventually, as my breathing slowed and the warmth from his body mingled with mine, his steady heart setting the pace of my own, I felt my eyelids flutter shut.

'Goodnight, Lottie,' he whispered. 'I'll be here.'

'Thank you,' I mumbled, squeezing his hand, finally letting myself go.

———

When I finally stirred, the light filling the room was muted, softened.

I stretched and my leg bumped up against something. Someone.

Awareness flooded over me and I turned to see Cole grinning, sitting up against the headboard, the bed already made on his side, sipping a steaming coffee as he read something on his phone.

'Morning, Princess. You stretch just like a cat, you know that?'

Temporarily speechless, I took him in, from the fitted plaid shirt, two buttons open at the neck and sleeves rolled up to reveal smooth, tanned skin beneath, to the perfectly fitting Wrangler jeans, hatless dark hair and heartbreaking smile that lit up those warm, deep eyes.

'You're here,' I breathed, instantly feeling stupid. 'I mean, you stayed.'

'I said I would,' he replied, his gaze softening as he looked me over. 'I've been up for a while now, but I wanted to be here when you woke up. You look pretty with your hair like that. And that dress is . . . uh, yeah. You always look this good in the morning?'

I looked at him in horror, hearing only sarcasm.

'I'll be right back,' I said, getting up and escaping to my ensuite, then staring at my chaotic reflection in the mirror to assess the damage.

My hair was . . . wild. An untamed mass of long curls, only somewhat hiding what was threatening to spill out of Bailey's strapless dress. Mercifully it hadn't worked itself down, but the amount of cleavage it did show was a long way from modesty. Since I had thankfully chosen waterproof mascara, only a little had smudged in the corners of my eyes. And somehow, the whole effect was more . . . party girl after a hot night of sex, rather than emotionally wrung out.

So . . . Cole had meant it. He thought I looked pretty like this.

Frowning at my lack of ability to differentiate between sarcasm and sincerity, I stripped off and had a quick shower, aware during every second of it that he was next door. The door wasn't locked. The thought of him coming in here . . . stripped naked like he had been on the moonlit night by the pools . . .

I turned the temperature to cold and stifled a scream before switching it off altogether.

Bundled up in a big bath towel, I let my hair down as I wandered back into the room, half expecting him to have left. Instead, he was in the same position on the bed, a rigid stillness to his whole frame.

But now his eyes burnt as they watched me cross the room. I sat on the edge of the bed, using the corner of the towel to dry the droplets of water that ran down my collarbone to my chest.

'Time for me to get the day started,' he said, slowly getting up and clearing his throat. 'Lil let me have the morning off, but . . . I'm pushing it now.'

He slipped on his boots, still by the side of the bed.

'Okay,' I replied, heart falling. I'd had no idea what to expect, but somehow the idea of time apart was not it.

He turned, hearing the change in tone.

'Lottie, I'd spend the whole day with you, but honestly, Lil would kill me. And I know I wouldn't be able to keep my hands to myself. I'm just not sure that's what you need right now.'

I nodded, accepting the words, the thoughtfulness behind them, but my heart fell even further.

'Well, I'm not sure how much I like you being a gentleman,' I murmured, earning a gravelled chuckle as he came round to my side of the bed and paused by the door.

'Don't you have a job interview today?' he asked, his voice suddenly quiet.

I groaned.

'Fuck, yes. Ugh. How did I forget?' I said, standing too quickly and almost losing my grip on the towel.

He blinked, turning on his heel and opening my door.

'All right, I'm out. I'll be down at the barn if you need me, okay?'

'Okay,' I replied, watching as he seemed to change his mind and turned and marched back over, my heart fluttering as he pressed a kiss to my forehead before retreating. As he left I felt a tug in my gut, as though a string bound me to him, pulling taut as he walked away.

Sighing, I resolved to pull it together, for the interview. All thoughts of my dad, Cole and Kyle would have to wait – let alone the thoughts that questioned whether I even wanted the job I was interviewing for.

But, true to my conditioning, I got ready anyway, turning from curly-haired bed siren into marketing professional in less than an hour, even rustling up a smarter, non-western shirt from Lil's wardrobe.

As I prepped for the interview in the home office, resisting the urge to check the ranch's social accounts to see the ever-growing following, the distant sound of a growling engine approached, wheels crunching to a stop on the gravel outside.

Dad again?

A falling sensation hollowed my stomach as I walked over to the kitchen, peeking out of the window. An insanely ostentatious car had parked, all sleek lines and tinted windows, and a man in a suit and grey cowboy hat emerged from the back as the driver opened his door.

I ran to the front door, pulling on my boots.

'Can I help you?' I said, slipping out onto the porch then walking down towards him. My stomach dropped as I realized who he was.

He narrowed his eyes, raking them over me.

'You're not Miss Dean, are you?' he asked, his polished transatlantic accent closer to mine than the Wyoming drawl.

'No, she's my cousin. Lottie Wright,' I said, offering my hand.

He took it, still studying me.

'Zach Sinclair. You're not from here, then?' he asked, leaning on the side of the car as his driver got back inside.

'London,' I replied. 'Can I pass on a message, or—'

'I'd rather speak directly to her,' he interrupted, in a manner so reminiscent of Cressida that I felt an instant swirl of anger. 'But I'm guessing you have no way of getting hold of her or knowing where on earth she might be here. At Elk Creek we are a more . . . efficient operation.'

I stilled, as though a cold hand had laid itself on my shoulder.

'I see,' I replied, my clipped British accent intensifying as I crossed into cold, professional mode. 'Well, considering I don't know when she might be back, perhaps it'd be *more efficient* if I just relay your message to her on your behalf.'

He paused, one eyebrow raised at my tone.

'Well, I'll get to the point. I was made aware that some of your guests had posted a video on social media. Our marketing manager sent it over. Apparently there's some kind of health and safety issue here, or maybe it's just a lack of professionalism. Either way, it hasn't gone down very well.'

Frozen in place, I waited as he pulled out his phone and pulled up the app, turning the screen towards me.

It was a clip of several riders, one of them falling off, screaming in pain and blaming an unsafe horse. Then a cowboy, face hidden, accusing city folk of having no idea what they were doing, wishing Wyoming had never opened to dude ranching.

A shot of adrenaline ran through me; the voice sounded a little like Jesse's – and I felt another jolt of horror as a Diamond Back jacket came into shot.

'The comments are fairly damning,' Zach continued casually, as though we were talking about the weather, closing his phone and slipping it into the inside pocket of his suit. 'I wouldn't be surprised if bookings dry up.'

'I don't know how . . .' I started, wracking my brain, trying to remember the guests we'd just had. Jesse had said nothing about any problems, and nor had Lil. 'I don't think—'

'It doesn't really matter what you think, though, does it?' he said, tilting his head. 'It's what other people think – potential guests. Social media is all about perception, isn't it? We thought, seeing as you've taken such a bold move into attracting visitors by using it, you must know that?'

It clicked. A small smile pulled at the corner of his mouth and his dark, shark-like eyes stayed perfectly still, fixed on my expression, as the truth dawned.

They'd faked it. Elk Creek were going after us on social media now.

'Lottie?' Lil shouted, approaching up the drive with Cole, shotgun dangling at her side. Then, as they approached, they both turned their attention to the car, and the asshole leaning on it.

'Miss Dean,' he said, eyes fixed on her gun. 'Charmed to meet you properly, I've heard so much about you. I was just telling your cousin here that your social media experiment has backfired somewhat.'

'They've faked a video of a riding accident, of Jesse being rude to a guest,' I hissed, all but snarling at Zach. Lil's mouth opened in shock. Cole moved closer to me, an uncompromising stare fixed on Zach. 'We could report you to the police, get lawyers involved,' I began, stepping up to him, sudden fury filling me up.

'I don't think you want to do that,' he said, moving to open his car door. 'I have enough lawyers on my payroll to bury this ranch. Which is exactly what I'll do, if you don't sell to us.'

He leant inside, pulling out a brown paper folder and handing it to Lil.

'I've told you people already,' she said, shaking her head.

'Oh, I know that,' he countered. 'But time's running out. We're expanding, and this place is right in the way. You'll sell to us, now, for a fair market price, or we'll destroy your place and pick up the pieces for pennies. It starts with this,' he said, tapping the phone in his pocket. 'And who knows . . .' He gestured at the trees around us. 'Terrible wildfires this year in the south of the state — have you heard? I know for a fact you have no insurance on this place. What if one swept right through here?'

Silence fell between us, the implication of his words sucking the oxygen from the air.

'You've got a week,' he added, nodding at the folder.

Cole stalked towards him.

'And you've got about ten seconds to get off this land before I throw you off the side of that mountain there,' he growled, his hand resting on the car door. 'Now get in and get the fuck off this ranch.'

'I look forward to your answer.' Zach winked at Lil, daring a glance back at me before Cole slammed his door closed, only just missing his foot.

We watched as the car drove off, throwing up a cloud of dust in its wake.

CHAPTER 15

Somehow, I got through the interview.

Retreating to my room and adopting my professional veneer, I'd excused the unprofessional backdrop as the interviewers came on screen, only to be greeted with warm understanding and a story from one of them about fond memories of an earlier trip to Yellowstone.

'Well, Charlotte, it's been a pleasure to meet you today,' said the main interviewer, just over an hour later. 'I also wanted to acknowledge that anyone capable of working in your previous team and maintaining a professional composure has already proven themselves in my eyes.' She smiled. 'I know Cressida from university, so please know that I fully appreciate what your experience must've been.'

Desperately trying to maintain my poker face, I thanked her, not missing the amusement in her expression.

'You'd find it quite different here,' she added. 'In any case, we'll be in touch very shortly to confirm. Could you start straight away?'

I nodded on autopilot, thanking them for the opportunity and hanging up.

An absolute silence gathered in my room, as the realization of how events were transpiring dawned on me. I looked over at the bed, where just hours earlier Cole had lain next to me, as close as another human could be, a half-step from a whole other situation. My whole body ached with need, the thought of it overwhelming, even in abstract.

And now . . . it seemed the ranch was over. My social media experiment had seemingly just sped up the process, leaving Lil, Cole, the others, all . . . where? Had I just signed a death warrant for the ranch and the livelihoods of everyone I was coming to love and respect so much?

I felt sick.

Putting on my hat and shrugging on my jacket and boots, I headed out to the back deck for some fresh air, the sudden need for solitude hitting me squarely in the chest. The thought of Lil and the others trying to put a brave face on the situation was more than I could bear. The muted light of the cloudy sky dulled the colours of the ranch and its surroundings, as though the Elk Creek threats had sapped the life from the landscape itself.

I listened out for sounds of the others, and heard the faintest murmur of voices from the kitchen rising and falling. Taking a few steps closer, I listened for a moment and heard all four of them in there, including – I realized with a stab directly to my heart – the sound of Lil in tears.

Unable to listen any more, hating myself with every step as I walked back around the deck, I headed towards the barn. Toying with re-watching the video, I forced myself to think through ways we could respond and set the record straight with viewers and followers, but shamefully, I was scared. What if whatever I created just made it worse? Would it provoke another visit from Zach Sinclair, or worse, force him into making good on his threat to burn the place to the ground?

I glanced at the home screen as I approached the stalls, two missed calls from Mum popping up. Dad had told her about the argument then, I supposed. Reaching Jasper, stroking his soft, sweet nose as he crunched through some hay, I knew I needed some time to think, to give the others some space to decide what to do. I'd caused more trouble than I'd helped. But before I went, I had to give Mum my side of the story.

'Oh, thank goodness, I've been trying to reach you . . . Oh sweetie, what happened? I mean, I've spoken to your father, but . . . tell me, in your words.'

I swallowed hard, more grateful than she would ever know that she hadn't just taken his side or his words at face value.

'It was awful, Mum. He just started laying into me about being here, saying I was running away from my responsibilities and Kyle, that I owed you both for paying for uni, and how I was trading a good life for this place.' I took a breath, knowing the next part would be hurtful for her to hear, knowing that Dad wouldn't have left it in his account of the argument. 'He completely trashed this place and everyone in it. Said he'd dragged you out of it, and insulted Aunt Carrie and everything she's been through.'

I could hear her moving in the background, saying nothing as she took it in.

'I thought as much,' she said finally, her quiet anger singing through the words. 'He gave me his version, but I could hear the kinda thing he'd say.'

'I really lost it with him,' I murmured, feeling shame wash over me, despite knowing he'd deserved everything he got. 'I swore and raged . . . I've never said anything like that before to him. He just . . . he laid into people that don't deserve that kind of treatment. I was so embarrassed, Mum, that Lil and Cole – he's one of the cowboys here – had to hear that.'

'Yeah, I heard about that,' she replied, a hint of amusement under the seriousness. 'You take after my mom like that – she always had a fire in her, passed it onto Carrie and Lil too, I think. It's not necessarily a bad thing that you told him your truth, however it came out. I wish . . . sometimes I wish I'd had the same courage. Maybe things would've been different for you, for both of us. He wouldn't have pushed you so hard and maybe I . . .'

I gaped at my phone screen. This was the first time I'd ever heard Mum admit anything like this.

'Don't blame yourself, Mum,' I said gently, gathering myself back up. 'Dad's . . . difficult. I'm not sure I understand where it all comes from, but it's not your fault. I should've told you sooner about Kyle.'

She sighed.

'Your dad is complicated,' she began, slowly. 'He holds a lot of regret about not making it as a pro-golfer, about settling for a lesser career on the tour and watching younger and better golfers do what he couldn't. So when you grew up and became the bright and clever woman you are, he channelled all that frustration into you. As for Kyle . . . well. You know I still don't understand the British obsession with class,' she admitted, her voice becoming wry. 'But being involved with a family like that was everything he wanted for you. I know, especially after the way I imagine he spoke to you, that it might be impossible to believe, but he does care about you, sweetie.'

'Right,' was all I could manage, aware that any other response would sound too sceptical.

'I just want you to be happy, Lottie,' she added, clearly trying to keep a grip on her emotions. 'I'm not sure running away will fix things, but time and space are important. And honestly, being away from Kyle sounds like a good call. I'm so disappointed he'd treat you like that; it must've been so horrible for you.'

I thought back to the moment I'd found out, the shock of it. But I saw it for what it was now, my perspective having shifted. It was just Kyle treating me as he always had, as a bit of fun, someone to show off to his friends and buy gifts for in return for my affection.

'I did run away,' I agreed, looking up from my phone for a moment, watching Jasper chewing on the hay and trying to ignore my swirling thoughts about Elk Creek. 'But it's turned into some-thing else. You were right, I do love this place. Nothing's changed.'

'I thought as much,' she said, the sound of a smile behind the words. 'Anything I should know about any cowboys? Your father mentioned something about it, but I didn't want to assume, given his way of seeing things.'

Debating whether to tell her straight out, I decided against it until things were straightened out with the whole social mess.

'I've been getting to know everyone here. That definitely includes a cowboy, for sure.'

Mum chuckled.

'You've always been the same,' she replied, her voice soft but knowing. 'Okay, my sweetheart. As long as you're doing okay. I'm going to speak to your dad myself, when he's home. There's some stuff we need to get out in the open. Avoid this kind of thing ever happening again.'

We said our goodbyes, and as I hung up, I was plunged back into the quiet of the stalls. Watching Jasper for a moment, I continued with my reason for coming down here in the first place.

After brushing him down for a few minutes and tacking him up, I swung myself onto his back, conscious that it wouldn't be long before one of them came out here. Not wanting to cause panic, I messaged Lil to let her know I'd taken Jasper out for a ride and not to worry.

Then, before I could change my mind, we set off, sedately at first until we got through the gate to the long wildflower meadow that ran right up to the beginning of the ridge. Jasper sensed it even as I did, as though my thoughts shifted my balance in the saddle, the subtle pull on the reins. His walk lengthened, and as I urged him on, he broke straight into a canter, then on into a flat gallop.

I grabbed onto my hat, feeling the brim lift in the whoosh of air past my ears, watching as we passed the landscape at fierce speed, Jasper as keen to move as I was. The tightly coiled low bun I'd stuffed my hair into for the interview suddenly untwisted, the hairband flying off. In seconds my hair billowed out behind me, whipped back in the wind that threatened to take my hat with it.

Jasper made it the whole length of the pasture before tiring, gradually slowing to a walk as I patted his neck. The sun emerged from behind a cloud, casting long rays across the mountainside, the snow glistening in the far distance like ice fire. It was unfathomably beautiful, almost too much to take in.

Desperation hit again. The thought of Lil losing all of this, another bully winning in this world. Ripping apart all she'd known, everything she'd worked for. Any potential future I might've had, the idea of a choice that glimmered in the distance, just out of sight.

Of me and Cole. Here.

Gone.

Tears fell as we walked, almost at the gate that led up to the higher pastures, the same route we'd taken for the cattle drive. I decided to keep going, not knowing how to go back, but as I did, another sound built in the quiet, despite the wind, and I glanced around, wiping my tears.

Cole thundered towards us, Domino flat out, her black spots and white coat blurring. Jasper stepped sideways as he heard, turning to face them.

'Steady,' Cole said as he approached, pulling Domino up as she fought him.

'What are you doing?' I asked, wiping roughly at my face, the urge to grieve alone fighting with the equally strong urge to be as close as physically possible to him.

'Honey, you can't just ride off like that,' he said, bringing Domino closer to us, Jasper's ears flattening as she approached. 'Jesse spotted a black bear and her cubs up here just a couple of weekends ago.'

'Oh,' I said, suddenly feeling just like the 'city folk' he'd once accused me of being.

'Look, it's okay,' he said, face creased with concern as he caught my expression. 'If you want to be alone, I get it. I'll ride behind, leave you be. I just . . . I need to make sure you're safe.'

I nodded, aware of the tug of my heart, trying to capture my attention.

'I'm sorry,' I said, taking off my hat a moment, the wind whipping my curls up and around me. 'For all of it. I've made this whole situation a lot worse, haven't I? And now . . . you and Lil, everyone . . .'

His jaw tightened. 'We'll find a way to fight it, Lottie. Ain't no rolling over here – that asshole will get what's coming.'

'Don't do anything stupid,' I blurted, a sudden image of Cole being led off to jail flashing through my head. 'I want you to be safe too.'

He didn't reply, just looked down at his saddle.

'You still want to ride, or go back?' he asked, not quite able to meet my eye.

'Ride,' I said, wanting to reach over to him, hold him. 'Come with me, though, don't hang back.'

He nodded, moving off but keeping Domino at a safe distance from Jasper. I rubbed my horse's neck.

'Quit being grumpy,' I said, almost smiling as he snorted in return, ears flicking back to my voice as though he understood.

'Where you headed?' Cole asked as we went through the gate, looking up the hillside. 'Much further and there won't be a lot of daylight left to ride in.'

'I don't know,' I admitted, desperate not to turn back. 'I just want to keep going.'

He nodded, then paused. His face was hesitant, his eyes fixed on mine.

'Unless you want to stay out? We keep a few supplies at the top, where we camped before, by the pools.'

At the mention of it, a warmth spread through me. I knew what that meant.

He knew what that meant.

My lips parted, willing instinct to bring the right words to the surface, feeling the knife edge we walked along. He stared at them, eyes darkening.

'Let's go,' I whispered, words lost to the breeze, but the intensity of his stare didn't let up as he read my lips perfectly, as though I'd whispered them right into his ear.

Without another word, he turned Domino in one smooth motion and spurred her on up the hillside, Jasper reaching after her, his long legs covering the ground with ease.

Within a couple of hours, sun blazing between the jagged peaks in the distance, we made it to the river, the steam from the pools already visible. Taking his lead, I jumped down and secured Jasper just far enough from Domino to prevent them from fighting.

'Why do they dislike each other so much?' I asked, enjoying the sight of a smile appearing on Cole's face, breaking the pensive expression he'd held all the way up here.

'Well, Jasper here only tends to like who he likes and Domino just ain't one of them. She's the sweetest girl,' he said, rubbing her neck as he loosened her cinch, 'but she likes to be in charge and he won't have a damn bar of it.'

I scratched Jasper's neck, wondering at how this gentle soul could kick up such a fight.

'You're a natural with them, aren't you?' he said, walking up the slope, past where the campfires had been lit for the drive. 'Not many cowpokes know how to whisper to horses.'

I rolled my eyes but smiled at his tone, waiting as he returned, his arms full of supplies, rolled up canvas and a huge bag that jangled as he walked.

'Whole camp in one. We built a shed up here a few summers ago, just in case.'

I watched him dump it down, right in the spot he and Jesse had camped in before.

'I'll do it later – come with me.'

We walked up to the lake, the wind rippling across its surface, the sun reflecting across it, flames dancing in unison over the water.

'It's something, huh?' he murmured, waiting for me to catch up. I stopped a few feet short of him and the sun caught his jaw, his whole face lit up in golden light.

I felt it again. Right there. Three words forming in my heart that would change everything, born of nothing but pure feeling, as deep in my gut as the call to fly out here in the first place had been. I knew he would go anywhere, do anything for me and without question, I would do the same.

He turned to meet my gaze, his brown eyes turned amber in the light.

'What now?' I said, only just daring to ask, my heart picking up pace as he walked towards me with measured, careful steps.

'Whatever you want,' he replied, voice soft, close enough to lift my chin with his finger as my hand came to rest on his shirt, feeling the ridged definition of his abs underneath. His heart was beating with a similar ferocity to mine, fuelled entirely by raw need.

Our eyes locked as I reached up and he leant down, and right there, the sun forcing my eyes closed, I found his lips. Soft but firm, opening to receive my tongue, meeting it with his as his hands grasped my waist and lifted me right up, pulling my legs back behind him until I was hooked around him.

I gasped, breaking off.

'No one to interrupt this time,' he said, walking us over to the pools. 'Shirt off.'

I raised my eyebrow at the new gruffness to his tone, his need loud and clear.

I dropped my jacket and started on my shirt buttons as he moved his lips up my neck, across my jaw, then gradually, slowly, found my mouth again, the urgency building for us both. I couldn't focus, my fingers sliding off the buttons and clasping his face instead, brushing the stubble on his cheeks, my other hand in his hair.

He groaned at the touch and as we reached the pools, pulled back and allowed me to finish the job, my shirt fluttering away to the ground beside us. Setting me down gently, his hands brushed up my waist and lingered over my breasts. He waited as I shivered, noting the goosebumps that followed with a lazy smile before he began to work on his own buttons until I intervened, moving his hands out of the way.

'I figure,' he breathed, moving to my jeans instead, my own breath hitching as I exposed his broad chest and pushed his shirt down over his shoulders, 'there's only one way to do this and stay warm.'

I glanced at the pools just as he did, biting my lip as I smiled.

'Remember when I found you here before?' I said, watching as his eyes fixed on my mouth.

'I haven't been able to think of much since, Princess,' he growled, pulling down the zip of my jeans.

'I couldn't decide if you hated me or not,' I breathed as his fingers skimmed across the waistband of my underwear, dipping just inside the lace at the top. His fingertips were cool against my skin, drifting back out to allow me to step back and take off my boots and shimmy out of the jeans, finally standing in front of him in just my underwear, my hair drifting across my face in the breeze. 'Or whether you really wanted to turn around when I was standing here like this.'

Before he could reply, I slipped down the straps of my bra, unhooked the back and threw it down onto my shirt.

Stunned, he simply stared. I moved back to him, reaching up to find his mouth, shivering under his touch, aching in every part of my body for him.

This kiss was deep, the line crossed. As his own clothes dropped away, his fingers snagged on my pants, working them down slowly, letting them fall.

We stood perfectly still for a moment, pressed together, each dip and curve of my body in line with his. He kissed me again, one hand running slowly down my side, slowing over my breast, continuing down to my hip.

'You really are perfect,' he whispered, voice stripped raw, drawing in a breath as I did the same to him. 'I knew you were perfect that night too. And fuck yes, I wanted to turn around and watch you strip.'

He turned me to the side, lifting my hand and guiding me into the bigger pool. The heat of the water was a welcome relief from the lake's cool breeze, but as he climbed in after me, I stopped noticing anything else at all.

There was just Cole, drawing me into him, dropping down into the water to level out our height difference.

'I never hated you,' he began, his breath uneven as our bodies aligned again. 'I think I just knew how hard I'd fall for you. How I couldn't avoid it, wouldn't be able to cope, if you didn't feel the same.'

I gazed at him, my words falling away as his arms locked behind my back. This time I wrapped my legs around him myself, smiling as I did it.

'And what if I do feel the same?' I whispered, forgetting how to breathe as he kissed my collarbone, then moved down further, his hand and mouth on my breasts. The sensation was overwhelming as I gave myself entirely to him. I knew how I felt about him, had known for a while.

'Cole, I—'

But he put a gentle finger to my lips.

'Why don't you just show me, honey?'

So I did.

Mouth on his, I reached down between us, grinding my hips as my hand gripped his cock. He moaned as I stroked him, slowly, moving him ever nearer to me, the sound in our mouths driving him harder until he slid into me with ease.

The feeling was unlike anything I'd ever known. To be this attracted to someone, to know what was building inside and now to have him on me, in me, groaning as we moved together was a kind of intensity I'd never felt before.

'You are so fucking beautiful,' he whispered against my ear, his tongue tracing the edge of it, kissing the soft, sensitive skin behind.

I shuddered, hearing him moan as I gripped harder with my legs, returning his kiss, starting at the top of his jaw and working slowly down his neck. I wasn't able to put into words the way he looked to me, the way I felt like I was being slowly dissolved by him, becoming part of him. That I wanted nothing and no one else.

We drifted towards the edge of the pool, my back against the smooth stones, and every thrust he made was intense, a kind of wonderful agony against the feel of his tongue in my mouth, the way his finger idly circled my nipple.

'Don't stop,' I whispered as I felt him begin to slow, knowing that if he came, I would too. There'd be time for moving slower, but now wasn't it. Not after what had felt like an eternity of waiting. 'Cole, I want you . . .'

'I'm yours,' he breathed, our movement building, desperate. I gasped as it happened, gripping his hand, his fingers slipping between mine as they had before, leaning back as my eyes closed, an explosion of heat and fire ripping through us both.

As it faded and I tried to catch my breath, he pulled me to him, holding me like we were the only two people in the world. I rested my head against his shoulder as I slowly returned to myself, turning to lay a single kiss on the smooth skin there. His heart was beating as fast as mine as he returned it, his lips pressing against my temple.

We said nothing, but there was no need.

We both knew what it meant.

CHAPTER 16

I had no idea how much time had passed in the tiny tent, I only knew that I never wanted it to end. With just a thin bedroll beneath us and two sleeping bags opened up on top of us, trying to sleep and stay warm would've been difficult anyway, even if we'd been able to stop touching each other.

But we couldn't.

Totally wrapped up in each other, we slept intermittently, only to be awoken by the feel of the other's lips, or a hand tracing the lines of a body, lighting a whole new fire and starting another wave of need. When the first light finally surrounded the canvas and we could make each other out again, I knew the way he looked at me had changed. Deepened.

There was pure, feral lust there, the force behind the way he kissed me, working all the way down my body until I almost passed out from the sensation, his hands as skilled as his mouth. But there was something else, something more profound, in the moments before and after. I stroked his cheek, wondering if it was the same thing I felt, wishing I could get inside his mind as well as his body.

'Can we stay here?' I whispered, smiling as he wrapped himself tightly around me, his face pressed to my hair, breathing it in as he kissed my head.

'As long as you want,' he murmured, his voice rumbling deep in his chest.

'What if I want it for ever?' I asked, feeling him pause and move back so he could look into my face.

He let a silence fall as his eyes moved over me and he took my left hand in his, stroking my fingers.

'I want you to stay for ever too,' he began, his eyes holding mine. 'But it's your call. I know you have a life back home and with everything here as it is . . . I'd understand if this was just a one-time thing.'

I smiled, despite myself.

'One-time? That ship sailed a while ago.'

He laughed, the tiny dimple above his lips forming, his eyes alight.

'You know what I'm saying,' he replied, stroking my hair, letting the curls run between his fingers. 'I'm Wyoming born and bred, and here, however things look with tough guys and cowboys, it's women that make the real calls. Behind every decent man in this state is a much better woman, and if he's lucky, she might be half as fine as you.'

I smiled, waiting as he drew closer on our makeshift pillows, kissing the corners of my mouth.

'I don't think I'll ever stop wanting you,' he said between kisses, the gaps shortening as I responded, pulling him down over me, wanting the weight of his body on mine.

'Show me,' I whispered.

———

It was some time before he finished showing me.

In the quiet that fell across us afterwards, the sounds of the landscape filtered through as the mountains awoke. The low, soft rush of the river beyond, a growing chorus of birdsong and the occasional rustle of the canvas, whipped up by the breeze.

'Come with me,' he whispered eventually, as our heart rates had returned to normal. 'Brace yourself, though.'

Before I could protest, openly ogling his completely naked and utterly mouth-watering body, he pulled me up and led me by the hand out of the tent.

'What the hell are you doing?' I giggled as he pulled me with him, wearing nothing but a mischievous smile as we walked across the grass. The lack of modesty had me looking around us, but other than the trees and a couple of birds of prey far above, we were completely alone. He held me next to him, keeping the cold at bay as we looked across to the mist shrouding the valley below us, the light still tinged with receding night.

'C'mon, rite of passage, you must've been skinny dipping before,' he said as we approached the river. The very cold river.

'I have but . . . oh fuck no!' I shouted, but before I could escape, he'd picked me up in his arms and, my legs kicking, dunked us both in the freezing mountain water.

It was cold enough to take my breath away, and his too.

'Give it a moment,' he said, teeth clenched as I clung to him.

As I did, giving myself over to trusting him, knowing he'd never do anything to hurt me, the initial startling cold wore off, leading to a strange sense of accomplishment.

'It's actually okay, I think,' I gasped after a moment, laughing as he grinned. 'As long as we're not about to get jumped by a couple of grizzlies.'

'They don't tend to come up this way too much,' he explained, teeth gritted against the cold.

'Okay, okay. Fuck the bears – can we get out now?' I begged, so cold that I couldn't even think about anything else any more.

'All right, I guess so. It's doing no favours for certain parts,'

192 • GEMMA MORR

he added, glancing down and making me laugh so hard that he dipped me in further, sparking a fully fledged splashing war.

Drenched and starting to freeze, when he held out his hand again, I took it without hesitation.

We ran back to the hot springs and jumped in.

'You're never gonna trust me again, are you?' he said, grinning as he lay back against the edge. I dipped my hair back in the water to stop the freezing drips running down my back.

'I trust you with all my heart,' I replied without thinking, watching as his face changed, a seriousness taking over.

Taking a deep breath, he pulled me to him, right up against his body.

'What have you done to me?' he asked, searching my face as though the answer lay there. 'Just walking into my life like that, turning up out of nowhere and turning it inside out.' I ran my fingers through his hair and kissed his forehead as he closed his eyes. 'I know it's your decision, honey,' he continued. 'But if you want to know where I stand, then I never want to let you go. I've never had this, felt like this, not even close. But it's not just about me – you've only just ended a relationship, so . . .'

Desperate to say how I felt, I bit my tongue, knowing there were things that needed remedying first.

'I have just ended it,' I began, holding his gaze. 'But it's only this, between us, that's made me realize there was never anything there to begin with. I want to stay,' I whispered, running my fingers across his cheek. 'But first we need to fix this whole Elk Creek situation. I'm not sure how yet, but there's no way I'm letting them have the last word. I didn't spend a whole fucking year with a bunch of asshat lawyers without picking up a few things. And when that's done, then we'll see about *this*.'

His smile widened suddenly, a wicked glint in his eye.

'Well then, you're gonna love what I did,' he said, taunting eyebrows rising to match mine. 'I recorded the whole conversation with that asshole on the drive, got the whole thing on my phone, clear as a fucking bell.' My mouth popped open in shock. 'As soon as the car pulled up, I figured they were only there to make more threats. Only thing we need to do is figure out how best to use it.'

Mind turning over, I bit my lip, concentrating.

'Princess, you've got to stop doing that with your lips,' he growled and just like that, he was grabbing my ass with both hands, ignoring my giggles as I wriggled away, giving in as one of his hands traced up my thigh and kept going until I gasped, melting into his touch.

'Fuck . . . Cole,' I said as I lay back against the opposite side, giving in to his hands.

'Yes ma'am,' he replied. 'I'm on it.'

———

In my exhausted state, still damp and feeling somewhat delicate, the ride back was a slightly uncomfortable but peaceful respite to the previous twenty-four hours.

We rode as close together as Jasper and Domino would allow, their occasional bickering making both of us laugh. But really, my mind was turning everything over: Lil's situation, the fake video, all the traction gained so far on social media.

I risked a glance at my phone as the ranch finally came into view. Opening my email, I ignored the latest two from Kyle and deleted them immediately. There was another, though, from the company I'd interviewed with just the previous day.

Offering me the job. And the salary . . . I raised my eyebrows. Holy shit. Twice that of my old job.

'You okay?' Cole asked, pushing Domino to catch up with us, Jasper's long stride always keeping us slightly ahead.

'Kind of,' I replied, not wanting to lie, but not wanting to hurt him either.

'Is it your ex?' he asked, keeping his voice neutral.

I shook my head.

'I mean, he is still emailing me, but I just delete them. No, it's a job offer, from the place I interviewed with yesterday.'

He nodded, trying to gauge my reaction.

'A good one?' he asked, the neutrality struggling to stay in place.

I blew out a breath.

'Yeah, it is,' I answered, shaking my head. 'But it'll have to wait.'

He nodded, jaw clenched. The conflict between heart and head was intense: my stomach flipped at the thought of fixing the situation at home, being able to maintain my life far better than before; but as I looked over at Cole, at the face that'd filled my thoughts, been pressed to mine in every possible way . . . the prospect of the job, of going home, felt . . . empty.

We got to the stalls and took the horses in, setting them up with a decent feed.

'I'll take over,' he said, leaning over the door as I started to brush Jasper down. 'You go in and wash up, rest for a bit. I'm used to being outdoors all the time, but I'm guessing you'll be wanting a hot shower.'

I put the brush down, giving Jasper one last stroke and smiling as he leant his head into my shoulder for a moment.

'You sure?' I asked, coming out and standing in front of him. 'I'm not a prissy city girl, you know.'

Cole smiled, his hand reaching for mine and squeezing it. I waited for the banter to follow, but instead, his face became serious as he took me in with an intensity that made my throat constrict.

'Whatever happens now,' he began, raising my hand, closing his other hand over it, 'I want you to know I'll never forget any of this. Not the time up there in the mountains, or the weeks before it. I knew when I saw you in that bar that you were . . . different.'

He placed my hand to his lips, kissing it so gently that tears sprang to my eyes. His sincerity ran so deep and he expressed it so naturally that I didn't know what to say.

'But I called you an asshole,' I blurted, blinking back my tears.

His seriousness broke, that same beautiful, self-conscious smile making his eyes come to life.

'Go on, go up to the ranch. Before we end up christening the stalls in front of the horses,' he said, reaching out for one last touch of my hair, making my scalp tingle.

———

I made it back up to the house without encountering anyone, grateful to be able to decompress alone, to try and sort through the jumble of practicalities and emotions. It felt as though Cole had opened up a deep well – one that was potentially dangerous, but the feelings pulled from it coming up pure and untainted.

A hot shower did feel particularly good, tinged with unexpected sadness at washing away the remnants of the searing cold of the river, and the earthy-mineral smell of the hot springs. I'd got used to Cole's smell, catching it on my shirt, my jacket, and without it, I felt . . . wrong. Back in my room and grabbing my shirt from the washing pile, I held it to my face, closing my eyes as his scent hit me again, creating an immediate, now familiar ache across my body.

Reluctantly I put it back, shaking my head and trying to focus. What I needed to do was find Lil and sit down with her, put our heads together to figure this out. There was a solution just out of reach, I could feel it. Like a reflection disturbed by waves on the surface; still there, just fractured.

As I dressed, I scanned my phone again, not quite daring to re-read the email from the company but spotting a series of messages from Hestia instead.

> Are you around today, Lots? I
> need your icy-calm dealing-with-
> shit brain. I think I might actually
> end up killing Cal. And I'm just
> not up for jail yet, so call me
> when you get this?

Frowning, doing a quick mental calculation of the time difference, I called her.

'Are you riding that cowboy yet?' she said as soon as she picked up.

'Hi, Hes.' I smiled. 'No cowboy chat until you tell me what Cal's done now.'

She sighed, her voice unusually downbeat as she explained what'd been happening, how they'd been slowly growing apart until it had all finally snapped the previous weekend, how he'd now officially moved out for good.

'I know we weren't perfect, but . . .' She stopped herself, an occurrence so rare that true anxiety for her bloomed. 'Oh, I don't know, it's stupid.'

'Don't be a dick,' I said, using an imitation of her own technique for preventing me from spiralling. 'Just tell me. You know I'm not going to judge anything you say.'

She groaned. 'But it sounds really fucking stupid now I've said it in my head . . . even if it's a little true.' When I didn't respond, waiting for her to continue, she groaned again. 'Okay, fine. I just thought that . . . well, you know that Cal is even more of an emotional wreck than me. So, in my stupid, twisted logic I thought that if I couldn't make it work with Cal, then it wouldn't work with anyone. And now we've finally broken up . . .'

'Oh, Hes,' I murmured, wishing we were face to face, that I

could give her a hug. 'That's not true. You must know that, deep down?'

'But what if it is? What if I'm too fucked up to really let anyone in, Lots? What if Cal was it and I just chucked it away because we've been too busy to make it work?'

I sighed, clutching my phone as though it was Hestia's hand.

'No, I just don't buy it. You do let people in – you let me in. And I was dressed as a giant cock when we met.'

She snorted a laugh despite herself.

'I know, I know. But it's not the same. I mean, I asked if you wanted to hook up, but seeing as you only like men – and frankly, fuck knows why right now – it means I have to look elsewhere.' She paused, the amusement fading. 'Maybe it's sex that complicates everything,' she mused. 'The minute there's any romance or intimacy involved, bang – it becomes messy and complicated, and seemingly, whether it takes five years or five days, eventually the outcome is the same. Over.'

I considered the short but memorable list of Hestia's boyfriends and girlfriends since uni. Most had been fairly similar to her, at least in one aspect. They'd had either a shared aesthetic or interest – one had even been the tattoo influence that'd tipped Hestia into discovering her talent for creating them, and her love of collecting them on her own body. But emotionally . . . I'd never seen a deeper connection, not even with Cal.

My mind drifted to Cole, knowing that below our explosive physical attraction was that depth – it wasn't just a sexual thing, although it was strengthened by that. I wanted the same for Hestia, badly.

'Listen. Relationships don't always have to work out, right? They just weren't the right people for you. Come on, you'd be the first one to tell me the same. Maybe you just need a proper break from things. You guys have worked so fucking hard on the studio in the last couple of years, it's hardly surprising that it's become too much.'

Hestia sighed.

'Oh, Lots. You've got real Yoda energy, did you know that?'

I chuckled.

'I miss you,' I replied.

'Don't give me that,' she mumbled. 'I know you're well occupied over there . . . and I love that for you. Anyway, the other part of it is not wanting to fuck up the studio. It's doing really well – we've got a massive waiting list, so I don't want to screw that up as well.'

'I know,' I said, wishing there was more I could say to reassure her, knowing how down she must really feel if she sounded this low. 'But the studio is just business, right? Surely you can separate that and set it aside?'

'Yeah, I think so,' she replied, another sigh escaping. 'I just feel fucking exhausted by the whole thing, you know?'

'You could always try my tried and trusted method,' I joked. 'Come over here, try ranch life instead. It's working for me.'

She paused and I suddenly realized how fun that would be.

'Really?' she said, seeming to be genuinely taken aback. 'No, I couldn't. I've got too much on, can't trust Cal to handle things at the moment.'

'So call his mother and make her deal with him,' I said, remembering how Hestia had always commented that only Cal's mum could handle his manic moods. 'What's her name? Diane?'

'You're right, actually,' she replied. 'She always did deliver the best verbal bitch-slapping.'

Something clicked as she said it, a light flicking on in my brain. A solution to the Elk Creek problem.

'Oh shit, you've just given me the best idea,' I said, putting her on speaker so I could finish dressing and drying my hair.

'What? Does someone over there need a verbal bitch-slapping?'

'Yep,' I replied, cursing at my hair, desperately trying to pull a comb through it.

'Hang the fuck on.' She paused, her voice suddenly charged. 'You haven't even given me any juice on this cowboy! I want names, facts, measurements . . .'

I laughed.

'Cole; tall, dark and ridiculously am-I-fucking-imagining-it hot, oh and . . . just right.'

'CHARLOTTE WRIGHT! You *have* ridden a cowboy!' she screamed. 'Please can you inform Kyle in front of me, I beg you – I'll pay?'

Still laughing, I grabbed my hat.

'Want to know something even better?' I teased, grinning at her breathless response. 'He's got a friend. Also a cowboy. Also hot.'

Silence.

'Does he have tats? Big dick? Emotionally unavailable?'

I laughed, shaking my head at the phone. I considered the tats question for a moment, wracking my brain to remember, for a few seconds only able to recall Cole, the memory of his body etched on my mind permanently.

'Yeah, he does have tats – two that I've seen, anyway,' I said, remembering when I'd filmed Jesse at Elk Creek. 'Both on his back. I haven't seen his dick and I don't plan to . . . and as far as I can see, he's pretty well adjusted. Although, he's an ex-bull rider. I'm not sure you can do that without having a few screws loose. Plus, you won't be able to intimidate him.'

'Interesting,' she hummed, the sounds of city life in the background. 'I'll consider that ticket. But when are you coming home?'

As I left my room, heading for my boots by the door, I realized I genuinely didn't know. Home was beginning to take on an entirely different meaning.

'Honestly . . . I don't know. It's rebooked for the end of next week but there's stuff I need to do here first.'

'Like your cowboy?' she asked.

'Amongst other things,' I replied. 'Listen, I need to take your idea to Lil. I'll fill you in, I promise.'

We hung up and I headed over to the cabins, knowing Lil would be cleaning up after the most recent guests' stay. The idea Hestia had given me battled with the image of her meeting Jesse. She'd either eat him alive or he'd charm the fuck out of her.

Regardless, it'd be quite something to watch.

'Lil? You there?' I called, eventually meeting her in the biggest cabin.

'You're back.' She smiled, noticeable dark circles under her eyes detracting from the cheeriness of her greeting. 'You finally returned my ranch manager? I was worried I might never see the two of you again.'

I grinned, not bothering to hide it, giving a mock shrug. 'He was just keeping the bears away, that's all.'

'Uh-huh,' she began, going back to wiping over the bedside tables. 'And . . .'

'And – I've had an idea,' I deflected. 'About how to deal with Elk Creek.'

She stopped, frowning.

'I don't think—' she began, but I waved it off.

'Hear me out, okay? It's a bit out there, but I think it might work. It's not exactly conventional, but then . . . this is Wyoming, right?'

She stopped, putting down the cloth.

'Am I going to need a drink?' she asked, and I smiled.

'Several.'

CHAPTER 17

'So, even if we can fix the Elk Creek problem, what about our image problem online?' Lil frowned as we drove up Elk Creek's long, winding drive the next morning. We'd only just escaped Jesse and Cole's insistence that they come along, 'for backup'. But this conversation was just between us women. 'Can't you just make a video and tell everyone their video was faked?'

I shook my head, wincing as I recalled the comments, the way followers had dropped away. The emails and booking enquiries had all but dried up.

'No one will take my word for it,' I said as we climbed, the huge ranch house coming into view, a smaller, older building just up the road from it. 'If I had a whole bunch of followers who knew me, knew I wouldn't lie, it might be different, but . . .'

I shrugged. Lil was pensive for a moment.

'Would it take time to build followers up? We seem to have built a whole bunch real quick for the ranch?'

I smiled back at her. 'They're mainly following for videos of Jesse, Cole and Bailey. They're the real reason people want to come and stay. I mean, people love the sunsets and seeing the horses at work too, and Jackson will always be super popular, but people connect with people, you know?'

We pulled up outside the big house and as Lil turned the engine

202 • GEMMA MORR

off, looking around to see if any trouble might be approaching, the solution smacked me right between the eyes.

'Oh shit, I totally didn't think of that,' I murmured, as Lil turned back to me. 'We should get influencers, people who already have a following, to come and stay on the ranch. They'll make videos, persuade people way better than I can . . .'

Lil's forehead creased.

'What, pay them?' she asked. 'Can we make sure their videos are positive?'

I nodded, conscious of the financial outlay this might require. After running a few influencer campaigns at my old job, I knew what it could amount to. But this was my mess to fix and I wasn't about to put the financial burden on Lil.

'Lots of them will take a trip somewhere as payment in itself,' I lied, knowing there would be no way she'd agree otherwise. 'We wouldn't need to pay anything else.'

'And that would turn things around again, get the bookings coming back in?' she asked, so much relief in her face that I hesitated, not wanting to give her false hope about what could be another risky venture.

'Definitely. In fact' – I pulled out my phone, flipping to the app and finding the video I'd saved a while ago with a thought to future plans – 'this is a beauty influencer I follow. A brand paid for her to go out to Nashville recently when they launched a product.'

We watched it, and I pointed out the engagement it'd received, scrolling through the comments where countless people had said they'd bought the products or were just about to, solely because of her video.

'I don't know if we can get something this big, she's got millions of followers, but even the micro-influencers hold a huge amount of sway. If we got maybe three or four of them over, planned out a weekend to really show them what the ranch is all about, let them get to know you guys . . . it might just change the whole game.'

Lil clutched my hands, and for the first time, I saw a real gleam of optimism in her eyes. But before we could start planning, a sharp rapping on the window made both of us jump.

'Can I help you, ladies?'

———

'Thanks for seeing us, Dotty,' Lil said, setting her hat down on the seat next to her as I did the same.

Dotty Sinclair, the eighty-year-old matriarch of Elk Creek ranch, one time barrel racer and best friend to our own grandma, Liza, sat across from us in her office. Still whip-smart, her white hair styled and pinned up, she looked as glamorous as ever.

'You haven't changed at all,' she said to me with a small smile as I glanced at Lil. 'It sure was a shame when Carrie and John couldn't figure things out – turned a lot of things upside down. You should be proud of yourself for keeping going, Lil. I had my doubts when Carrie left for Colorado, but I'm happy to have been proved wrong.'

Lil nodded. 'It's been hard in places, but no one ever said ranching was easy.'

Dotty nodded as her housekeeper came in, setting a pot of coffee down next to us.

'Thank you, Jennifer,' she said. 'Can you make sure we're not disturbed? It's been too long since I've seen these young women; the ranch will just have to live without me for a while.'

'Yes ma'am,' Jennifer replied, nodding to us as she left and closing the door behind her.

'Now, what can I do for you?' said Dotty. 'I assume it's not just a social call?'

I hid a smile, enjoying her blunt approach. It caught Lil, normally so composed and ready with a quick comeback, off guard, but then Dotty was renowned for her ability to unseat anyone, especially the biggest male egos in a room.

'Well now,' Lil said, clearly debating how best to approach things. 'We had a visit from Zach a few days ago.' Dotty narrowed her eyes a little, pouring a cup each for us first, then herself. 'He . . . uh, he made it pretty clear that he wants to buy the Diamond Back, and he's not that keen on accepting my answer, which is still no.'

Dotty nodded, tilting her head to the side.

'Zach has always been stubborn like that,' she replied. 'I'm afraid he was indulged by his father, God rest his soul. The eldest boy and all of that.' She sighed, giving Lil a hard look. 'I know what he wants and I know just how long Carrie, and now you, have said no. It's just business though, Lil. And like all men, you've got to just keep firm. I'm caught in the middle here because I want to make sure we keep doing well, expand as a business. But your grandmother was my dearest friend and Carrie's still my goddaughter. So, you're as close to blood as it can get.'

Lil pulled her phone out at that, opening the voice memos app.

'I appreciate that, Dotty, I really do. It's why this hurts so much, to hear someone I consider as extended family come up onto my property and threaten Lottie and me like this.'

Dotty opened her mouth to protest, shock plain across her features as Lil pressed play and Zach's words reverberated through the room.

'. . . *time's running out. We're expanding, and this place is right in the way. You'll sell to us, now, for a fair market price, or we'll destroy your place and pick up the pieces for pennies. It starts with this . . . and who knows. Terrible wildfires this year in the south of the state – have you heard? I know for a fact you have no insurance on this place. What if one swept right through here?*'

As the recording finished, both Lil and I let the silence linger. I studied Dotty's face, pure shock registering there as she held her hand to her mouth.

The only thing I'd been worried about, the thing that could take us to a darker place was if she already knew, had sanctioned it herself. Then this recording would be our leverage to go to the police. But there was no way she'd known.

'I'm rarely lost for words,' Dotty began, gathering herself.

'It was a shock for us too,' Lil said, keeping her composure. 'I just didn't think it was the way we did things here. Not amongst old families, farming this land for generations. We've both been here for what – almost a hundred years now? Sinclairs and Deans, side by side?'

Dotty nodded, taking a long drink from her coffee. The tops of her cheekbones were tinged pink.

'Elizabeth, Charlotte,' she said eventually, looking to each of us. 'You have my word when I say that there will be no repeat of Zach's behaviour. You're quite right, that is not how we do business here – with anyone, let alone old friends. In fact, I'll go one better: I'll have my lawyers change up my will. There will be no purchase of Diamond Back without forfeiting the right to inherit Elk Creek.'

Lil's eyebrows were lost to her hairline.

'I'm ashamed that my boy would do such a thing,' she added, shaking her head. 'But this is why we don't ever leave the men in charge.'

Lil's shoulders sagged with relief.

'Thanks, Dotty.'

'No, no, come on now. There's no thanks needed. Although, I do thank you for coming to me on this. You had every right to take something like that to the sheriff, and then we'd all be in a whole other position.'

'It won't leave my phone,' Lil replied, keeping her back straight as she held Dotty's rigid gaze.

I held my breath; the implication was clear. She wasn't deleting the recording. It would remain in her phone for safekeeping.

Dotty nodded in understanding.

'Carrie raised a smart girl,' she said, holding up her coffee in a small salute.

'It was Lottie's idea, actually,' Lil said, giving me a sly look. 'She reminded me who really calls the shots here. Took someone from outta state, outta the whole country to make me remember.'

Dotty's clear blue eyes fixed on mine.

'Well, your momma took quite a turn in moving all the way across the world, but it looks like the biggest piece of her came right back home, huh?'

————

As soon as we were halfway down the drive, a cloud of dust obscuring the back window, we turned to each other, grinning.

'You did it,' I said, relief overwhelming me in waves.

'YOU did it!' Lil yelled, letting out a loud whoop of celebration as she smacked the steering wheel. 'Holy shit, Lottie. Just like that, years of those assholes bullying us. Over. Thanks to you, honey. I was just so buried in trying to work through it, stay outta their sight . . . I forgot all about going to the source.'

'It was Cole that actually reminded me, yesterday,' I began, returning Lil's suggestive smile and raised eyebrow. 'He said behind every decent man in this state was a woman. I wouldn't call Zach decent, but Cole was right about the rest of it.'

Lil paused as we rode over the cattle grid and out onto the main road, headed for the interstate.

'So . . . am I going to lose my ranch manager anytime soon?' she asked. 'Or am I gaining my cousin full time?'

I stared at her, mouth half open with an answer, but knowing I couldn't bullshit her or leave her with half-truths.

'I . . . I want to fix this problem I've created, make this influencer idea work. The job I interviewed for in London a few days ago has offered me the role . . . but honestly, I don't know yet. I'm . . .' I shook my head, trying to find the right words. 'I'm fucking crazy about him, Lil. But I'm also really scared of fucking up again, you know?'

Her face changed, and she reached over to rub my arm.

'Honey, we all fuck up, every last one of us. But given what happened between you and your dad, I think you just need to listen to your gut on this one rather than anyone else, right?' I nodded. 'So I won't try and persuade you of anything, but you need to know that Cole would never hurt you, not in the way that asshole did in London. And, Lottie, that man is head over heels into you, sugar. I've known him for what . . . more than ten years now, since he was fifteen or sixteen. I've never seen him like this over anyone, not even close. And I'm talking about even *before* you went on up the mountain.'

At her sudden grin, I couldn't help it. We both started laughing, relief and lightness mixing with schoolgirl humour as we reached the turning for the interstate.

'Wait, wait,' I said in between gasps. 'We need to brainstorm this influencer plan. What do you say to going into town instead? We'll get lunch and drinks to celebrate, I'll make some calls and get things organized, then reclaim my title.'

Lil hiccupped back a laugh.

'Okay, it might be good to have a few hours off anyways. But – title? What do you . . .' Her eyes lit up, a fresh smile broadening across her face. 'Oh, okay, guess I know which bar we're going to then.'

'Challenge accepted?' I asked as she swung right onto the road, foot on the gas.

'Oh honey, you've got no chance.'

———

Several hours, about a dozen calls and emails later, we had a plan and a potential influencer line-up, with just a few details left to confirm. The Cowboy Bar was buzzing with people, music and the feral whooping of Miss Elizabeth Dean of the Diamond Back Ranch.

The mechanical bull had started nice and slow, Lil giving a cocky smile and a wink in my direction as she moved easily with it. But as it sped up, chucking her from side to side, she grabbed her hat and really concentrated, a group of tourists yelling encouragement as Lil's work-hardened, experienced legs gripped the bull for dear life.

I knocked back the rest of my whiskey – the second one, thanks to happy hour – and gritted my teeth. The bull-riding title was mine to lose, last won way back on my last visit. Back then, the loser had received a dunking in the ice-cold water trough by the side of the corral, a forfeit we'd agreed to retain.

Eventually, with a particularly violent lurch, the bull flung Lil off to the side, the timer registering twenty-two seconds as the bell went off. Uncurling herself from the mats and dipping her hat to applause, she came over to the side, vaulting over it.

'C'mon then, cowpoke, up you go.'

I mock eyeballed her, the whiskey doing its work, and as I reached out and mimicked her vault over the side onto the mat, someone wolf-whistled.

Turning as I grabbed the strap on the bull, I saw Bailey at the front, raising her glass with a cheeky grin. Next to her were Cole and Jesse, wearing matching expressions of amused curiosity.

'Any tips, cowboy?' I shouted at Jesse, watching as he laughed.

'Just hang on, hotshot.'

I nodded, trying to ignore the hungry look I received from Cole as I threw my leg over the bull in one smooth motion, prompting some yells and cheers from the tourist crowd. His gaze had deepened, as though he was imagining something quite different.

'It's bath time!' yelled Lil, her face alight.

As the bull began to move, I realized how long it'd been since I'd seen her look so relaxed and happy. I smiled to myself as I realized what I needed to do.

Leaning back and keeping the plastic gripped between my thighs, my hips loose, it almost felt too easy. That was until it switched direction with such ferocity that my hat flew off, hair flying wild. I checked the clock: eighteen seconds down.

Bailey whistled again and I gripped harder as the movements became increasingly erratic, my knuckles white until I loosened my legs a fraction and *slam*, I hit the deck.

On my back, breathing heavily, I looked up at the clock. Twenty seconds.

Amongst the clapping and whistles, I looked up to see Cole at the side.

'You okay, cowgirl?' he asked, holding out a hand.

Grabbing my hat, I flicked my hair back and walked over to him, feeling an instant spark as I touched his hand. All of a sudden, the only thing I could see was him, everything else blurring into the background.

'I lost,' I said, breathing heavily, calculating whether I could kiss him without it becoming something we'd need a room for. 'My turn for the forfeit.'

He smiled down at me, reaching for my waist. Before I could ask what he was doing, he picked me up, his hands firm but gentle, and set me down on the other side.

'It was worth it,' he whispered in my ear as Lil approached. 'That image of you up there will stay in my mind for a very long time.' I turned back to him, resisting every urge to pick up where we'd just left off, my body instantly pressing against him.

'Just practising.'

He groaned, hands gripping my hips as Lil came to a stop, dangling her truck keys in my direction.

'Oh, it's about to get real cold, girl. I can't wait to see this.'

———

Back at the ranch, floodlights on in the gathering dark, I stood next to the water trough.

'Come on, no chickening out now or I'll make the ranch manager dunk you.'

I arched an eyebrow at them both.

'Already done it once,' Cole told Lil, a smile breaking out. 'Up at the river.'

'Romantic,' she replied, elbowing him as I laughed.

'Actually . . . it was,' I said, not missing the change in Cole's expression, from playful to serious, and the sappy smile Lil returned. 'But this is . . . not.'

I turned back to the trough, taking off my jacket and boots. And slowly, excruciatingly, lowered myself into the icy water. Biting back a scream, I went in up to my neck.

Lil counted down from ten, and after one, I shot up, gasping.

'FUCK ME that's cold!'

'C'mon,' Lil laughed, 'here's a towel. Get yourself in the shower.'

I made it back up the slope as they followed, Cole eventually appearing at my shoulder. 'Come here,' he said, scooping me up as I protested, Lil chuckling behind us.

'Oh my God, I'm too heavy for this, seriously!'

He laughed as we approached the porch and he strode up the steps and took us into the warmth inside, walking down the corridor and turning into my room.

'Princess, I've carried saddles heavier than you.' He sat on my bed, propping me up and rubbing the towel against my arms to warm me. 'I'll let you wash up. Jesse and Bailey are cooking — hope your stomach's feeling strong.'

'Wait, don't go,' I said, eyeing the wet patch on his shirt where I'd leant against it, the way it clung to his abs. 'We've got a few minutes, right?'

I got up and closed the door, pulling off my wet shirt and jeans and walking back over to him.

'Come have a shower with me,' I said, taking his face in my hands, my lips finding his.

He responded instantly, his mouth opening as he stroked my waist, one hand working its way around my back towards my bra clasp. Then, gradually, he stopped.

'Princess, I . . .' he said, pulling back. 'Fuck. You have no idea how much I want that shower, but here's the thing.' My heart fell, sudden fear crashing into me. He took my hands and looked straight into my eyes. 'I meant it when I said this is all your decision to stay or go or whatever you choose. I think . . . I hope you know what I want, but until you make that call for sure, I might need to keep to myself a little . . . Well, self-preservation, you know?'

Frozen, I felt the first shimmers of a crack in my heart, a glimpse into what *real* heartbreak might look like. The depths of it yawned ahead of me, deep and black and unending.

'Okay,' I whispered, nodding. 'I . . . understand. I think.'

He stood slowly, holding my face in his hands.

'I know why it's difficult to decide on this. Lil told me about the influencer idea, the whole thing. I understand fixing all that first and making a call after, but if you do decide to go home . . .' He paused, taking a breath. 'I'm not going to blame you. Not one bit. But I think . . . I need to protect my heart a little.' I felt tears rising at the unquestionable sincerity in his voice, the pain that leaked into his expression. 'Because if you do go home, I'm not sure I'm gonna cope too well. That's not on you, but the further we go with this, the more it's gonna hurt.'

I nodded again, taking his hands from my face before the tears could fall.

'I get it,' I said, stepping back. 'I just . . . I need to make the right call. I'm scared of fucking everything up again.'

His hands balled into fists as my voice broke, then in one long stride he closed the distance between us, pulling me up to him, his grip gentle. But his kiss was not.

It was fire and promise and every emotion we'd experienced together in the last few weeks. I clung to him, my hands grasping at his shirt, willing him to give in to the way it made us both feel, even though I understood his reasoning for backing off.

'This isn't it,' he said as we broke away from each other for a moment, trying to gather sense and breath. 'It's a pause. Whether it's saying goodbye on the other side, or . . . more.'

I nodded, resting against him for a moment, breathing him in.

'Warm up now, okay?' he said, walking over to the door and opening it. 'I'm gonna go supervise, see if I can't prevent them poisoning us all, right before the new guests get here.'

I nodded, grabbing my towel from the bed.

'Cole?' I said, my voice quiet. Too quiet. He'd slipped away, closing the door softly behind him. I stared at it, feeling the tears gather and fall freely.

'I've fallen in love with you,' I whispered.

CHAPTER 18

With contracts signed and most of my savings committed, we had three days to make the ranch into the most social media-ready version of itself. Lil and I ran around getting the right supplies in, meal-planning and adding extra touches to the cabins – even ordering in personalised Diamond Back Ranch jackets for the incoming guests.

'So tell me how this all goes,' Bailey asked. 'I mean, I get the idea but what's the strategy?'

We were next to each other in the tack room, a saddle and bridle each, cleaning and oiling the leather. I'd had the influencers provide their height and riding ability in advance, allowing Bailey to choose which of the horses would suit them best.

'The strategy? You're making it sound like a military manoeuvre.' I chuckled, watching as she smirked in return.

'Tryin' to corral city folk into saying exactly what you want about the ranch? I'd say so. I'm always thinking strategy,' she added, finishing one bridle and moving on to the next. 'Barrel racing is all strategy.'

I nodded. 'Yeah, you're right, I guess. Well, the first thing is choosing the right people. This bunch have similar but slightly different audiences, all into travel in the US. That way we stand to reach out to as many of the people who are most likely to want to come and stay here as possible. The second thing is giving them the experience they really want, and making it look good. They could have the best time of their lives but if the cabins don't look bougie enough or it rains the whole weekend, the content won't work.'

Bailey considered my words, her well-practised handling of the bridle, the methodical way she used the cloth to get the oil into the leather appearing somewhat meditative.

'So it was you that arranged the good weather we've got forecast for this weekend?' she said, smiling and finally turning to me, eyes crinkling. 'What we gonna do with these cowpokes then? Anything you need us to know?'

I nodded, grateful for her understanding. This whole thing would only work if they all played their parts. I'd already briefed Jesse and Cole and received a mildly bemused, albeit supportive response. But Bailey held the key role; she was the grounding influence in the whole thing.

'Well, Jesse and Cole are going to be, uh, occupied with their own tasks.' She raised her eyebrows but didn't venture anything, just waited for me to go on, her expression calm but her eyes still glimmering. 'So I need you and Lil to tag team-leading them through the itinerary.' I raised myself up from the bench and reached into my back jeans pocket, pulling out a folded piece of paper. 'Your focus in particular is to show them what can be done with the horses, give them a barrel riding demo – maybe even coach them to do their own, easier version.'

I unfolded the paper as she chuckled, setting down her cloth to reach for it.

'Well, jeez, it's sure packed full.' She nodded as she read through the list and paused as she got to one of the activities. 'Cold-water swimming in the mountain river? You sure a bunch of city folk are gonna go with that?'

Smirking, I carried on with the saddle I was working on, buffing out a mark near the pommel.

'That one's tried and tested by another city girl. It definitely got the endorphins going and it'll be fucking hilarious to film.'

Bailey side-eyed me.

'I don't want to know.' She laughed. 'No shooting on here? We do that with some of the regular guests. Jesse has a whole range set up that he can get out.'

I shook my head.

'Nah, one of the influencers is really anti-guns. I was scanning through her feed and she made a couple of really strong opinion videos on it. We'll just leave it – I don't want to create any kind of negative vibes.'

'You really have thought of everything, haven't you?' said Bailey. She waved the piece of paper. 'Can I keep this?'

I nodded. 'Oh – and the two women I've invited, they've both ridden before, but they're both a little intimidated. One of them – Kendra, I think, but I'll double-check for you – had a bad experience once; her horse bolted and she was okay, but it really dented her confidence.'

Bailey narrowed her eyes, thinking.

'Okay, I'll swap her out for Jasper, if you don't mind. He's our gentleman – well, except around Domino. But he always behaves beautifully for greener riders. A little slower these days, except when you're on him.'

I grinned, remembering the speeds we'd reached on the way back from the cattle drive.

'Now, not to rain on the parade or anything, but what're the chances of this not coming off?' Bailey asked, frowning. 'I mean, I can see how you've thought all this through, but how do we know it will work?'

I shrugged. 'Hard to say. I mean, I know it *can* work – I've seen it happen in my own job, and with other brands and products on social, but there's no guarantee. But if we show them the best of the ranch, if you guys give them every last bit of your western charm' – I smirked at her, receiving one in return – 'then it'll work. They're all super influential, so if they give it their approval, we'll be back on track.'

She nodded, looking thoughtful as I held my breath. The real truth was, we were walking a very fine line. If they didn't have a good time or something went wrong, it'd likely come out. The fees weren't a golden ticket to wholly positive reviews, especially as I'd chosen them all based on their authentic approach to creating sponsored content. It was one of the reasons why they all had really engaged followers that listened to them, but it was also a bigger risk to the ranch.

'Lil said one of them's British, right?'

I became still, then tried to cover it. She'd homed in on the biggest risk of all, the one I'd hidden part of the truth about.

'Yeah, that's right – Leo. He's from the UK, lives in New York now but . . . uh, I kind of know him, through an . . . acquaintance. It's the only reason it happened, actually – he'd be too expensive otherwise. He's got a huge following that seem to do everything he tells them to. I got mates rates.'

I scrubbed at Jasper's bit, trying to distract myself from the way I was connected to Leo: he was one of Kyle's oldest friends from school. They only saw each other once or twice a year at most, but they were still close enough.

'Huh,' said Bailey, swapping cloths as she moved on to Penny's conker-brown saddle. 'I didn't realize they got paid *and* got a free vacation. Maybe I'm in the wrong business.'

I paused, cursing myself. I'd been meaning to keep the fees part to myself and hoped Bailey wouldn't mention it to Lil, for now at least. I knew Lil didn't have the spare money and I wasn't about to let her get into debt for an experiment. Thanks to having no life outside of work in London, and Kyle spending most of our relationship trying to buy my affection by working his way steadily through his family money, my savings had been pretty extensive.

But, between keeping my flat in London and now the influencer fees, the moment where I'd have to decide between the new job or staying here had very nearly arrived.

'I reckon you'd make a great influencer,' I deflected, noting her incredulous look. 'What? You'd be great. I just wish I'd filmed you at the rodeo – that riding was insane.'

She shrugged, looking faintly embarrassed at the praise.

'I'm not cool enough for social media,' she teased, nudging my arm with hers.

'You are genuine and amazing, and these influencers are going to love you and have a lot of fun.'

'So . . . are you gonna be okay with Cole being part of this charm offensive?' Bailey asked after a pause. The question was innocent enough, but somehow it felt like a stab in the heart.

'I asked him to be his usual charming self,' I said, receiving a calculated glance in response, my voice not quite able to hide my internal conflict. The thought of Cole looking at someone else the way he did at me, of having it returned by one of the women – both straight, both beautiful – was acutely painful. But, if it led to the kind of content the ranch needed to get bookings in again, to help build the business to secure Lil's and everyone else's future . . . then the sacrifice had to be worth it.

That's how I justified it, anyway. Despite the physical ache of missing Cole's skin against my own. Of never having been quite so aware of him being on the other side of the house, the other side of a door. Twice now, I'd wandered down the hall towards his room, hesitating as I drew closer. The thought of touching him again was all that occupied my thoughts, in between preparation for the influencers' arrival this evening. But I knew it wasn't fair to him, to either of us.

'I hope you don't mind me saying so,' Bailey began, pausing to choose her words carefully. 'But it sure would be strange here without you now. If you go on home to London after this.'

I nodded, swallowing.

'I didn't expect it to be such a difficult choice.'

'Yep, well,' she said, finally getting up and stretching, her final bridle now finished, 'these things always happen when you least expect them, right? I never expected to become a barrel racer, get a sponsor or two, make something of it. But sometimes life just happens and you've gotta trust your gut.'

I took a deep breath. Two days. We just had to get through two days. And then, if everything went okay, if Lil would let me stay, then maybe . . .

'What about you?' I asked, needing to get the hell out of my head for a while. 'Anyone catch your interest round here?'

'Aw, no one really.' She grinned. 'I'm not much of a commitment type, y'know? I don't mind a little fun now and then but it's just me and Dunkin against the world right now.'

———

Five minutes before six, I spotted headlights curving up the bottom of the drive.

'Lil! They're here, I need you out front. You seen the others?' I shouted, grabbing my hat as I ran out of my room, right into Cole.

'Woah there,' he said, voice low as he steadied me, his hands on my arms. 'You all right?'

I looked up, startled. His touch set my heart racing, ratcheting up a notch as his eyes grazed my face, rested on my lips.

'Yeah . . . I just . . . I think so,' I stumbled, wanting to step into him but also step away; to resist the urge but also feel him again.

'It'll go fine,' he soothed, thumb stroking my arm, sending heat through my skin. Then, as though he could feel it, he withdrew. 'I promise we'll do everything we can to make this work, okay?'

'Right, just two days,' I told myself, half under my breath.

He nodded, still staring into my face. Then, as if reassuring himself too, he said, 'Okay. Let's make this a show they don't forget.'

'I forgot to ask, ma'am,' Jesse said as he approached, shirt unbuttoned at the top and a lazy grin on his face. 'Are the two of us allowed to wear shirts this weekend, or . . .'

I dead-eyed him.

'Get outside and charm the fuck out of them *with* clothes on,' I instructed. Moving past us, Jesse touched the brim of his hat in response.

Cole said nothing else, just adjusted his hat and strode away with Jesse. I tried to gather myself, hearing Lil calling Bailey over from the kitchen. I hung back, wanting the first introductions to be with the four of them, the true ranch reps.

I stepped out onto the porch to find the two women already out of the taxi, shaking hands with Lil. Both on the taller side, one brunette, Ashley, and one pale blonde, Kendra, were both staring fixedly at Cole and Jesse. They were even more stunning in real life, clearly not needing any of the filters on social.

I couldn't blame them for ogling the cowboys; I'd done the same. But as Kendra approached Cole, doe-eyed and smiling, I felt sick. He smiled in greeting before taking her hand to shake it, ducking his head with the shy smile that pulled on every feeling at my core.

'Well hey, Cole . . . the videos don't lie, right, Ash?' she said, turning back to her friend, hand over her heart.

But Ashley was already preoccupied, giggling as she borrowed Jesse's hat and tried it on. He looked delighted, indulgently watching as she posed for him.

'Wait, wait – let me get that,' said Alix, the guy that'd emerged with them, laughing at Ashley with Bailey and Lil. He pulled out his phone, tapping the screen and moving closer.

I waited, letting them capture the flirting, grateful, despite my heavy, sick feeling, that everyone was playing their role. Jesse was in his element, embracing the role I'd briefed him on, posing with Ashley, taking his hat but promising her the opportunity to win it back. Their backdrop was the old, pretty ranch house, the setting sun setting the back of it ablaze in golden reds.

'Hi there, I'm Lottie. I was the one in touch with your agency,' I said, introducing myself to Kendra, who was mid-flow, talking to Cole about her hometown.

'Oh, right, hi,' she replied, her handshake as insipid as her greeting. 'Wait, are you on social too?' she asked, narrowing her eyes as though she recognized me.

I felt my old self, my corporate veneer settle into place. Cole watched us with interest, careful to stay a step back.

'No, not my scene,' I said, suddenly sounding more British than I had for some time. 'But it's great that you could make time for us this weekend. Lil will show you to your cabins.'

Kendra nodded.

'Right, great. I think maybe you just look like someone I recognize – the whole dark-haired, light eyes thing, plus the accent . . . Yeah, it's definitely a look at the moment.'

I raised an eyebrow but smiled, noticing more lights approaching on the drive.

'That's our last guest – excuse me,' I said, taking sure, deliberate steps past them, nodding to Lil to get them moved on. Slowly, she rounded them up, her and Bailey taking their bags.

As the taxi approached and rounded the top curve of the drive, I noticed two people in the back, hidden by the glare of the sunset on the back windows. Confused, I wondered if perhaps it wasn't Leo after all, but some other tourist couple, chancing their luck at finding a place to stay. When it pulled up and Leo emerged, I stopped.

Because emerging from the other side of the taxi was a tall, slim, dark blond-haired man with a sense of style so out of place on the ranch that it was identifiably him from a full mile away.

Kyle.

All of the breath left my body and I stood, rigid, as Leo greeted me.

'Lottie! Oh God it's been an age! When I told Kyle I was doing this he jumped at the chance to come and surprise you — said you hadn't been home in weeks. It's shit about your job, eh? I was saying to him that you should do content creation — you've got the face for it, he always could pick the hottest woman in the room.' He chuckled, waiting for Kyle to walk around the taxi and join him.

'Oh God, no . . . I'm better behind the camera, I think. But thanks so much for coming,' I finally managed, fixing on his face, his wild brown wavy hair swept back. 'Would you be able to just head over to my cousin Lil? The blonde over there? She'll show you to your cabin. I just need to have a minute with Kyle.'

He laughed.

'I'll say! After that much time apart,' he added, winking back at Kyle.

My shock was rapidly turning to rage, a slither of anxiety underlying it. As Leo walked away, cheerfully calling out to Lil, I looked up at Kyle, his face impassive, eyes all over me and my clothes. The lack of designer anything, the dirt on my boots, my loose curls and the hat keeping them back off my face.

After one more glance over at the cabins, noting that everyone was now almost inside, I stepped up to him.

'What the actual FUCK are you doing here?' I hissed, unable to help myself as I used both hands to push him back.

Steps behind me made me pause.

'Lottie, what's going on?'

Cole's voice was worried; he was still too far back for me to feel his presence, but close enough for me to feel safe.

'I don't know, Kyle,' I snapped, taking in his surprised, submissive expression. 'What the fuck *is* going on? Why are you here?

WAIT – hold on,' I said as the taxi started to move away, stopping as I banged on the window. The driver rolled it down. 'Could you wait a moment, please? This man needs a ride back into town.'

'Lottie, we need to talk,' Kyle said, shaking his head as though I was a toddler, mid-tantrum, that needed to be reasoned with via a firm voice and a guiding hand. 'It's all been a misunderstanding.'

'You're damn right it's a misunderstanding,' I replied, my voice shaking. 'You were not invited here and have absolutely no fucking right to just turn up uninvited and try and justify what you did.'

'Lottie, for goodness' sake,' he said, taking my arm and moving me away from the taxi. 'Let's just talk and—'

'Get your hand off her.' Cole's shadow fell across us both, close enough for me to be enveloped in his scent, and feel the threat in his voice. 'Get in that car and get off this ranch. If she wants to talk to you, she'll come to you herself. Right now, if you don't leave, I will personally escort you off the property.'

Kyle dropped my arm, frowning, glancing between us.

'I'm at the Four Seasons,' Kyle said, glancing across to Cole but not quite daring to hold his gaze. 'You owe me a conversation, at the very least.'

'I don't owe you shit,' I whispered, trying to stop the sob lodged in my throat from rising up. 'I can't believe you did this.'

'What was I supposed to do?' Kyle hissed back, flinching as he caught Cole's glare over my shoulder. 'Your dad said you were here, and then when Leo told me he was coming over—'

'Oh my God, my dad put you up to this?' I replied, trying to turn but coming up against Cole instead. He held firm, body tensed, ready.

'Cole, c'mon, let them be,' Jesse said, his voice just behind us.

'No, it's fine, Jesse. Kyle's leaving,' I said, willing him to go.

Kyle shook his head.

'Not until you agree to meet me to talk, tomorrow, when they're all busy entertaining your influencer guests.'

His eyes flicked over Cole, now pressed against me, my body blending into his. I hesitated, feeling the crossroads we stood at. Taking the wrong turn could end up with the weekend ruined, with Cole knocking ten shades of hell out of Kyle and God knows what else.

'Fine,' I snapped. 'I'll come to your hotel. Just go. Now. Please.'

He glanced at me, then at Cole, seemingly satisfied; then he climbed into the taxi. We watched in silence as it took off, disappearing quickly down the steep curve of the drive.

'I'll stall the guests a little, give you a minute,' Jesse said, jogging over to the cabins, looking back at us once and nodding to Cole.

I stared blankly at the dust gradually settling back onto the road, trying to grapple with what the hell had just happened.

Without a word, Cole turned me around to face him, holding me tightly for a moment. The relief of touching him was almost too much as I tilted my head up to him, finding his eyes.

'You don't have to do a damn thing,' he said, his voice hard, his expression bleak. 'Like you said, you don't owe him anything and I don't trust him with you, not for a fucking minute.'

The implication was clear. Cole's fear that Kyle would somehow talk himself back into his previous role, explain away what'd happened and somehow make it all right again was obvious. An echo of Cole's pain, from his earlier life, flickered through his expression. Losing someone he cared for, knowing how that felt. But he didn't know Kyle like I did.

'I know. But he's persistent. If I don't explain, he'll just—'

'I'll fucking kill him if he touches you again,' Cole snarled. 'I'll drag him out of the Four Seasons by his fucking fancy jacket and send him back to London with my foot up his ass.'

'Cole,' I said, daring to break our pact in order to touch his face, my fingers stroking his skin, watching as his anger melted under them. 'It'll be okay. Forgiveness is not on offer, not for one second. I just need him to know that it's finished.'

He scanned my face over and over, desperation in his eyes, his hands grazing my neck, my waist, drawing back as if he couldn't control himself if he let go.

Jesse's voice filtered back over to us, talking loudly, as if in warning. They were leaving the cabins, ready for the tour of the rest of the ranch. Kendra's voice became audible, her laugh breaking the tension around us. This was not what she needed to see.

'I need to go,' I whispered, memorizing his face again. 'Just stick to the plan. Please.'

'I need you,' he whispered back, hands on mine.

But I stepped away, walking quickly to the side of the house, taking myself around the back, fighting tears all the way.

CHAPTER 19

I stayed in the background, not trusting my emotions.

As the influencers settled in, the team embraced the plan and fell into their roles with ease. Utterly on edge, I watched as they entertained them beautifully and I . . . wore my corporate mask. It felt so alien, yet so familiar: muted responses and crafted smiles, swimming at the surface and never reaching deeper. How could I have lived like this for so long in London? After almost a month here, I realized I felt like I'd ripped off a Band-Aid that couldn't be replaced, the wound below now healing after exposure to the realness of this place, as fresh and raw as the mountain air.

'Are we going to the Cowboy Bar?' Kendra asked, draped over the sofa arm nearest the fire, the huge hearth allowing for a small bonfire that lit the whole living area. It was the largest, but somehow also the most cosy room at the ranch, rarely used day to day, when the kitchen and smaller seating area there was the focal point. But for guests, with its deep, soft, tan leather sofas, throws and cushions, it was perfect.

'Oh my God yes,' Ashley mouthed, mid-way through filming Alix giving a room tour.

'Are you a regular, Cole?' Kendra asked, swirling the ice in her drink, looking up from under her eyelashes at him on the other side of the same sofa.

Ignoring it, swallowing down all feelings, I turned to Leo.

'So, how's New York?' I asked, wondering if my fixed smile looked as fake as it felt.

'It's fun, I'm liking it,' he answered, his own smile slow, curious. 'But . . . I've got to ask, what's going on? Kyle didn't tell me why you were here and now he's been sent packing to his hotel . . .' He raised his eyebrows, holding up his hands as my expression changed.

I felt frozen, stuck between wanting to tell the truth and wanting to glaze over it all.

'I needed a break. We're having a break,' I admitted, keeping my voice low. 'I spent a lot of time here as a kid and it's the first place that came to mind when I needed to feel safe somewhere, you know?'

He raised an eyebrow.

'You and Kyle are having a break, or a break-up? Oh my God, this is huge, you guys are the hottest couple!'

His voice carried across the room during a lull in conversation, almost every head turning in his direction, including Cole's.

I could feel the weight of his stare on the side of my face as my stomach dropped. The urge to be anywhere other than this conversation was overwhelming. How could I have been so stupid as to try and keep to innocent small talk with one of Kyle's friends?

The choice felt impossible. Tell Leo it was totally over and risk him not helping the ranch, maybe somehow turning this weekend into making some kind of reconciliation happen; or hurting Cole.

'I'm going to speak to Kyle tomorrow,' I said, not giving a direct answer and shooting a look at Lil that begged her to take the attention away from me. 'I guess we'll see.'

He opened his mouth to ask more, just as Lil announced the itinerary for the next day and started to take orders for another round of drinks. Excusing myself before he could ask any more, I headed to my room, careful not to look at Cole as I did so.

'Thanks again for inviting us,' Kendra drawled as I reached the door, forcing me to turn back to look at her. 'I think it's going to be a fun weekend.'

She glanced at Cole, biting her lip as he looked back at her for a moment.

'You're welcome,' I replied, feeling and hearing the steely corporate barrier rise once again. 'Have a great day tomorrow, and I'll join you all in the evening at the Cowboy Bar.'

As I left, I felt Cole's eyes follow me out, right as Kendra launched into another story, demanding his attention. As I walked back to my room, I knew I had to make this work.

There was too much at stake.

———

Almost no sleep later, I overapplied my make-up in the morning, bemused that this had been my routine for so long before arriving here. It felt like an age of dabbing and squinting, then styling my hair into something smooth and tamed. I'd got used to my natural hair, letting the curls fall casually across my shoulders, but that wasn't going to cut it at the Four Seasons.

I needed Kyle to see me as I had been, to say no to him as the version of myself he knew. His reaction last night had spoken volumes, and now I needed to make this conversation with him count. I'd willingly walk in there, make myself very clear and leave.

Even my clothes were London-coded, the things I'd been wearing when I arrived, making me feel entirely out of place. Everything felt uncomfortable, the jeans that'd cost a small fortune from some new designer label at Harvey Nics now paling in comparison with the fit of my Wranglers.

Grabbing the keys to Lil's truck, as we'd agreed the previous night, I headed out. Waiting until everyone was prepping for their ride, loading up with supplies for a picnic, paid off. After last night, I decided keeping talking to a minimum was the best course of action.

As I drove past the corral, Cole and Jesse turned towards me, already mounted. Cole's jaw was set and his eyes dark, calling something out to Lil as I passed. I knew he wouldn't like what I was about to do, but I had to do it. Alone.

———

The lounge at the Four Seasons was busy, with early summer guests heading out for hikes, rides and trips up to Yellowstone. It only took a few seconds of surveying the area to see Kyle, talking to another tourist, the two of them mirroring each other's confident swagger.

I approached slowly, waiting for Kyle to spot me from the corner of his eye.

'Ah, Hugo – this is my girlfriend, Lottie. You won't believe it, Lots – Hugo's another old Etonian, works just up the road from your old place in the City. Anyway, good to see you – maybe a drink later?'

I nodded as Hugo offered a hello and goodbye, managing to avoid Kyle's hand on my arm as he guided us towards some chairs near the tall window overlooking the mountains beyond.

With simmering rage, I sat opposite him, letting him order for me, knowing there was no point fighting the habit of a lifetime.

'Kyle, I'm not your girlfriend,' I began. 'Flying all the way over here and then pretending nothing has changed is completely delusional.'

He eyed me for a moment, as though considering the best tactic to use, how to *manage* me.

'Okay, okay. Look, here it is.' His hands were open, eyes beseeching. 'I won't deny that I made a big mistake – a monumental fuck-up, okay? I'm not pretending about that at all. Total honesty from me, all right?'

I folded my arms, keeping my lips clamped shut. The only fuck-up had been on my part, thinking that we were ever right for each other. Compared to how I felt now, to what Cole had shown me, my relationship with Kyle had been exposed in all of its ugly true colours. A surface-level nothing.

'But no one is perfect. Everything we had was so good, Lots, you can't deny that? It's our one-year anniversary in a few weeks. That means something. I mean, Christ, I've never been with the same person for that long.'

'You weren't,' I replied, unable to help myself. 'You were with me *and* her.'

Our drinks arrived and he made a ridiculous show of over-tipping, the waiter falling over himself to thank him before leaving.

'The real question here isn't about all of that,' he said finally, sipping his coffee and grimacing. 'God, Americans never know how to make real coffee, do they? Lottie, this is really about whether you're willing to throw away everything we had for one silly mistake. It's bad enough that you got sacked, let alone creating all this mess with us.'

I clenched my hands into fists, my knuckles aching as I forced myself to keep it together.

'I didn't get sacked, I got made redundant. Two different things.'

He shrugged.

'Minor details,' he replied. 'Surely you don't want to give up that easily on everything? On us? Lottie, I don't want this to be it. We work well, me and you, everyone thinks so. I mean, God, even Mother sees it and she loathes everyone.'

And here we were, at the part I knew we'd reach eventually. The bit I'd imagined all too easily in those long hours awake last night, when I'd pretend to be talked round, start to go along with things like the good little girl he'd petted and bought for the best part of a wasted year.

Kyle would never willingly let go of something he felt he had a right to; it would need to be taken away, irretrievably. So I'd figured there was only one way to play this out and not ruin the influencer weekend, much as I loathed the idea of it. Leo was integral to the success of it all, and I didn't want any of his focus on Kyle.

For now, I'd play the part of the wronged girlfriend, but be forgiving and grateful for Kyle's efforts to win me back. When they'd all gone, however, their experiences cemented and content secured, he would be officially dumped in no uncertain terms. I wasn't sure how I wanted this to go yet; that probably needed another sleepless night to figure out.

The only part I couldn't reconcile with this plan was the inevitable pain it would cause Cole. It would be temporary, explained away in less than forty-eight hours, but it would be pain nevertheless. It'd brought tears to the surface, imagining how he'd feel, thinking I'd gone back on my promise not to forgive Kyle. I'd even toyed with telling him my plan, but I knew how perceptive Kyle could be, knew it had to appear real. Cole was many wonderful things, but a poker-faced strategist wasn't one of them.

'We did work well,' I said slowly, eyes downcast. 'That's why it hurt so much.' I found his eyes, saw the sudden light of optimism sparking.

He moved his chair closer, launching into his vision of how things would be from now on, the key he'd already had cut for me, for his house. I let him talk and talk, agreeing where required, until his version of events was reality, for him at least. The thought of the life he painted for us, of the grey, unforgiving London I'd struggled against for so long, felt unfathomable.

'Oh, Lots, I've missed you,' he added finally, reaching over to stroke my hair.

Barely repressing a shudder, I gave him a small smile.

'Let's take it slowly,' I said, treading carefully around his ego. 'I need time to adjust, I think.'

He pouted for a moment, then nodded.

'So where are the influencers today?' he asked, leaning back, satisfied that the charm offensive was complete. 'I can't believe the money Leo gets paid for this kind of thing,' he scoffed.

I felt a stab of panic, needing to get us somewhere public, somewhere where he wouldn't try his luck physically. The thought of having to kiss him, let alone anything else, turned my stomach.

'Well, they're heading over to the Cowboy Bar soon, actually. Happy hour and line dancing this afternoon. It's a Jackson staple. We should go, it'll be fun.'

He raised his eyebrows, finishing his coffee.

'Suppose there's not much else to do round here out of season,' he said, shrugging. 'This place is only good for skiing, and even then I prefer Aspen. It's all a bit rough and ready, isn't it? Anyway – lead the way.'

———

We'd been in the bar for barely an hour when the group arrived. Although I was sitting with Kyle, his arm casually lying across the back of my chair as we watched the dancing, seeing Cole enter with Kendra hanging off him was a gut punch.

'Oh, look!' Leo called, waving at us from the bar.

Everyone turned, Cole last of all. In one movement, his entire body bristled, standing straighter, arms flexing. Jesse held his arm, whispered something over his shoulder.

We exchanged no words as they came over, Kendra holding on to Cole's arm as she led him straight into the dancing, Jesse and

Ashley following. Bailey, Lil, Alix and Leo were chatting, faces animated as Leo filmed everything.

He waved us over and whilst Kyle stood up, I stayed seated, three strong cocktails having taken effect.

'Go ahead,' I said, smiling sweetly. 'I'm dreadful at this – I'll watch.'

Smirking, Kyle joined Leo, throwing himself into it.

Immediately I glanced over to Cole, just as he did the same. Our eyes locked, his over Kendra's head as she moved into him, around him. His gaze was careful, pained. He glanced to Kyle and back to me, confused.

I looked down at my drink, wanting to reassure him but not knowing how without raising Kyle's suspicions. Gradually, as the afternoon gave way to evening, Kyle and Leo's antics increasingly took centre stage, other tourists joining in.

As I plotted how to sneak away, calculating that Kyle was gradually becoming too drunk to notice, Jesse sidled over. The top buttons of his shirt were open, his tan glowing with the exertion.

'Having fun?' I asked with a smile, trying to mask the strain in my voice.

'I'm keeping up.' He returned it, but his expression lacked his usual warmth. 'Listen, Lottie. You can tell me to back off, I know this isn't my business, but . . . this situation with your ex. It's got Cole all twisted up. I know you and him have something going on . . .' He paused, reaching over to put a hand on my arm as I flinched at his words. 'And I know it's big. I don't want to put my foot in it and speak out of turn, but Cole is totally gone for you. I just . . . I can't stand by and watch him get his heart broken, you know?'

I gritted my teeth, fear and shame curdling in my gut.

'I . . . I know how things look, but I'm not planning on that, okay? You're a good friend for risking a conversation about it,' I said, trying to give him a reassuring smile, but feeling it was more like a grimace. 'But Kyle is only here for the weekend. That's it.'

Jesse frowned, but nodded.

'Does he know that?' He glanced over at Kyle, mid-conversation with Leo. 'He sure isn't touching you like that.'

'I swear to you, Jesse. I don't feel anything for Kyle. I've just got to keep things on a level this weekend. I can't risk ruining this whole thing because he ends up having a tantrum and making this whole weekend about our relationship drama. The ranch is on the line, your jobs.'

Tears threatened again as I swallowed hard. Jesse squeezed my arm as I turned to him, his eyes softened.

'Okay, okay. I get it now. Don't fret, Princess, we've got you. They're having the time of their lives and we'll keep it that way, all right? I've even promised Ashley a one-on-one private roping lesson, clothes optional.'

'Jesus,' I croaked, knocking back the rest of my drink. 'Tell me you're joking.'

He just smiled, turning back to the bar.

'Things sure got a lot more fun since you arrived. You want another drink?'

I shook my head, glancing at Kyle again.

'I'm gonna head back. Alone.'

Jesse winked, adjusting his hat as he sauntered over to the bar.

'I'm tired,' I said to Kyle as I reached him through the mass of bodies on the dancefloor, shrinking away as he grabbed me around the waist. 'I'll see you tomorrow, okay? We're having a cookout at the ranch in the evening – come and join us?'

'Go back to my hotel,' Kyle said, cheeks flushed. 'It's the penthouse. I'll meet you there.'

'I'm staying at the ranch,' I shouted above the music. 'Let's take this slowly, okay? We can talk more after everyone's gone.'

Kyle rolled his eyes, but nodded as he ran his hands over my ass before kissing me, hard.

I pulled back immediately, turning before he could try anything else and stalking off the dancefloor, almost making it to the exit before someone grabbed my hand.

'Don't tell me he's talked himself into your life again,' Cole growled, barely caged anger rolling off him in waves.

'I can't talk now,' I said, not daring to keep speaking to him, just walking out into the faded light, hearing Kendra's voice behind me, calling him.

———

I kept it together on the drive back to the ranch, keeping my thoughts purely practical. I scrubbed at my face once home, trying to erase Kyle from it, getting straight into my pyjamas and then bed, lining up my headphones to get stuck into an audiobook. It felt futile, but I needed to escape and knew a book would be the answer, but also knew hearing the voices would stop my attention wandering.

As the narrator began, I shuffled back against the headboard, closing my eyes. It started to work: muscle by muscle I felt myself unclench, the complexities and frustrations easing away until—

A hand touched my shoulder and I jumped, my eyes flying open as I removed my headphones, relaxation swallowed by anxiety.

Cole.

His eyes were wild and he was running his hands through his hair.

'What? What's happened?' I asked, pulling back the covers to move my legs out, the desperation in his eyes scaring the shit out of me.

'I can't lose you,' he whispered, lowering himself to kneel in front of me.

I froze, stunned, as his expression became one of pure pain. Guilt struck hard and I scrambled to make my thoughts into coherent words, to take it away.

'Cole, I need to—'

He moved closer, pulling me to the edge of the bed so my body was aligned with his.

'I lied. I said I'd let you make this choice without interfering, but I can't. I can't just let you go like this. I've never felt like this about anyone, Lottie. Seeing him touch you, kiss you—'

He shook his head, hands clenched, fighting with himself. I wanted to explain, but I knew he wouldn't hear it right now. So I did the only thing I knew would make him listen.

Crossing my arms, I took off my T-shirt.

Stunned, he looked from my chest to my eyes, his own wide with shock.

'I'm playing a game, Cole. I've given him hope to keep him quiet and stop him fucking up this weekend,' I said, reaching over and undoing his shirt buttons. 'But that's all it is. Because I don't want to be anywhere without you.'

I held his gaze, confusion still marring his handsome features as I ran a finger over his cheek, the prickle of dark stubble making both of us shudder.

He shrugged his shirt off, letting it fall to the floor.

'So you're not . . . together? You're not leaving?'

I shook my head vehemently as he gripped the side of the bed, bowing his head in relief. Moving forwards, I lowered myself off the edge of the bed, kneeling in front of him. Finally, as though waking from a nightmare, his body came alive. His hands trailed across my breasts, then moved up to my face, my neck.

'I'm so sorry if I hurt you,' I whispered, my lips brushing his as he brought his face to mine. 'I needed to convince him, but nothing happened. I can only think of you, I only want you.'

Then his mouth was on mine, tongue claiming me, hands lifting me onto the bed, removing my shorts.

'I've been picturing you like this since the mountains,' he said, voice raw as he unzipped himself, barely free of his jeans as he leant over me. 'I'm yours, Lottie. Any way you want me.'

He started with slow kisses from my neck, slowly working down and down, over my breasts and down, one hand on my hip as his stubble grazed my thigh.

Voices in the hall startled me, and I grabbed at the cover just in case.

He stopped, head above my legs, glancing back at the door. Then, looking back at me, shrugged off his jeans completely and held out his hands to me.

'Bathroom,' he whispered, gently pulling me up, kissing me as I reached him, skin on fire as our bodies touched. He half carried me into the bathroom, closing the door behind us and locking it with a reassuring click.

'Where's that shower you promised me the other day?' he asked, eyeing the large waterfall-style shower in the corner.

Smiling, I stepped over and turned it on, leaning against the wall as he entered, frowning as he knelt down again. 'What are you . . . oh . . .'

His hands moved lower, spreading my legs. Slowly, as the hot water ran down his shoulders, rivulets gathering in the defined muscle of his back, his tongue traced a line of fire from my hips. As one hand reached around and gently squeezed my ass, he pulled me closer still, his tongue searching lower and lower until it was in me. I gasped, unable to keep my eyes open to the feeling he created, leaning my head back against the cool tiles. As the steam began to build, the noise of the water only just covered my moans until I had to put my fist in my mouth to stop myself from screaming.

'Not yet, Princess,' he said, kissing back up my body, then, picking me up gently, one hand on my waist and resting my back against the wall, he guided himself into me as I locked my legs behind him. 'Yes, honey, use me. I want you to come on me, show me how I'm yours.'

'Cole,' I murmured, beginning to lose it as he thrust into me, gripping onto the hard muscle on his back, my fingertips slipping on his wet skin. 'Don't ever stop.'

He laughed, his voice husky.

'I won't. I can't. You're all I ever want, Princess.'

And there, in the water, he held me until the end, until his end. Until the hot water ran cold and he bundled us up in towels, moving back into my room and dragging the huge, solid wood chest of drawers in front of the door in one easy movement.

'Once isn't enough for my girl,' he said, eyes gleaming as I fell back onto the bed, looking over his body with wonder as he walked back to me.

'I want to lose count,' I whispered as he got in with me, knowing, loving that another sleepless night lay ahead.

CHAPTER 20

'We just have to make it through the cookout tonight, then they'll be packed up and leaving first thing in the morning.'

Cole nodded and I smiled as he tried to tame his mussed-up hair, evidence of the complete lack of sleep he'd promised and very much delivered.

'And Kyle? How are we gonna deal with that? I mean, I would happily send his ass packing the old-fashioned way, but you choose, beautiful.'

I considered it, craving the satisfaction of seeing Kyle laid out flat on the deck, but the risk of him becoming nasty, getting lawyers involved or finding some other way to ruin Cole and the ranch was too great.

'Why don't we just fuck in front of him?' I suggested, keeping my voice casual, enjoying the sudden surprise, then the grin that sprang up.

His gaze was feral.

'I love that mouth,' he said. 'I love all of it.'

I became still, suddenly aware of how close he'd been to saying the words with a whole other weight of meaning behind them.

We stared at each other in silence as Cole's face became serious and he opened his mouth to speak—

'Lottie? You up yet? I could do with a hand in getting all this food prepped for later if you don't mind? We can take it all down to the lake ready and set up? Looks like a clear night out.'

'Okay, Lil,' I shouted back, still holding Cole's gaze. 'Be ready in ten.'

The silence returned between us, but I sighed, knowing the day couldn't be put off any longer.

Before I could move off the bed, he took my hand in his.

'I don't want to hide or pretend after this weekend,' he said, emotion welling in his voice. 'I want everyone to know how I feel about you; I want to start a life together.'

I wanted to say it. My gut response was begging me to just say it. But not with Kyle and the others around. Not yet.

'Me too,' I replied, chickening out. 'They'll be sick of seeing and hearing about it soon enough.'

He squeezed my hand before starting to pull his clothes back on, my eyes snagging on his perfect ass.

'I'll do my best to avoid Kyle,' he said, pulling up his jeans and ruining my view. 'But I've never met anyone that needed a beating as much as that asshole.'

I nodded, getting up and pulling on western clothes again, my real clothes.

'Just think of Lil and the ranch,' I said, trying to be firm, but crumbling as I watched him tuck himself into his jeans and zip up.

He caught my gaze, smiling as I looked away, trying not to blush.

'Princess, I'm only ever thinking of you,' he said, pulling his shirt on. 'Damn, the way that pretty pink colour lights up under your freckles like that . . .' I bit my lip and his hands stopped working on his buttons. 'You trying to make me late?' he growled, stepping around the bed despite my protestations.

'I can't,' I gasped, half laughing, half refilled with need despite having spent half the night tangled up with him. 'Lil needs me – she's going to know you're missing too if you don't get down to the barn . . .'

He paused, fingers on his zip, narrowed eyes on my mouth.

'Then it's a date, after the cookout. Those lips and my cock.'

I raised my eyebrow, as though considering a deal.

'I'll think about it,' I said, shrugging. 'All day.'

He laughed, finishing the buttons and brushing my chin with his fingers before striding to the door and moving the chest of drawers back over, then checking the hallway was clear.

'Not as much as I will,' he replied, disappearing, closing the door softly behind him.

———

The day passed in a haze of nervous tension. As Jesse, Bailey and Cole entertained the guests with a roping contest, Lil and I set up at the cookout area. It was down by the small lake, towering fir trees giving way to a clearing and a thin strip of pebbled beach. A covered deck was strung with fairy lights, a couple of rocking chairs, a hammock and a long outdoor sofa right opposite a giant fire pit.

An industrial-sized grill and stone-built pizza oven were positioned on the other side, put into place on the last visit my parents and I had made out here together.

'Seems to be going well, I think,' Lil said, breaking the silence. I'd been so deep in thought at how to handle the situation with Kyle, as well as fighting back replayed passion from the night before, I'd barely said a word all morning. 'They're having a good time. Leo said he'd love to come back for real, bring his girlfriend and her family in the fall.'

'That's great,' I replied, suddenly wondering if he still would, given what was about to go down.

'So . . . umm . . . what's the deal with you, Cole, Kyle . . . I don't want to push you, honey, but you've hardly said a word. You need me to do anything?'

I paused, not knowing how much to tell. But her open face, the genuine concern in her eyes made the decision for me.

'I want to get today out of the way, to have them all leave with the best content and get things on track for you. But after that . . . Lil, if you'll have me, I'd like to stay, help you run things here.'

Her mouth popped open and she put down the burger buns in her hands.

'For real? You wanna stay here?'

I laughed at her surprise. 'If that's okay? I'll pay my way, I'll help you make it work – get another job in town if the payroll can't stretch to include me.'

'Oh honey, I'd love that,' she said, moving over in a rush to grab me into a hug. 'We'll find a way. I know it's been a bit up and down, but it'd be so . . . empty without you.' She stood back, frowning. 'But what about Kyle? The job in London?'

I shrugged.

'They can't compete,' I started, trying to choose my words carefully, then giving up. 'Because I'm in love with Cole and there's no way I can live without him.'

Eyes bulging, Lil gave an ear-splitting squeal and squeezed me so hard I stopped breathing.

'Holy cow, Lottie! When did you—'

'I haven't told him yet, not in so many words,' I said, fighting back a smile, thinking of all the action that'd said it instead.

'And Kyle's coming over for the cookout?' she asked, finally gathering herself to give me a last squeeze and carry on with getting the food ready.

'Yeah . . . that's the last test. If we can survive that, we can survive anything.'

———

My own words were ringing in my ears a few hours later, when we finally lit the grill and everyone descended. Ashley and Kendra decided to get some footage by the lake, posing with their wine glasses as I topped them up.

'Hey, Lottie?' Ashley said, moving her phone around for the best light. 'Can I ask you something?'

I glanced back at Kyle. He'd arrived not long ago, hungover and sulking, insinuating that we should get out of there, go somewhere nice and 'get to know each other again'. My stomach churned at the thought of it.

'Sure, shoot.' I smiled, wishing I could drain the rest of the bottle right here and now.

'I hope it's okay, but I kinda showed one of my friends some of the content – don't worry, she won't share anything yet, I just knew she'd be crazy about this place. She makes travel content too, but more on weddings and girls' weekends, that kind of thing.' She leant over, pulling up her friend's channel, scrolling through a couple of videos. I held my breath, realizing it was one of the influencers I'd wanted to invite over, but with a following of over 5 million and fees to match, I hadn't even bothered reaching out. 'She wondered if you were up for offering a free stay for a few of her followers, running it as a competition on her channel. I think she'd visit too, just for herself, to check it out – no fees.'

I blinked, trying to play it cool but unable to stop the grin spreading across my face.

'Umm, yeah, I'm sure we can do that.' I smiled at her and looked back for Lil, wanting to include her in the conversation. 'That's amazing, thanks for sharing with her.'

Ashley waved it away, glancing at Jesse.

'Oh no, you're welcome. It's been the best weekend, right, Kendra? You guys are awesome and this place is like a little slice of heaven.'

Kendra hummed, her eyes in the distance. I didn't need to

244 • GEMMA MORR

follow her gaze to know who she was watching, but after last
night, I couldn't be less concerned.

'Where's the wine from?' Kyle drawled, pulling a face as he
swirled and sniffed it, finally braving a sip as Lil attempted a smile
in return. The happy feeling building inside me evaporated. I
could sense Kyle's irritation, his patience dangerously low.

'It's Californian,' I stepped in, shooing her back to the others,
hating myself for bringing him on them all.

He didn't reply, just proceeded to down the whole glass, as Leo
caught sight of him and laughed.

'Steady on,' he said. 'Where's the race?'

Kyle shrugged, eyes on Cole as he strode across the deck to
help Lil.

'Wine like that is only good for chugging back,' he replied,
suddenly glancing at me as I hovered nearby, stoking the fire. His
eyes were beginning to glaze, the tips of his cheekbones becoming
pink. 'Plus, no use staying sober, is there? No need to *perform* later,
so what's the point?'

Conversation quietened as everyone heard the undertone.

My stomach dropped. *Fuck*.

'Steady, mate,' Leo said, frowning.

I felt it, like a tremor across the water in front of us. The
impending storm. Kyle wasn't getting what he wanted, when he
wanted it. I glanced at Cole, his whole body shaped by concern,
turning as though he was about to walk over to me.

Kyle noticed, his face turning dark, sour.

He started laughing, but the sound was bitter.

'Oh God, that's why,' he said, halfway to standing, steadying
himself on the back of the sofa. 'I was so busy seeing how the man
mountain was looking at *you* that I didn't see you returning it.'

Fear took over as I saw Kendra, Ashley and Alix's eyes
widening.

'Kyle, can we talk for a moment please?' I said in a low voice, gesturing for him to walk with me, away from here. Cole was rigid, eyes blazing.

'No, no, no,' Kyle said, wagging his finger at me. 'I've admitted my mistakes and God knows you've got on a fucking high horse about them, but look here, at what *you've* been up to!'

I locked on to Cole's eyes, begging him to stay calm.

'Don't fucking look at him when I'm talking to you, you slut,' Kyle hissed, drawing gasps from the women, especially as Cole strode forward suddenly.

'No, Cole, please,' I begged, running to stand between them, but Cole reached Kyle first.

'Go on, say it again, I fucking dare you,' Cole said, barely a foot from Kyle's face. 'If you insult her one more time . . .'

'And why does she matter so much to you?' Kyle replied, stepping up to him, arrogance carving a nasty smile across his mouth.

'Cole,' I whispered, heart in my mouth, the horrified expressions all around us evidence of the end of the illusion.

'It matters, asshole, because I'm not standing for it any more. You are speaking to the woman I love. And I'm gonna be spending every day for as long as she'll let me, proving to her that not all men are selfish, hypocritical pricks like you.'

Undiluted silence rang out across the space, every single mouth popped open.

Except mine. All I could hear were his words, ringing around and around in my mind. He loved me.

Which is why I missed Kyle spinning around and marching towards me, locking on to my arm with a vice-like grip.

'I don't think so,' he said, yanking my arm, his fingers gripping hard enough to bruise as he began to walk us away. 'Lottie, enough of this fucking hillbilly trash.'

'Ow, Kyle, you're hurting me – stop!' I yelled, hearing but not seeing the pounding footsteps behind me, only aware of Cole as his hand clamped over Kyle's arm and wrenched it off me.

'I warned you, asshole,' Cole snarled, and as Kyle turned back, fist already raised, Cole swung his own and smacked Kyle hard, in the face.

Chaos reigned.

Jesse and Lil were with Cole in seconds as Kyle bellowed with rage.

Bailey pulled me away gently. 'You okay, sugar?' she asked, her words barely registering as she checked my arm. 'He grabbed you pretty hard there.'

'Stop them fighting, please!' I shouted, watching as Leo pulled Kyle back as he yelled a string of obscenities. Jesse and Lil hung on to Cole, forcing him back.

'Is this what you really want, you little bitch?' Kyle yelled at me, a red welt growing on his cheek. 'You know what, if he's already had you, I don't want to know. God knows what you're riddled with now.'

'Kyle, stop, you're embarrassing yourself,' Leo said, fighting him back until Kyle pushed him off. 'It's not dignified, mate. She's moved on, just leave.'

Throwing Cole one last, hate-filled look, Kyle shrugged as though none of it mattered.

'Good luck with her – she's a manipulative little bitch and a fucking nobody, just like you,' he spat. 'I've had enough of this bullshit, this fucking trash town. You're welcome to it, to her.'

Bailey hugged me tightly as he stalked off, the implications of this whole sorry episode dawning rapidly on me.

'I'll take it from here,' Cole said, appearing on my left, letting me fall against him as the tears started.

'I'm so sorry, Lottie, I just lost it,' he said, tilting my face up to him. Aware of the others, all openly staring, I could only think to say one thing in reply.

'It doesn't matter,' I whispered, holding his eyes in mine. 'I love you too, Cole.' I said it softly, watching as it registered, the anger and violence of the last few minutes dissipating into something else entirely. 'You don't have anything to prove to me. You've already done it.'

He held my face in his hands and slowly, leaning down, he kissed me. Gently at first and then more firmly, only breaking off when Bailey wolf-whistled.

'Oh my God, that is the most fucking romantic thing I've ever seen,' Ashley cried and as I looked over, Cole still holding me tight, she and Kendra were clutching each other, both with their hands over their mouths. 'You guys are the cutest,' she added.

'Hold up, when did you both meet?' Alix asked, bringing his phone over. 'This is too good – were you on vacation here, Lottie?'

'Umm . . . sort of,' I replied, glancing at Cole for reassurance, not sure what was happening, but as long as it didn't involve the guests running off and reporting what a disaster their trip had turned into, I didn't care.

'She came here to get away from that asshole, after he cheated on her,' Cole said, pressing a kiss to my forehead, 'and found herself a cowboy instead.'

'Holy shit, that is one hell of a marketing strategy,' Kendra breathed.

Suddenly overwhelmed with relief, I started laughing at the sheer ridiculousness of it all. In a moment she was laughing too, then the others joined in.

'Seriously though, this is an amazing story,' Ashley said, eyes alight. 'Can we include some of it in the content? I mean, not Kyle's temper tantrum, but the whole finding your cowboy thing? My followers will be *obsessed*.'

I looked up at Cole, waiting before he nodded.

Leo walked over, hands up in apology.

'Lottie, I'm so sorry I let him barge in on the trip, I can't believe the way he just spoke to you. Look, I'll make sure he gets on the plane home. I never would've said anything if I'd known this is what he'd be like.'

'It's okay,' I said, shaking my head. 'It's not your fault. I just didn't want this weekend to become about him, or us . . .' I looked up at Cole, staring at me with such intensity that my stomach filled with butterflies.

'Oh it's all about you two,' Alix said, grinning. 'C'mon, let's get some shots by the lake before the sun goes down. This place is stunning – look at how gorgeous the water is!'

The surface of the lake was still, a mirror reflecting the burnt coral sky, while the mountains watched over us from a distance.

Cole and I walked, hand in hand, down to the shore. The stillness was beautiful, utter calm after everything that'd just happened.

'So what are the chances of getting you skinny dipping in there with me, huh?' Cole asked, smiling at my reaction as he straightened and flexed his right hand, the beginnings of a bruise beginning to bloom across his knuckles.

'I'm more of a hot springs kind of girl,' I said, then as I considered his face, his smile at the sheer magnitude of what had just happened, I added, 'But give me some time to get used to it and maybe I'll change my mind.'

'How long have I got?' he asked, his fingers squeezing mine.

I reached up to his mouth and brushed my lips against his.

'Always.'

———

A month down the line, I'd already relented with the lake. Three times.

Not only that, but the lake was central to the plans for the position of the new cabin, something Cole had surprised me with just a week earlier, with Lil's *very* hearty blessing. Living just down the hall from a couple that into each other was . . . a lot.

It'd be entirely mine, my own little piece of my family's ranch, and Cole was building it with Jesse's help as a gift. The extra work was a challenge to squeeze in alongside all the extra bookings since the social media content had blown up, but now that we'd hired someone to manage the admin and bookings, as well as another two cowboys to help with the horses, the path was clear.

Ashley had been as good as her word and her influencer friend, Kinza, had already visited just two weeks after the others had left. The competition to win a stay at the Diamond Back blew up on social, alongside everything Ashley, Kendra, Alix and Leo had posted.

So much so that I'd been added to the payroll as marketing and guest experiences manager to deal with the trickle, then the flood of bookings that had followed. It was a fraction of what I'd earnt in London, but enough for all I needed. In fact, I'd never imagined I could ever have so much; I wanted for absolutely nothing.

I'd even managed to force Lil into taking some time off and going on her first holiday in four years, giving her time to see her mum in Colorado and then visit London for the first time ever. There were still two weeks left on my lease, and given I'd rented it fully furnished, it made for perfect free accommodation. Hestia had already cleared out and sent over what little remained of my things after I'd asked her to just donate my whole wardrobe to local charity shops. The old Lottie had officially gone, morphed into this new version of myself, permanently dressed in Wranglers and my now truly worn-in tan boots. And as well as my clothes, I'd never felt as comfortable in my own skin, especially when it was up against Cole's.

Leaning on the corral fence, I was watching him and Jesse marking out the new fence line for the road down to the cabin when a small cloud of dust on the drive up announced the final part of my plans. The last seal of approval needed to make all this official.

Bailey's truck rounded the corner by the barn, coming to an abrupt stop.

'Lottie, where the hell did you find her?' Bailey asked, jumping down from the driver's side and adjusting her hat, grinning. There was a pretty pink tinge to her cheeks, as though she'd spent just a little too long in the sun.

I grinned back, waiting as the passenger door opened and a maelstrom of red hair and black clothes sprinted across the drive to me.

'Lottieeee! OHMYFUCKINGGOD!' Hestia yelled, slamming into me with a force that almost knocked us into the dirt. 'This place is incredible and Bailey is just fucking GREAT and holy shit . . .' She stopped, looking up, hand raised to shield her eyes against the sun. Cole and Jesse walked towards us, Jesse's shirt undone under the intensity of the late June weather. 'Is that . . .?'

'Yeah,' I replied, laughing, waiting for them to reach us. Cole's expression was warm and amused, his eyes flicking between me and Hestia. Jesse's eyes were wide, taking in everything about my friend, from the multitude of tattoos to the way the sun caught her hair, like spun flames. 'Cole, Jesse, this is Hestia.'

They both tipped their hats to her, smiling as she shook her head.

'Well fuck me, Lots – I know you said they were hot but . . . holy hell. What the fuck are they putting in the water here?'

I tried not to laugh, failing miserably at Jesse's surprised expression.

'It's good to meet you,' Cole said, extending a hand, now his turn to be surprised at Hestia's firm return handshake. 'I've heard a lot about you.'

'Well, annoyingly, Lottie has been very coy about you,' she replied, narrowing her eyes at me. 'But from what I do know, it sounds like I'm going to know you for a very long time to come, so I'm looking forward to finding out more.'

Cole ducked his head and smiled, moving over and reaching out to pull me to him, his lips instantly on my forehead.

'But you,' she began, stepping up to Jesse, hands resting on her hips, 'you, I know almost nothing about.'

His lips curved as he looked over her, his expression just as brazen as hers.

'Happy to change that, ma'am.'

She raised her eyebrows at me.

'I should've come to visit weeks ago,' she said, smiling up at Jesse, then back at Bailey, leaning on her truck and watching the whole thing. 'Now, c'mon and show me around, cowboy.'

She looped her arm through his and together, they started walking up the drive as if they were old friends.

'I'll take you into town later, get you a hat,' I called after them, not willing to move out of Cole's arms just yet.

Hestia just looked back over her shoulder at me, smiling. Without a word, she reached over to Jesse's hat and transferred it to her head, peering over at him as he stared at her, mouth half open, smile forming.

'No need.'

BONUS CHAPTER
COLE

From the moment that woman first looked at me across the bar, I knew I was in trouble.

Hell, I even tried to convince myself I was just being a gentleman by getting that slimy asshole, Jim Randall, to leave her the fuck alone. But I knew that wasn't it, best intentions aside. Even from the other side of the room Lottie stood out. Not just because of the city clothes – hell knows Jackson Hole sees enough of *those* year-round – nor even the shit-eye she was giving everyone in range. No, it was just . . . her, something magnetic, something I hadn't felt before. More than just fucking beautiful. The minute I imagined her in some tight Wrangler jeans and a cowboy hat . . . well, that was the moment I got off my ass and went over to her at the bar.

And then . . . that sexy British accent. The way she'd levelled me with a single look.

I was almost hard just thinking about it.

But then my phone rang, my brother's name flashing up on the screen.

'You've got two minutes or less, Jay – I've got a dozen cowboys and a whole herd to move this weekend,' I said, shoving my hat on roughly and adjusting my jeans as I left the old barn. I needed to get a fucking grip.

'When did you get so busy and important, little brother?' he said, chuckling. He loved any opportunity to remind me of our five-year age gap, even though I now dwarfed him. 'I've got a question to ask.'

'This better not be something you can Google,' I sniped, striding across the grass. I instantly scanned the property, seeing the trucks and trailers already gathered at the back of the barn, a couple of guys already raising their hands as they saw me.

But I knew who I was looking around for, and it wasn't them.

Jay barked a laugh.

'Who rattled your cage today? Well, does Google know whether you want to be my best man or not?'

I stopped, snapping right out of my thoughts. He and Lianne had got engaged at Christmas, but somehow I hadn't figured I'd be a part of the wedding in *this* way.

'Your . . . Oh, shit – really? Wow. I thought . . .'

'You thought I was gonna ask Riley, didn't you?' he guessed, his footsteps and the sounds of horses in the barn back home echoing in the background.

'Well yeah, he's your oldest buddy,' I admitted, reaching up to rub the back of my neck. 'But, fuck, I mean, I'm honoured, man. Of course.'

There was a pause, masking what I knew would be one of his quiet smiles in return. We'd been close growing up, especially after Mom left and shit was rough for a few years. But once Jay had finished high school and took on running the ranch with Dad, I started with rodeo, getting good real fast, and we'd drifted apart.

'Well now, I'm not going to pick a friend over my own goddamn brother for something like this, am I?' he replied. 'I'm gonna warn you, though, Lianne will be dragging you to suit fittings, rehearsal dinners and hell only knows what else.'

I groaned, setting off again and heading for the gate.

'And a speech, right?' I said, shaking my head at what I'd just agreed to.

'Yep. Oh – and watch yourself around some of her girlfriends. A couple of shots and they're gonna be climbing you like a fucking jungle gym.'

I snorted, reaching down to place my hand on the gate and vaulting over.

'Those days are in the past,' I muttered as I lifted the phone back to my ear. My attention was drawn yet again to searching through the people around the corral and barn, slowing as I finally spotted long, dark, curly hair.

She turned at the same moment, in conversation with Bailey. My heart all but stopped when she smiled, watching as it lit her eyes. I wanted to smile with her, despite knowing it would fade if she saw me, knowing I could kick myself for being an ass the other day.

'You still there?' Jay asked as I approached Domino and untied her from the fence, leading her around the side of the trailer. 'What's with you? Wait – I've heard there's a new girl up there at the Diamond Back. Don't suppose that's . . .'

'Gotta go, brother,' I said, cutting him off. 'Tell Lianne to call me about fittings or whatever she needs, okay?'

I swung onto Domino, pocketing my phone and smiling as I heard the end of one of Carter's jokes. One of the ex-Elk Creek managers, now at a ranch over the border in Montana, he'd brought a bunch of guys to help out. Thankfully his riding was better than the jokes.

'Hey man, thanks for coming along,' I said, pulling up alongside him.

'You've got it,' he replied, turning in his saddle along with everyone else as the sound of galloping hooves thundered across the field.

Bailey and Lottie had taken off, dust rising in their wake. Lottie was lowering herself, hair streaming, letting Jasper extend himself fully, ears pricked forward and the kind of youthful energy I'd never seen in him before. Lil had told me she was a natural with horses, that they responded instantly to her, but I realized how quickly I'd dismissed it – dismissed her – the minute she'd talked about the city. But it was clear how much Jasper loved her, that even Bambi, the most skittish baby girl we'd ever had here, had all but fallen asleep after Lottie had brushed her down.

Fact was, this was my shit to deal with. And, more than that – given how I couldn't stop thinking about that girl, about that kiss – I was gonna need to do something pretty fucking drastic to turn it around.

'Say, that the new girl?' Carter asked as a couple of the others started whooping and laughing. 'Diamond Back really does have all the good views over this side, huh?'

'Knock it off,' I growled, before gesturing for everyone to start moving. 'That's Lil's cousin and she'll have your hide for talking that way.'

'Whose hide?'

Lil strode over on Penny, tipping her hat to the guys as they moved off to follow Bailey and Lottie, all of them nodding to her. Carter gave me a knowing grin as he left.

'You know how nothing stays quiet in a small town. They were just talking about Lottie arriving.'

'Huh.' She arched an eyebrow. 'And did they mention the fact that a certain cowboy was spotted sweet-talking the new arrival at Shelby's Bar?'

Fuck.

'Hey, I was just stopping Jim Randall getting his dirty hands on her. Made sure she got back to her motel, okay?'

I received my second dose of Dean shit-eye in as many days.

'And yet somehow you said nothing about meeting each other when I thought you first met by the wood store?'

Double fuck.

I shrugged.

'I didn't want to embarrass her, she was roostered.'

She paused for a moment, then shook her head.

'Listen,' she said, drawing closer. 'That girl's got steel at her core, but she's not nearly as tough as she looks right now. She's having a shitty time – no thanks to a man – so whatever's going on here with you two, you ease the hell up on her, okay?'

I frowned, instantly wanting to know who'd done that to her, feeling even more like the asshole she'd accused me of being.

'Yes, Mom,' I replied, unable to help myself smiling with her and realizing with an uncomfortable jolt how similar her smile was to Lottie's.

'Cole Miller, I love you dearly, but so help me God . . .'

I held my hands up.

'I'm just messing with you, okay? I'm gonna make it up to Lottie. We'll be the best of friends by tomorrow.'

She groaned as I moved Domino on, glancing up at the others, now way up the field.

'Cole,' she warned, doing the same with Penny. 'I know your way of making friends with hot women—'

'Race ya,' I grinned as we moved into a lope, picking up speed once in the longer grass.

'Asshole,' she laughed, holding onto her hat as Penny sprinted to catch up.

I gritted my teeth, all too aware that she was the second woman to give me that title recently.

———

After setting up camp, finishing our food and settling down for the night, Jesse and I sat on the log outside the tent.

As Lil approached Lottie with a new hat in her hand, I doubled down on Jesse's words, determined to focus, despite having spent the last twenty minutes distracted by the way the firelight had reflected in her hair, turning it gold.

'. . . So I don't know. The doctor said another break might stop me riding again, period, bulls or not, but . . . I just think I got unlucky that time. You hear how much JB earnt at World Finals last year?'

I nodded.

'Three million.'

'And then some with all the sponsors,' Jesse added, shaking his head, finally noticing my distraction as Lottie put on the hat and smiled at her cousin in a way that twisted my insides. 'Damn, that girl is something,' he added, under his breath.

As Lil left, we watched as she took it off and replaced it, twirling gracefully on the spot as if testing whether it might fly off. It was fucking adorable, but Jesse's enthusiasm had my hands clenched into fists.

'She's right, you sure do pass for a fine cowgirl,' Jesse called out, chuckling to himself as she startled, those beautiful blue eyes now trained on us. 'Just be careful no one else takes it and puts it on, y'hear.'

I, wingman to Jesse's tired-old lines for longer than I could remember, almost rolled my eyes.

'I'm sure you're going to tell me why,' she said as I tried not to stare, watching as her hands moved up to her hips as her expression turned full-Dean, but her voice . . . that accent turned the words into sharp little knives. I looked at her, unable to help myself smiling as I felt Jesse take the hit.

'Wear the hat, ride the cowboy – or cowgirl, Princess.'

Smooth bastard. Unflustered as ever, he added a smile – the one that usually resulted in the same outcome each time. My fists clenched at the thought of those two hooking up . . . but it wasn't my choice.

'Best be careful, then,' she answered softly, her eyes flicking to mine, just for a moment, as she turned. Jesse missed it as he reached back into the tent for something, leaving me to watch her approach the campfire. I willed her to turn around, wondering if I should go after her.

'I'm turning in,' Jesse yawned. 'Still hate the early starts. Think I'd be used to them by now.'

'Yeah,' I agreed. 'Never gets any easier.'

———

Two hours later, I was still wide awake. Jesse was really getting into his stride, snoring loudly enough to keep the resident black bears at bay.

But I couldn't blame him for keeping me awake – my own thoughts were doing a damn good job of that.

Sighing, I got up, swiped the towel from my bag and headed out into the night. The moon was almost full, lighting the short path up to the pools, and the promise of hot water and maybe some sleep to follow was enough to grit my teeth against the cold.

Stripping down and climbing into the smaller pool, the heat and the quiet combined into the kind of relief I hadn't felt all week. Settling back, I found a comfortable position against the smooth stones and closed my eyes.

Almost immediately I could feel her hand against my chest, the way she'd pulled me into her, the taste of the whiskey on her lips . . . the way they had turned cherry red after we'd kissed again, just before she left the bar.

Opening my eyes and almost groaning out loud in frustration, a light from the camp suddenly caught my eye. As I watched, a figure approached in the darkness, towel clutched under their arm.

My heart damn-near stopped. Lottie. Right here, whilst I lay in here, naked as the day as I was born and the beginning of another goddam boner under the surface.

'This your way of saying you're sorry?' I blurted, somehow imagining humour might help the situation, but regretting it as soon as her face turned cold.

'Sorry? For what?'

I kicked myself, desperate not to blow it this time. What would Jesse do? Fucking ride it out. Be smooth.

'For calling me an asshole?' I said, trying to keep my voice light, the same kind of innocent *who me?* bullshit that seemed to work when Jesse did it.

She paused, and some of the hardness melted.

'But you . . . I didn't actually call you an asshole. I said your assumptions about me made you come across like an asshole.'

I hid my smile, ducking my head a little. Damn, I liked this girl, that fucking smart, beautiful mouth. And unless I was wrong, there was a little bit of . . . guilt, maybe, in her words. Or was that wishful thinking?

'Right, same thing,' I said, careful to keep it neutral. 'You getting in, or you going to freeze yourself half to death out there?'

She hesitated, but before I could say anything more I saw her eyes flick over me, from my face and down over my chest, further down to where I hoped to fuck she couldn't see the effect she was having on me.

But . . . shit, she was checking me out, no mistaking it.

'Well, I can't,' she said, suddenly stepping back as our eyes met, as though aware of my thoughts. 'I'm not just stripping off in front of you. If you were any kind of gentleman you'd get out and leave me be.'

Jesus H. Christ. Stripping in front of me.

She began to turn away and I had to force myself from launching out of the pool after her.

'Wait up, wait up,' I called, not wanting to wake the camp but desperate for her to stay. 'I'm sorry, I'm only teasing. How's about I turn around and keep my eyes to myself, then you let me know when you're safely in and tucked away?'

Her eyes narrowed and her hand motioned for me to turn around. I did it without thinking, knowing in the same instant that I'd do whatever she wanted me to, knowing how much fucking trouble I was really in.

I had to close my eyes to the sound of her clothes falling onto the stones, able to imagine what her peachy ass would look like outside of those fitted jeans all too well.

'Why are you awake anyway?' she asked, stepping lightly over to the other pool.

'Jesse snores,' I replied, barely able to hold it together as I heard her towel drop, vaguely aware that this felt like some kind of personalized torture. 'And I like sitting out here like this, it's . . . peaceful. Usually.'

'I'm in,' she replied, and I made the mistake of looking straight at her, the way she'd pulled her hair off her neck, the slope of smooth skin that faded under the surface. Her eyes were doing the same to me, meeting mine.

I cleared my throat and forced myself to look up instead, focusing on the moon, feeling the rush of blood to everywhere other than my brain. I had to get it together. This was Lil's cousin, for fuck's sake. Anyway, I'd seen plenty of pretty girls before, *been* with pretty girls before. There was no reason this was any different. Plus, I had to fix the mess I'd made – I owed her that at least.

'So given that you're not a city girl,' I said, steadying myself as I turned back to her, determined to keep it cool. 'Then what's a country girl doing in the city?'

For a moment I saw the knives sharpen, waited for her to cut me open. Instead, she seemed to shrink back, more than a little hurt.

'Trying to make something of myself,' she said, her voice as soft and quiet as the night. 'Honestly, I don't know.'

She closed her eyes as she leant back, brow furrowed. I realized right then that all I wanted to do was scoop this girl up and hold her until she never looked that way again. Thoughts of sex aside, seeing her look that way was like a fucking knife in my heart. But much as I wanted to, I couldn't just reach out and touch her, not yet.

Time to own it, even if it hurt. She was worth it.

'My mom was a country girl in the city,' I said, suddenly unsure as the words came out. 'She . . . felt the same thing, I think.'

My heart was pounding. I never spoke about this shit, not to anyone. Lil was the only one, other than family, who really knew.

'And how did it work out for her?' she asked, her voice the same gentle tone as the one she'd used with the horses.

I wanted to answer her, to let her know the way I'd been that day in the corral wasn't her fault, wasn't really me. But . . . fuck if this didn't hurt so much. I found her eyes, holding them, seeing the kindness there. There were echoes of Lil again, that fierce exterior and just about the kindest, softest soul underneath.

'I don't know,' I replied eventually, having to break eye contact to make it through the next bit. 'She rarely visited me, my brother or my dad after she left us. Last I heard she was running some tech company in San Francisco, found herself a whole new family over there.'

'Shit, I'm sorry,' she whispered. 'No wonder you're not keen on city people. I had no idea.'

I tried to smile, but from her expression I knew she didn't buy it.

'How would you know? It's okay. I mean, it's not, but I'm a grown-ass man.' I sighed, shaking my head, really hearing the words now I'd said them aloud. 'I need to let this shit go, you know?'

She was silent for a moment, completely still in the water. I could almost hear the thoughts churning in her mind before she fixed her eyes on me again.

'Or live with it, recognize it for what it is. You don't have to be defined by her actions. From what Lil tells me, you're defining yourself in the opposite way. She told me what you've done for her, for the ranch. I get the impression you're about as far from selfish as it gets.'

I was unprepared for the compliment, for the kindness in her words that she held out like a hand. It was beginning to feel fucking dangerous, like I was walking right into the sun, my eyes blind and skin burning, but I didn't care. I wanted more.

Shit.

'So, what do you want to make of yourself?' I asked, wondering if there was any chance, any at all, that she might be staying here for a while. Maybe just long enough to get to know her more, persuade her to stay in whatever way I could.

'I just want to be good at what I do, whatever that is. If I could do that away from the city then . . . that would be the dream. But that's where all the opportunities are. Maybe it's just a temporary thing,' she paused, glancing at me. 'I'm not sure I can live surrounded by concrete my whole life.'

It was like she'd heard me, even though I knew, deep down, that was beyond delusional.

But fuck it. She'd started that kiss, drunk though she was . . . and there was absolutely no mistaking the way she'd checked me out by the wood store – hell, the way she'd done it a couple of minutes ago. There was something here, right now, and it wasn't just one-sided. I knew it.

Heart pounding, I took the chance.

'You and Lil kinda look alike, you know?' I said, pushing off against the stones and coming right up to the edge nearest her. 'Makes it difficult.'

Her eyes widened, blinking as she took in the change of tone.

'Makes what difficult?'

Jesus. Her voice was all breath, her chest rising under the surface of the water. I tried not to smile but failed, just fucking relieved I hadn't misjudged it. I'd have to make this moment count.

'I think of Lil as family,' I began, bringing my hands out of the water to grip the side, tensing my arms in preparation. 'But the thoughts I've had about you, well, they're not things you ever want to be thinking about family.'

Her blue eyes even wider than before, beautiful lips popping open, I couldn't help laughing as I pushed myself up and out of the water. It was totally shameless, but fuck it.

'Holy shit, Cole,' she said, turning her head to the side, but not before I knew she'd taken a good look.

'That's what they all say,' I said, smiling as she kept her head turned. 'What I mean to say is, no hard feelings, Princess. I've got no problem with you, never have. It's just what to *do* with you.'

I grabbed my towel up, wrapped it loosely around my hips. She didn't reply as I started to walk away slowly, the total opposite of what I wanted to do. In my mind I'd already got into her pool, turned her around gently and lifted her legs around my waist.

Glancing up at the moon, I made myself a promise. If that's where this was headed, if she wanted to, we'd come right back here and do just that.

'Don't stay out long,' I called back, knowing full well that I'd be waiting up until she came back to her tent, but would also knock the ever-loving shit out of anyone who even looked at her. 'The other cowboys will be up soon and I don't fancy starting my day knocking skulls together.'

ACKNOWLEDGEMENTS

My first and most heartfelt thank you must go to the inimitable Judith Murray. After a lifetime of writing in near isolation, I'm so incredibly grateful for your warmth, support and a belief in me that I didn't wholly have in myself. Thank you doesn't fully cover it, but I am so very glad our paths crossed. Kate Rizzo, Imogen Morrell, Mia Dakin and team, I so appreciate all of your efforts on my behalf – it's an honour to have a home at Greene & Heaton.

To my insightful and talented editor, Kinza Azira – thank you for supporting me to shape the book into the story it's become. It's been such a genuine pleasure to work with someone that *gets it* and shares my soft spot for cowboys! Huge thanks also to Katie Loughnane – how wonderful that our paths have crossed again after all these years – and the wider Pan Macmillan team: Kate Tolley, Charlotte Dixon, Rosie Friis, Anna Shora, Mairead Loftus, Lloyd Jones and Siân Chilvers. From my own time in publishing I know all too well what it is to bring a book to life and the sheer graft involved – please know how much I appreciate all you do.

Thank you also to my international publishers for believing in Lottie and Cole so early on; I'm so glad their journey gets to travel beyond Wyoming and into other languages and territories.

I've been incredibly lucky to work with amazing people, past and present, who've supported and encouraged me through my writing. In particular: Hannah B, Alesha, Ben, Suzanne, Laura,

Gavin, Aimee, Niamh, Emily, Liv, Kirsty and Val – thank you for your generosity and time, it's made all the difference.

To my family, and extended family, thank you for your support always. Mum and Dad – who knew that trip to Wyoming would lodge itself so firmly in my mind? Thank you for giving me a sense of adventure – albeit more mental than physical! – and for introducing me to the Wild West and so many amazing places.

Ellie Willis – you are such an inspiration to me, from your own incredible writing talent to your keen editorial eye, I just know I wouldn't have got to a place of creating this without you. Lizzle – our friendship is ingrained in everything I write. Almost forty years (dear *God*) since we squabbled at pre-school, at this point it's more than friendship. I've always thought of you as my sister, and the only friend I've ever truly been able to look in the eye . . . ! I'll write our story one day, I promise.

For Elle, my ride-or-die, eternal cheerleader and quickest wit in the west. Girl, this is the uni meet-cute we never quite had. There's a big chunk of our friendship woven into Lottie and Hestia's, and I'm more grateful than you can ever know for your support and friendship.

Finally, to Rich. Ironically, there aren't the words to thank you for your unending love, support and encouragement through this whole process. This really is for you and our boys.

READ ON FOR THE FIRST CHAPTER IN THE
NEW DIAMOND BACK RANCH NOVEL
COMING SOON . . .

CHAPTER 1

'So tell me, cowboy, what's your favourite thing to ride?'

I pinned Jesse with my eyes as I said it, but it was Cole that almost sprayed beer over his cards, the poor fucker still adjusting to my delivery.

Lottie smirked, shaking her head as Bailey slapped the table, issuing a dirty cackle. 'Hestia, girl, you're a damn riot. How can someone who sounds just as ladylike as Lottie here come out with shit like that?'

I shrugged, still focused on breaking Jesse's stare. There wasn't even an inkling of a smile, nothing. Damn. Fucking hot *and* a good poker face.

'Oh don't be fooled by the accent. Lottie's just the other side of my coin, as Cole's been finding out.' I glanced up at him, raising an eyebrow. He was grinning now, glancing back at Lottie with the same besotted expression he'd worn ever since I got here. 'It's just that where she chooses dignity, I always choose violence.'

There was a pause, everyone waiting for Jesse's response. Lottie gave me a knowing smile, which I returned.

'I know what you're trying to do here,' Jesse drawled, taking his time as he looked back at his cards, utterly unruffled. 'And there's no way you're getting one up on me through distraction.'

It'd only been a few days since I'd arrived at the Diamond Back ranch for a few weeks away from all the shit back in London, but

I was getting impatient. The flirting had been hardcore, even by my own standards. Trouble was, this guy was a little too much like me. He was willing to push it further than others would, utterly sure of himself and very aware of just how fucking tasty he was – from biceps that strained against his shirt sleeves to the old Hollywood, all-American chiselled face.

He was also all too aware that he was making me wait, despite having already fucked me with his eyes about a dozen times.

So I decided something on the spot. When we got to it for real, which I guessed would be any time in the next hour or so, I'd make him beg for it.

'Answer the question then,' I replied, leaning in against the tall-backed chair, elbow on the armrest. 'Or I'll give you a real distraction.'

That did it. His dark, smoky grey eyes flicked onto mine then dipped down to my chest, where I knew the top buttons of my shirt were taut against my breasts. Shifting in his chair, he refocused on his cards.

I had him. A surge of triumph coursed through me, and I tingled with the urge to rip his shirt open with one hand and rip his belt off with the other.

'Well, let's see then,' he said, just as slowly as before, but this time he wasn't quite able to stop himself from giving me a quick glance, the corner of his mouth curving up. 'We've got bulls, mean sons-of-bitches but over pretty quick – kinda similar to the broncs.' Cole snorted as he studied his own cards. 'And then there's the regular old horses here on the ranch, but that's nothing. I've been riding 'bout as long as I've been walking, so . . . that leaves buckle bunnies, I guess.'

'Okay, I'm out,' Bailey announced, shaking her head with a smile in Jesse's direction as she stood up, glancing between us. 'I'm training with Darcy tomorrow, so I'm gonna leave y'all to it.'

Lottie started giggling, waving to Bailey as she rounded the table and headed across the vast living room.

I paused, focusing on my best friend for a moment. The lightness in her laugh was unlike anything I'd heard from her in years, maybe even since uni. Her whole demeanour had changed in the couple of months she'd been here, as though she'd finally shaken off the weight of London, a job she hated and Kyle, ex-boyfriend and professional knob.

It made me so insanely happy to see it.

Cole pulled her up onto his lap, his own expression matching her joy as he brushed a thumb over her cheek, watching her laugh. I almost had to look away – the love in their touch was so intense that it felt wrong to intrude.

I'd never known that kind of love, not even with Cal, my ex of five years. Passion, yes, friendship and a shared love of tattoos and music, definitely, but somehow, nothing deeper. We were both messed up, I knew that, products of dysfunctional parents and traumatic childhoods. Somehow I'd hoped – tried – for a while to connect through that. As it'd turned out, neither one of us had been brave enough to bare our true selves, so the soft, vulnerable and breakable bits had remained locked down, tighter than ever.

This time, when I caught Jesse's eye again, I could've sworn his thoughts mirrored mine. He quickly smiled in a way that reset my thoughts firmly back on him, on what that mouth would feel like on mine.

'Anyone want some snacks?' he asked, placing his cards face down. 'Another beer?'

Cole and Lottie put in their orders before Cole resumed his poker tutorial. I could tell Lottie wasn't really listening by the way she was watching his lips, playing with one of her curls absent-mindedly.

'Hestia?' Jesse asked as he rounded the table towards me,

circling his shoulder as he did so as though it was bothering him. 'Drink? Snacks?'

I pushed my chair back and stood, moving just far enough into his personal space to make myself clear as I flicked my hair over my shoulder.

'I'll give you a hand,' I offered, keeping my voice low. He raised an eyebrow, fighting another smile. 'With the snacks, you perv.'

He laughed then, unable to hold it back. Lottie and Cole looked up together.

'C'mon then,' he replied, sauntering over to the door and glancing back to me, eyes darting from my shirt to my black denim mini and down to my Doc Martens – which I had so far stubbornly refused to swap for cowboy boots. 'I think I've come up with a way to describe your look, you know,' he added, turning into the hallway as I followed.

'Tread carefully, cowboy,' I warned, allowing myself an extra-long, fully gratuitous stare at his ass. His indigo blue jeans were fitted to perfection and, combined with his casual, confident walk, moved in a way that sent heat flaring right through me. 'These boots have kicked many asses in the last ten years.'

Entering the kitchen, with the light over the table on low and the sounds of Lottie and Cole's laughter fading as the door shut, the atmosphere changed.

'Kick any as fine as mine?' he asked, opening the fridge door, pulling out a couple of beers.

I leant against the table, folding my arms.

He turned as if to question my silence, eyes immediately resting on my breasts, barely contained by the buttons.

'Jessica Rabbit,' he began, undeterred, putting the beers down on the countertop, reaching up into one of the cupboards and bringing out several bags of chips. 'Meets Wednesday Adams. That's your look.'

I narrowed my eyes. Secretly, I fucking loved that. But this was my way in, so I wasn't about to tell him that.

'A cartoonish, psychotic teenager, then?' I said, voice low, as though he was walking a fine line.

His face changed in an instant, awareness flaring. I almost felt bad, even though this was all part of the game. It confirmed what Lottie had said though, that under the cocky exterior was a genuine guy with a big heart.

'Woah there.' He put everything down, rounding the counter with his hands raised. 'I meant it as a compliment. Damn, I mean, you've got the whole red hair, sexy thing going on with all the black clothes . . .' He stopped, clocking my eyes.

'No, no, do go on,' I purred, stepping closer, watching as he realized we were in touching distance, his eyes drifting down once again. 'Up here, handsome,' I added, waiting for him to look me in the eye again.

'I . . . I just meant . . . Wait, are you . . . You're fucking with me, aren't you?'

Dipping my head to hide my smile, I kicked myself, realizing how much harder I found it to do this with him. There was something about his energy, something insistent and relentlessly positive, that made it almost impossible to fuck with.

'Well, if I'm a sexy red-headed psycho –' I replied, snapping my head back up and noting his relief, followed by a flash of challenge in his eyes – 'that makes you . . .' I considered it for a minute, studying his features openly. To his credit he didn't flinch, just stared right back, only reacting as I bit my lip, painted as cherry red as my hair. His grey eyes widened at that, and his jaw flexed. 'I've got it: Chris Hemsworth in his Thor era meets the hot, ex-military one from Yellowstone, what's his name? Kayce?'

This time he stepped forwards, pushing his dark sandy hair back from his face. It was tanned from the intense June sun, and his eyes were brightened by the contrast. The shadows of the dim room highlighted his sharp cheekbones, sloping to darker stubble on his cheeks and jaw.

'The hot one?' he asked, reaching out and gently unfolding my arms, taking my hands instead. The brazen look in his eyes and the pure jolt of electricity that shot straight up my arms at his touch almost gave me pause. I knew I could handle myself, handle him in this scenario, but something felt . . . different. He paused too, turning my smaller hands in his, studying the white tattoo on my left wrist. 'What does this one mean?'

I hesitated, suddenly checking myself. It wasn't like it was a personal question as such, but all of my tats had stories, some deeper than others. I'd explained this one many times before, to many people, but I couldn't put my finger on why explaining it to Jesse suddenly felt . . . exposing.

'It's an old Norse compass,' I began, staring at my wrist, feeling his eyes on my face. 'Helps prevent you from losing your way. I did it myself when I was first starting out, just before I opened the studio with my ex.'

'And is he still in the picture?'

I looked up, the gap between us disappearing. But, remembering my earlier promise to myself, I deflected. Not this easily.

'Why don't you give me your own tat tour and I'll tell you,' I countered, slowly retracting my hands from his and stepping back to lean on the table again.

He gave another small smile, and then his fingers began undoing his shirt buttons, working slowly as he watched me.

'I've only got two so far. But . . . maybe I've got room for more,' he said, eventually reaching the last button and opening it up to reveal the tanned skin beneath. *Holy fuck* . . . Yep. Definitely Thor. Turning around, he slid the shirt off to reveal a tight, toned back, leading right down to that ass. 'So, what do you think?'

Momentarily stunned, I didn't get it together until he peered at me over his shoulder. There was a bucking bull, small but nicely done, on one shoulder, and a larger water dragon at the top of his spine.

'Nice,' was all I could manage, covering my shock by getting up from the table and approaching him, as if to inspect them. But, in truth, I felt like if I didn't touch him again in the next ten seconds I might just fucking implode.

So I touched him, reaching right out and stroking my finger down the dragon, letting my long, sharpened, gloss-black nail drag slightly on his skin.

'Plenty of space for more,' I breathed, feeling him shudder under my touch. 'Shame I didn't bring my kit with me.'

He turned then, fast enough that we were touching as I looked up into his eyes.

'I've shown you mine,' he growled, his finger grazing my chin, following the line of my neck and down, across my collarbone. 'Only polite to show me yours.'

I almost smiled, feeling as though he'd plucked a line from my own head. Except I couldn't, because my entire body was consumed with the thought of fucking this man until neither of us could stand any more.

'I think you're mistaking this accent again,' I murmured, beginning on my own buttons, teasing him by moving as slowly as I could, the first one popping apart to reveal an obscene amount of cleavage. He swallowed as he watched. 'There's not a single polite thing about me.'

As though unable to stand it any more, his eyes darting to the door as though weighing up the chances of us getting caught, he moved his hands over mine, popping the next two.

I shook my head gently, stepping back to bend over and untie my laces, kicking off my DMs and giving him an entire eyeful of my black lace bra.

'Fuck,' he breathed, shifting position as he leant back against the counter, the front of his jeans straining against the biggest fucking boner I'd ever seen.

'That's more like it,' I smiled, continuing to torture him with achingly slow pops of my buttons, now revealing my whole rack, the tats that stretched from the flames on my neck and down to the *Sleepy Hollow* scene on my chest. 'Explaining every one of these may take a while,' I began, letting the shirt fall to the floor, stepping up to him again.

'I've got time,' he answered, the gravelled edge to his voice growing as his fingers reached out to trail my flames. 'Although I'm having a hard time concentrating right now.'

'Ever fucked a woman with tats like mine?' I asked, failing to maintain my own game of making him wait and reaching out for his belt buckle, freeing it in seconds and running my hand over his zipper as I pulled it down. In the same moment I realized he wasn't wearing anything underneath, his cock straining to get out.

'Oh I've fucked plenty of women with tats,' he growled, circling his hand around my back and pulling me closer still, hearing the snap of the catch as he undid my bra. 'But no one like you, honey. You are one of a fucking kind.'

As my bra dropped and before I could move first, he made a sound between a groan and a growl, taking my face in his hands and running his tongue over my lips for a moment.

'Why do I get the feeling you might just undo me, Jessica?'

That was it.

I pushed my lips onto his and felt his instant response, his tongue against mine. One hand was on my breast, stroking my nipple, gently pulling it between his fingers. Moaning into his mouth, I found his jeans again and ripped them down, my hand closing around his cock.

'Fuck me right now,' I ordered, taking my lips off his just long enough to look down at the size of him in my hand, my voice too strained to be truly authoritative.

'You're in an awful rush for someone that was keeping me waiting back there,' he murmured as I reluctantly let go of him in order to undo the button on my skirt. 'Oh, no, no, Jessica, you leave that itty bitty skirt right there,' he whispered in that drawling accent of his, finding my mouth again, pressing me to him for a moment before his arms circled me, lifting me up onto his hips.

'What're you doing?' I gasped, his lips now against my jaw, working up to my ear as he walked us across the kitchen to a bare wall, his hands moving round to grab my ass. My skirt had ridden right up in the process, baring my flimsy lace underwear beneath.

'Do you remember when you arrived?' he murmured, his tongue now moving down to my breasts, teasing me as his cock brushed my thigh. I could barely answer, tilting my head back and only aware of where I was when I felt his hand on my head, gently cushioning it as we reached the wall. He pushed me up against it, his own breathing as heavy as mine. 'You took my hat clean off my head and wore it for yourself?' I nodded, almost whimpering as he lifted my skirt, his fingers tracing the thin lace, slipping inside them briefly. 'Well now, maybe you don't know the rules here, honey, but you wear the hat . . .'

'. . . you ride the cowboy,' I gasped as his fingers moved again, pulling my underwear to the side. He kissed me roughly again, pulling a condom from his pocket and ripping it open, swearing under his breath as I helped him roll it down, applying pressure as I did so.

He paused for a moment, his eyes wild, as though he wanted to say something else, but wasn't sure how I'd respond.

'Fuck me,' I demanded, saving him from any overthinking, desperate to feel him in me. 'Now.'

He smiled, edging closer, somehow able to support my weight against the wall with barely any effort.

'I want that mouth around my cock next time,' he demanded right back, waiting until I smiled, running my tongue over my bottom lip in answer. 'And then I'm gonna kneel right down between your legs and have you ride me that way too.'

Before I could even think to answer, he pushed into me, gently at first, and matched my own moan. It was louder than I'd intended, and I was suddenly aware that anyone could walk in and find us. But as he slid back out and pushed in again, harder, I knew I didn't fucking care.

'Harder,' I whispered, wrapping my hands around his broad, muscled shoulders, giving myself more leverage to move with him.

'Holy shit,' he groaned as I ground myself against him, knowing that there was limited time before we'd make each other explode.

I arched back, eyes closing. His mouth was on my nipple again, circling and sucking it with his tongue as he fucked me, harder and harder until I was biting my lip to stop myself from screaming out.

Slowly, very deliberately, he moved up to my mouth, slowing as though he was about to come, the kiss deepening. It began to change somehow, gradually at first, then all at once. His hand wove into my hair and his cock thrust deeper, pushing me against the wall with a whole new intensity.

Opening my eyes, I found myself looking straight into his. His expression mirrored how I felt, the realization of a shared feeling.

He paused, eyes now studying my whole face.

'How did I only just meet you?' he asked, his voice suddenly rough, as though emotion had ripped the edges.

For once, I had no idea what to say, too surprised by the way my own feelings seemed to wrap around his, wanting to comfort him somehow, or tell him how I'd never had an experience quite like this before, not even with Cal.

Instead, I was saved by the other feelings that suddenly rose up as he pushed into me again, making me come so hard that I almost saw stars. His mouth covered mine, wrapping me in a gentle kiss as I moaned, hardening as it was followed by his own.

I held onto him as he finished, my arms still circling his shoulders as I rested my head against his chest, eyes closed as I tried to catch my breath. We stayed there, just breathing against each other, one of his hands still in my hair, the other on my ass. He smelled incredible: a deep, warm, smoky scent.

'That was . . .' he began, breaking off as though realizing the next words might just take us into new territory, to somewhere I guessed neither of us was familiar with. I lifted my head as he tucked a loose strand of hair behind my ear.

His eyes blazed into mine, clearly deep in thought, as an unfamiliar but very definite jolt hit me square in the gut.

'Yeah, it was,' I whispered, wanting nothing more than to stay right here with him, and therefore knowing I had to leave immediately.

Shit.